For Glory and Gabe

Also by Stuart Jaffe

For more information visit www.stuartjaffe.com

THE WAY OF THE

BLACK BEAST

Book 1 of The Malja Chronicles

Stuart Jaffe

The Way of the Black Beast is a work of fiction. Names, characters, places, and incidents either are the product of the author's imagination or are used fictitiously, and any resemblance to any persons, living or dead, business establishments, events, or locales is entirely coincidental.

THE WAY OF THE BLACK BEAST

Copyright © 2011 by Stuart Jaffe
Cover art by Jeff Dekal

ISBN-13:978-1466321847
ISBN-10:1466321849
First Edition: September, 2011
Second Edition: September, 2013

Acknowledgments

If you've ever read an acknowledgments page, then you know that a lot of people help out an author in the creation of a book, many times without them even knowing it. Here are some of the people that helped make Malja's story come to fruition: Jeff Dekal, Stephen and Amy Ball, Garrett Place, Rich Sigfrit, and Tee Morris; McKenna Donovan, an excellent editor; the Magical Words team -- David B. Coe, Faith Hunter, Misty Massey, Edmund R. Schubert, and A. J. Hartley; and of course, my wife and son. But most of all, I couldn't write this without having people like you to read it. Thank you.

THE WAY OF THE

BLACK BEAST

CHAPTER 1

Malja had followed the killer for hours. She hid amongst the shadows of the forest pines and birches, careful not to alert him with any sound. Though he acted as if out for a stroll, all her instincts told her a confrontation neared.

He stepped into an open clearing. The broken macadam of a four-lane highway long dead cut through only to disappear in an overgrowth of weeds and vines. Insects meandered in the tall grass. A rusting signpost — NO FLYER LANDING — held a lonely vigil in the center.

The killer stopped near the sign and raised his face to the clouds. The hot Krysstaprime season neared its end, but the sun still cooked the ground.

"Don't you think it's 'bout time we talk?" he said. His dark skin obscured the brown eyes underneath his little round hat. He wore a strange suit — all black, trim cut, black shirt, gold buttons — and carried a beaten guitar on his back. Unusual clothes but not unheard of, not like Malja's long coat and black assault suit. "Or do you plan on following me forever?"

Malja cursed and stepped away from the trees. She stopped at the clearing's edge, reached behind, and pulled Viper from its custom-made sheath. The large sickle-shaped weapon with both its inner- and outer-crescents sharpened was unique amongst the world's fine straight edges.

"Weapons already?" the killer/guitarist said. "No talk?"

"We'll talk." She scanned the trees, searching for an

ambush. Light and shadow sprinkled the ground. He had picked this spot for a reason. "You killed two people before I could talk with them. Why?"

"It's my job. Why else?"

She saw movement off to the right — just a bird. The guitarist grinned as he pulled a sleek, balanced sword from the neck of his guitar. Sunlight glinted off its clean blade. "You want to kill me for those I killed?"

"I want to know who hired you."

He chuckled. "I can't tell you that."

"The two people you murdered had information for me."

"I imagine so. I was told to kill them before they could speak with you."

So it hadn't been a coincidence. Her body slipped from cautiousness to warrior with nothing more than a shift of her foot. Her grip on Viper tightened as anger heated her chest. Her senses grabbed every detail — the rustle of the leaves, the movement of his blade, the uneven macadam, the broken branches, the sweat trickling down his neck, the sun baking the earth.

With a sadistic grin, the guitarist pointed to the left edge of the forest. "Come out, boy," he said, his voice losing all of its playful tone.

Malja's anger boiled hotter. A lanky, twelve-year-old took three furtive steps into the clearing. He had scraggly blond hair and misfit clothes. *Tommy*. Malja had told him to stay at their camp.

"Doesn't look much like you," the guitarist said.

Now she saw why he had picked this place. He knew the boy had followed them, and he thought she was the mother. He had traveled such an odd, circuitous route in order to force Tommy's position — too far away for Malja's protection.

She glanced at Tommy. Despite the hot sun, he was shivering. She studied the guitarist, searching for the flicker of motion that gave an enemy away — a twitch of the shoulder, a change in attention, a lowering of the body. When she saw it, she knew he was about to attack the boy.

Like two wolves smelling the same meal, Malja and the guitarist broke into sprints to reach Tommy. Her straight black hair, braided to the middle of her back, slapped left and right. The thick heat made the run brutal. Malja's legs pumped hard only to travel a short way. Everything in her felt slow and labored while the guitarist appeared to glide through the grass.

Tommy stood his ground.

He thinks I'll get to him first, but he's wrong. Breathing in dust and heat, Malja found enough air to yell once, "Tommy!"

Her urgency cut through his confidence. Recognizing his miscalculation, he dashed towards her. Too late. He only managed a few steps. The guitarist grabbed his arm, yanked him close, and put the sword against his neck.

Tommy grunted and kicked, but the guitarist had a firm grip. Malja rushed up and snapped into a fighting stance. Tommy saw this and became still — quiet and cold. To Malja's surprise, his eyes dropped to the lightning arc tattoo on his forearm.

No, don't do that. "I'd love to kill you," the guitarist said, dripping sweat.

"Let the boy go, and you can give it a try."

"Not my orders, sadly, and I must follow my orders." Honest regret flashed across the man's face. "Of course, if you really are who you say — *the* Malja — well, maybe I ought to bend the rules a little."

Don't, Tommy. I can handle this.

The guitarist readjusted his hold on Tommy, breaking

the boy's concentration for a moment. A chilling sparkle lit in the guitarist's eye. "Y'know, if you really are her, then I know how to get you what you're after. Or should I say *who* you're after, hmm?"

No matter how much she wished otherwise, Malja's shock raced through her like a feverish disease. "You lie," she finally managed.

The guitarist shook his head with patronizing mirth. "You're looking to find two magicians. Brothers. Go by the name of Jarik and Callib."

Malja's chest constricted. "Anybody who knows even a little about me knows I'm going to kill those bastards."

"Not a very nice thing to call your fathers."

"I can think of a lot worse to call them. They ripped me from my mother's arms, taught me only to fight, and then tossed me away because I didn't turn out like they wanted. Left me in the woods to die. I was ten." Tommy would be ready anytime now. If he succeeded, she would have no choice but to strike. "Now tell me what you know or die."

"An empty threat while I have the boy."

"Never made an empty threat in my life."

With amusement, the guitarist weighed her words. "Perhaps I've said too much. Let's end this in the best way possible. We each go off on our own. You can go back to your camp, and I'll go a different direction. I'll send the boy when I'm safe. Then you —"

A ball of crackling electricity appeared before the guitarist. *No, not yet,* she thought as the guitarist stared, befuddled by its sudden formation. Angry understanding gradually creased his forehead. He looked at Tommy.

Before he could slash the boy's neck, the entire electric ball blasted into the guitarist. Violent shaking sent him a few steps backwards, throwing Tommy aside. Malja wanted to rush to Tommy — his body shook as well — but she could do nothing for him. The guitarist, however — with him she could do plenty.

She struck fast like another ball of electricity. Cutting upward from the knee, out across the forearm, and back through the neck. Three distinct cuts in one fluid maneuver as she stepped forward. She finished a pace beyond the guitarist and listened like an animal expecting another attack. Only when she heard his body slush to the ground in several pieces could she relax.

With careful, controlled motions, she removed a stained cloth from her pocket and wiped Viper. Her pulse calmed as she cleaned. When she finished with the cloth, she pulled out an apple.

Malja loved apples. She had grown up eating them and for her, they were the perfect food. Her blade was perfect, too. It needed to be sharpened and oiled but it did the job, slicing more people than she dared to think about. Easier to think about apples. Each bite calmed her, brought her back from the animal she had just been.

She tossed the core aside, spun Viper and settled the blade in its special sheath. She walked over to Tommy who sat in the grass playing with a rock.

"You okay?" she asked.

Tommy squinted against the sun, tapped his chest twice, and brought his hand to his forehead — a military salute. A brave face, but Malja caught the tremors in his hands. She also saw the tattoo on his arm. She often tried to forget that Tommy was a magician. Most of the time, she only saw a sweet boy who had suffered at the world's callousness. But when she glimpsed that tattoo, she glimpsed the other side of him.

Magicians bore one tattoo for each spell they mastered, using it as a focal point. Some said the magic came from the tattoo itself. If that was true, then Tommy could never be rid of it. Under her scrutiny, he rolled his sleeve down.

"Don't do that again," she said. "If he had realized you were conjuring, he would've killed you. He almost did."

Flashing a cute smile, Tommy pointed to Malja.

"You can't know I'll win. I make mistakes."

Tommy popped to his feet and skipped toward the body. Even after caring for the boy over several months, Malja found some of his behaviors disturbing. Maybe because of his abusive past, maybe because of his magician blood, maybe because he needed her protection — whatever the reason, he seemed to find comfort in her violence.

As she approached the dead guitarist, Tommy motioned for her attention. He held up the old acoustic and pointed to the pick guard. The word *Bluesman* had been etched in with a graceful hand.

"Means nothing to me. And don't think you're forgiven. No more magic. Understand?"

Tommy saluted, but his body language said he doubted her.

To hide her frustration, she inspected the body pieces. The first thing to strike her was the suit. This close up, she saw that it had been well made and well cared for — looked almost new if not for being slashed to pieces and soaked in blood. Nobody made clothes like this anymore.

Long ago, centuries maybe, before the Devastation, everybody wore such suits. The world thrived under the spell of success and civilization. Magicians provided unlimited energy, bountiful harvests, and all the raw power needed to fuel industry and technology. But some magicians grew too powerful. They abused their magic, striving to dominate people instead of helping society, seeking the secrets that might turn them into gods. And the Devastation leveled it all, casting the people into generations of scavengers and survivors. Yet another gift of the magicians.

The guitarist might have found scraps of a suit in one of the many city ruins, but a well-tailored, crisp and clean one? That stretched reality too far. Yet here he lay. The only answer she could think of was magic. But magic supposedly only worked in the natural realms. A magician could conjure a cotton plant or a herd of wooly torsles to sheer, but someone would still have to turn it all into cloth and tailor the suit.

Then again, Jarik and Callib had conjured her assault suit, and without a doubt, it was magic. She had worn it from her earliest memory — it grew with her, always conforming to her changing body. It stayed cool in the heat of Krysstaprime and warm in the icy rains of Korstraprime. It allowed her to move free and smooth.

"Look at this," she said, spreading open the Bluesman's coat. Tucked in his waistband, Malja found a small handgun — a relic from before the Devastation. Finding ammunition would be challenging, but in the right hands, a well-placed shot could end a fight very fast. The gun had a clean barrel and a wooden body with a minor crack down the side — and no trigger. That's why he didn't use it.

Malja considered pocketing the find. However, experience told her the weapon would never work well again. She'd be better off having one made from scratch, except no one did that. The magicians had made them. Like so many other secrets, the Devastation took that art as well.

"This man," she said, "was an assassin with a suit that could only have been conjured, and the only magicians I know who can do that are Jarik and Callib. So they hire him, kill off my way of finding them, but don't kill me? Maybe they have some feelings for me after all." Tommy grunted and shook his head. "No? Because they don't need to hire an assassin. So, who would hire this man?"

Tommy pulled his hand from the Bluesman's inside pocket. He held up a gold coin for Malja to see. On either side, the same name had been engraved — NOLAN.

Malja let out a disappointed sigh. "Wonderful."

Chapter 2

After the morning's excitement, neither Malja nor Tommy wanted to trek farther through the forest. They silently decided to take the rest of the day off in front of their campfire. Tommy played with some sticks, watched birds, and tended the fire. Malja pulled a tattered book from her pack and settled down to read.

Though just a torn cover and eight pages remained (numbered 127-134), the book never failed to capture Malja's imagination. It was called *Astronomical Wonders*. A two-page spread sat in the middle of the text, diagramming the solar system. The book explained that the stars in the night sky were actually enormous fireballs, and that people lived on a planet that circled one such fireball. Their planet, Geth, was second from their star and one of only four in the system, but that every star had planets.

Malja peered up into the night. As much as she believed the book to be true — it matched what she had been taught growing up — she found it difficult to comprehend. Corlin was only one of five large countries in the world, and if Geth could be big enough to hold five countries, why couldn't the universe be as big as the book suggested?

She put the book away. It made her feel small and insignificant. On some days that was a good thing. But not when she killed. She didn't want to think that taking the life of another meant so little.

From her pocket, she pulled out the Nolan coin. As the hours passed, Malja twirled the gold coin between her fingers.

"Teala Nolan," she said, barely raising an eyebrow from Tommy. She kicked dirt in his direction, startling him. "You almost died today. I don't want you in a situation like that again. Understand? If I choose to confront Nolan—" Tommy cocked his head and grunted. "Okay, when I confront Nolan, it'll be my choice. But you're stuck with me. It's not right for you to be in danger so much because of me. Violence follows me. You don't need that."

Tommy lifted his shirt to reveal the criss-cross pattern of scars left from repeated lashings.

"That's my point. You've already seen enough. Those bastards using you to power their boat, chaining you in that small room ..." She grew quiet as she recalled the blood on the walls, the raging storm, and her decision to save the boy. Shaking off the memory, she said, "I couldn't just leave you there. But I'm no mother, and this is no way to grow up."

Scowling, Tommy strode toward Malja. He snatched the Nolan coin away and began packing their travel gear. Malja closed her eyes for a moment, not sure if she should be thankful or sad.

"For the longest time, I've been on my own. I'm not good at being responsible for another."

Tommy slapped his hands against his sides and frowned. He pointed at her with one finger, at himself with another, and put the fingers together.

"We're a team, huh? A team has to be able to trust. You know I don't want you using magic. It's dangerous, and I can fight fine for myself. So, you want to be a team, you start by listening to the leader. Trusting the leader's decisions. And I'm the leader."

Tommy crossed his arms and produced a familiar scowl. Not only did this mean that he didn't agree with her, but it also added a connotation of *Go ahead, try to live without me. I'll just stand here.*

The boy had courage. Malja gave him that. He could brave the idea of facing Nolan or any threat without a visible hesitation. Moreso, he could stand up to her. And while she wanted to protect him, she had to admit that to survive in this world, one needed to be brave and strong. The safest way for Tommy to achieve that was by her side. Without her, he might get injured or die, and she hadn't gone through all the trouble of saving his life just to let the world rip him apart.

"Okay," she said. "But you listen to your leader."

With a happy double-tap salute, Tommy continued to pack their things.

* * * *

They stood before the iron gate. Drizzling rain did little to wash away the four grueling days spent hiking to the Nolan mansion. Torches burned in sconces on either side offering little light and less warmth. Four northern konapols growled at them. They were the smaller, domesticated version of the wild konapol, but like their relatives, they had thin gray fur that highlighted toned muscles, powerful front legs, and comical, wrinkled faces that hid vicious teeth. They were like pudgy, old men who would be glad to tear apart anyone dumb enough to cross them. Though tired and grumpy with hunger, Malja forced her mind to remain alert.

As the gate opened, the clanking of old metal died along the muddy ground. One man appeared. A burly fellow wearing a torn tunic adorned with a white sash — an attempted uniform.

"What you want?" he said, clearly unhappy at having to answer a night call in the rain.

Malja held out the coin. The guard squinted, harrumphed, and headed away. He herded the northern konapols into two cages.

"Come on," he yelled over his shoulder. "I ain't gonna carry ya."

As they entered the grounds, Malja observed closely — marking exits and ambush points. Everywhere her eyes fell, she saw the simple miracles of civilization that the world had lacked since the Devastation. The pathway leading to the house had not been thrown together from scavenged concrete but rather had been meticulously laid with red and brown brick alternating in a subtle yet lovely pattern. Four enormous columns, good for defense, reached from the ground all the way to the overhanging roof three stories above. The foyer did not have the marks of decay and neglect but rather showed the tender care of a house staff working with meticulous pride every day. Even in the huge main room where they waited, claw-shaped sconces buzzed with lightning balls pointing to the employment of magicians — just like in ancient days. They cast a brash, pale light on the stone walls.

Tommy took interest in a marble statue standing in an alcove. Two waterways in the floor trickled small streams down the center of the room, and Tommy hopped over them in several boyish bounces. The statue that had caught his eye depicted a hefty, bald man with a beard reaching to his feet — the Prophet Galot who learned the will of Korstra, brother god of Kryssta, and brought it to the enlightened. Malja knew nothing more of the story. She never had a use for religion.

"That's over two thousand years old," Nolan said, entering the room in a crimson gown as if waiting to host a grand ball. The lines on her face suggested she had been waiting a long time. Though stark and cold in demeanor, she had a disarming, pleasant voice. "My apology for the lack of welcome, but my staff is asleep. They work hard for me, keep this place running and I give them a roof and a full belly. But if I push too hard, they'd probably leave."

"I suspect people would put up with a lot to live here," Malja said.

Clasping her hands together, Ms. Nolan said, "So you're the great Malja. I half expected flames to burn from your eyes."

"That's a new one. Usually I'm ten-feet tall with the muscles of a betron."

Ms. Nolan's mouth opened in a hideous grin. "Stories of me are equally exaggerated ... mostly. Now, what do you want?"

"I'd like to know why you're trying to have me killed." Malja had not intended to be so blunt, but the old lady had a way about her that opened things up. Magic? Malja wondered. Other than in fairy tales, she had never heard of mind-controlling spells, but few people knew the full extent of magic and its uses.

Ms. Nolan appeared puzzled. "I assure you, I don't wish you dead. I have no reason to."

Malja reached behind her and gripped Viper, but a thought stopped her from pulling the weapon out. Nobody had frisked her. Nobody had even asked her to give up her weapons. Malja found herself, once again, wishing she had listened better to Gregor, her adoptive father. He had tried to teach her about magicians, but at such a young age and having been tossed aside by the bastard magicians Jarik and Callib, Malja had no desire to be educated on that topic.

"Why do you believe I want to kill you?"

Malja held out the Nolan coin. "I found this on the body of your assassin."

"I see," Ms. Nolan said with a distasteful frown. "Follow

me, please."

The two women walked through a hall lined with ornate paintings of the Corlin countryside. Tommy flitted around them, never taking his eyes off Malja for too long. This time the attention pleased her — it meant the boy would not notice the open booths built into the walls. She had never seen a focus booth before but had heard about them in every starving town she visited.

Before the Devastation, wealthy people owned private collections of magicians to provide electricity, food, heat, everything. These heartless closets were where the magicians slaved away their days — easy to access by the Masters but out of view to guests. One booth had its door closed. Malja thought Ms. Nolan was about to comment on this, but she closed her mouth while observing Tommy. *She's noticed the tattoo.*

"In here," she said and opened a heavy door carved with the Korstrian symbol — four lines intersecting to form an intricate M. At least, Malja always thought it looked like an M.

Ms. Nolan took one step, stopped, and faced Malja with a look of concern more unnerving than her contorted grin. "We call this the Dry Room. Perhaps," she said, tapping her lips like a worried grandmother, "the boy should wait out here."

"He goes with me."

"I understand; however, in this room—"

"He goes with me," Malja said, her patience dying.

"Very well."

As Malja entered, she saw the horrible reason Ms. Nolan wanted Tommy outside. An emaciated woman clung to the thick, wooden bars of a cage. The cage, shaped like an enormous egg, had wooden spikes pointing in and out — the woman could not escape and nobody could help her.

Madness drenched her. She howled as if calling the moon and followed the mournful sound with an abrasive cough. She tore a strip of gray cloth from her shredded dress and coughed mucous into it. When she attempted to reach through the bars, Malja saw the tattoo — a bluish swirling like the wind blowing through clouds or a tide splashing the rocks.

Malja glanced down at Tommy. He spied the woman from behind Malja — curious, but scared. Not for the first time, she wondered how old he really was. Based on his height, the little bit of fuzz on his upper lip, and his odor, she placed him at twelve, on the cusp of puberty. His reactions, though, ranged from the cold pragmatism of a seasoned warrior to the trembling fear of an abused child. The latter appeared to be winning out now.

"Enough," Malja said, her firmness snapping Tommy from his fear as well as re-focusing her own purpose. "Tell me why you sent that man, or I'll just kill you and forget about it all."

"Do you solve all your problems by killing?"

Malja held still. The question had plagued her thoughts for some time now. She hated killing. She believed that. Each time she cut open an enemy, part of her became less than before, made her smaller. Yet, if she wanted to be honest, killing did solve a lot of her problems. She often eased her worries by remembering that violence ruled the world around her. No governments. No laws. She killed to survive.

Ms. Nolan walked to the cage with an arrogant stride, but stopped just shy of the madwoman's reach. Speaking firmly but in a calm, controlled tone — a warrior's tone used to command but not agitate — she said, "I didn't hire anyone to kill you."

"This coin calls you a liar."

"No, it calls you naïve. Do you think I'm stupid? Why would I pay an assassin with a coin that identifies me?"

"You think someone wanted me to think it was you?"

For a breath, Ms. Nolan's eyes lost focus as if she had lost herself in some indulgent memory. With a sudden sadness, she said, "I wish you were right, but I think the answer is less tricky. The coin was the mark, the assignment. The killer was sent to kill me. You just got in the way."

Malja shook her head. "He was assigned to kill certain people before I could speak with them. But I had no reason to seek you out."

"Maybe not yet."

"I don't understand."

Ms. Nolan pointed to the cage. "That shadow of a woman in there was … is … my sister. Audrex was born two years to the day after me." Ms. Nolan paused, and Malja had the presence to wait quietly. From the side, she saw Tommy had the presence, too. "My sister was the wild one. She would run through the woods, yelling silly words, not worrying about whose attention she might garner. She would pick up a plant or eat a berry without worrying what it was or if it might be harmful. She never seemed to notice the painful lives we all led. We were struggling to survive, and she would play. If there was no food, she would sing a song. If there was no water, she would dance and twirl. And she was beautiful. When she hit her teens, men showered us with gifts — food, clothing, anything. Father had died and her beauty made life easier, so we let it happen. But no matter how generous the bribe, Audrex would only flirt or offer a little kiss. They wanted a wife; they got a memory. That all changed when the magicians came.

"There are so few people in the world now, and they're

spread so far apart. If you find a few good ones, you're lucky. But we had a whole town of good people — solid people, real law and order, all Korstrian, no magicians. Blissgar was a good town. Actually built the town ourselves rather than live in the ruins and rubble like so many do. Of course, here in Corlin, too many roving gangs want to destroy such towns. It's safer to be in the ruins. We found that out when a gang of them arrived. Magicians. Yes, I see it in your face. I thought the same thing — magicians don't form gangs. I knew something bigger was at hand. The two leaders stepped forward and declared that Blissgar now belonged to them. Two brothers. You know them."

Malja nodded. "Jarik and Callib."

"No other magicians are so brazen. We resisted, but it was a foolish thing to do. We had no hope of winning. They overpowered us the first day. It only took one week for them to notice Audrex and only one day to seduce her. They were handsome, powerful, and different from everything Blissgar had ever offered her. She willingly became their consort. The idea alone nearly killed Mother. The day she went off with them was the last I saw of her for thirty-four years.

"I went on with my life. What else could I do? I thought of her all the time, but it became like a mourning period, like I had to accept that she was dead. A few years later, I married Ven Nolan. We tried to consolidate the towns in the area — form a government, but there were never enough people. Still, my husband was respected and we ran several farms. When he died, I took control.

"Then, as the Korstraprime rains fell, she appeared at my door — changed. It's been hard. The cage protects her and us. But it's hard."

Audrex prowled her cage and stared at her tattoos. Whatever her magic needed, the cage kept her from it.

Malja tensed as a thought hit her with frightening force. "Magic ability is a family trait."

"And yet I'm not a magician." Ms. Nolan shuddered. As she spoke on, her voice cracked. "Nor were my parents. Nor our grandparents. That's why she's insane. They stole her from me and did Korstra alone knows to turn her into a magician. But we are what we are born to. It can't be changed."

"So they threw her aside," Malja said as the coals in her heart burned.

Nolan's eyes dropped to Tommy. "Your boy is a magician. Be careful around him."

"He's not like that."

"Not yet. But every magician is unique in how much talent they possess. He has one spell now. But as he grows older, if he learns more, well, magic takes its toll."

Malja knew that price. She had seen it first hand in Jarik and Callib. Each time a magician cast a spell, it ate away at the brain. Little by little. The more powerful spells took away more of a magician's sanity. The weakest magicians, the ones that could only create electricity, became feeble old men and women lost in delirium. The strongest magicians ended up mad long before they became old. That madness had led to the lunatic thoughts that brought on the Devastation. It led to two brothers stealing a little girl.

Malja glanced down at Tommy. *He's not like that.* Besides, if he doesn't use his magic, he won't suffer any damage.

With a sharp, cleansing breath, Ms. Nolan stepped away from her sister. "Your assassin tried to cut off a trail you have followed and his next target was me. If my information is correct, and it is, you seek Jarik and Callib. I can help."

"Then help."

"I want a promise, first. Promise me that whatever you

do to them, promise me you'll make them suffer extra for Audrex."

Malja bared her teeth. "With pleasure."

Chapter 3

Tommy clutched the saddle's pommel as they headed west through the forest. His tense heartbeat pattered against Malja's skin. She had tried letting him ride in back of her, wrapping his arms tight around her waist, but he near-wet himself. His anxiety subsided only slightly when seated in front, protected by her arms. How anyone could grow up not knowing how to ride a horse — never mind absolute terror of the experience — baffled her. Then again, a slave on a thief's boat had little call for horsemanship.

The chestnut quarter horse Ms. Nolan had supplied (Orla was its name, but Malja tried not to put names to horses — they never lasted long around her) did not react to Tommy's fear, although Malja swore the animal took care to provide a smoother ride than usual. She just hoped they wouldn't need to gallop. Tommy would have a heart attack.

The morning air smelled crisp as the sun poked through the trees. Already the heat rose, and Malja wondered how long the horse could endure. Later the air would be stifling. The horse better hold out. Ms. Nolan gave the impression that time mattered in this case.

Fawbry, she had said, was a minor nuisance in Terrgar. All the surrounding towns belonged to Ms. Nolan (according to her), but Terrgar remained a dark hole on her map. It caused problems getting supplies to the far-end towns, caused problems with communications, and caused problems forming a solid front to her greater enemies in the western countries. Allowing Fawbry to continue to disrupt her holdings or escalate his activities invited an attack.

"Fawbry knows who you need to see. Bring him to me, and I'll get the information you want," Ms. Nolan had said.

The politics didn't matter to Malja. Warlords, politicians, businessmen, magicians — all the same. They sought to rule over others using the laws of people as tools for their personal advancement. They hid beneath lofty ideals and utopian promises they never intended to keep. Or they simply bullied their way from behind a sword. Malja had no use for it. Anarchy worked just fine.

They camped in the shade of a fractured bridge. Half the bridge spanned the far side of a dry bed. The other half was a mere skeleton. Its concrete pillars rose to hold up nothing like musicians standing on stage without their instruments — awkward and wrong.

Malja let the heat of their campfire soothe her weariness. Tommy nestled by her leg, wrapping his arms around her calf and resting his head on her knee. With a tentative touch, she stroked his hair, recalling the first time he had hugged her knee — the night she rescued him. It was such a simple act of affection, the very act that had won her over, yet she found it difficult to reciprocate more than her gentle touch on his hair.

Like horses, people didn't stay with her long. If she managed to keep Tommy alive long enough to become an adult, she expected him to go off for a life of his own. She couldn't expect him to stay. And she refused to force him to be what she wanted — that was Jarik and Callib's way.

Before she could spiral down into blistering memories, Malja cleared her thoughts with several deep breaths. She watched Tommy's hair trickle through her fingers. She listened to his slumber. She fought off all other concerns until an hour later, she fell asleep.

After another day traveling, Tommy had relaxed a little around the horse. By the time they reached Noograff, he could act like he had been born riding. But it was an act. He put on a brave face for the townspeople, yet Malja felt his tensed muscles clinging to the saddle.

The town of Noograff looked like many towns Malja had seen. An amalgam of single-story buildings cobbled together with materials from the nearest ruins. Rock, wood, and concrete chunks formed the foundation of materials. Old pavement, metal bars and pipes, and sharp bits of glass were more typical for extravagant homes. Noograff appeared to be more foundation and less extravagant.

The two roads were dirt with the odd bit of macadam poking through. Food and labor seasoned the air with a savory, rich aroma. Two wells marked sources of healthy water. To Malja — all signs of hearty, honest folk who understood these wild lands.

Good, she thought. She wanted to be around people that made sense.

She had heard rumors about the North countries that they had many carpenters and stoneworkers. They had towns cleared of the ruins and even a city or two. But those lands were elsewhere and they were governed. She preferred these towns. What they lacked in beauty they made up for in heart.

When they reached the main road through town, Malja's initial assessment faltered. A crowd of forty men and women congregated in the road. Many were absent limbs. Some bore deep scars and one woman had lost a chunk of her left ear. They carried makeshift weapons and sweated under makeshift armor. Some wore animal hides and others wore stained and patched clothing from long ago. Everyone wore something bright yellow around the head, arm, or neck. Despite their roughened exteriors, they looked like children playing at war.

Standing on a table made from a door laid across four large rocks, a heavy-set man with salt-and-pepper hair spoke to the exuberant crowd. In one hand, he waved a pearl-grip handgun. In the other, he clutched a yellow cloth. "I say it is enough that we struggle to eat, it is enough that we labor our meager fields. Why should we pay this scoundrel, too?" The townspeople roared their agreement. "This isn't our first time facing some idiot that thinks we'll be easy to bully. Nor is it our second or even our third. Warlords come and go. We've faced them, fought them, and in the end, we remain. What makes this different—" The crowd roared and hooted again. "What makes this different, what makes this unique, is that for the first time we will bring the battle to them. We will not wait for the evils of the world to pick upon us, to try to tear us apart. We will not watch our children shiver with the fear of what might come our way. No. We will take on the evil where it lives. And when we're done, Mayor Fawbry and all his ilk will never bother the town of Noograff again!" The loudest explosions of support erupted complete with the banging of swords, stamping of feet, and fluttering of yellow.

Malja had seen plenty of armies do the same. She had even stood before a few, spouting similar lines about how great they were and how righteous their cause. In the end, blood flowed the same color.

The heavy man paused in his speech and squinted toward Malja. "You there. You've picked the wrong day to visit."

"I'm passing through, but I think I can help you."

"Help us? Why would the mother of a young boy want to help fight with strangers?"

"Ms. Nolan has sent me after Mayor Fawbry."

All eyes were on Malja and Tommy. The faces were firm but not threatening — not yet. The man on the table made a show of his confusion. "Don't know any Nolan, and we don't want your help."

Damn. Ms. Nolan's power had appeared authentic, but obviously she claimed more than she truly held. That clouded the matter of Mayor Fawbry. If Ms. Nolan's claim of information turned out to be a lie, Viper would make her pay.

"Go away," the man said. "Pass through tomorrow."

With one hand, Malja eased Tommy to the ground. He didn't want to let go at first, but Malja shook him off. Pouting, he scampered to the side as she urged the horse forward.

"My name is Malja," she said, noting the stunned look on a few faces. "Those who know of me, know that I am an army within myself. We have a common enemy today. I will be in Terrgar. I will fight to get to the Mayor. There is no changing that. The question you face is whether to fight with me or to get in my way."

The man scanned the crowd. Malja felt his confidence drain away like snow melting in her hands. "Y-You're a liar," he said. "You could be anybody. You could be one of Fawbry's people. Prove you're Malja."

"No."

The man waited for her to say more, to justify her refusal, but the longer he waited, the stronger she became. She sensed the shift as it rippled behind her. A lackey of the enemy would stage some kind of display in order to prove herself. The angry crowd understood that Malja would do what she said, that only the real Malja would attack a town by herself, that they had no choice.

"I'm Pressig," the man said, trying to regain some ground through bluster. "You may join us, but do not impede us or you'll be brought before our judges."

Malja smirked. "Nice to see a town with some laws."

Pressig frowned, unsure if she mocked them. A second later, with smooth political ease, he broke into thick laughter. The townspeople followed suit, and Malja withstood the onslaught of merriment like a small animal caught in a storm. Another wave of yellow followed and more hollers. When they finished, Pressig raised his hands and said, "We have an ally, and that's good. But the battle still waits. Get what you can. Prepare your hearts and souls. We leave at second bell."

The town rushed to life as everyone handled their final business before war — providing for loved ones in case the worst happened and saying goodbye. Though she knew Tommy could take care of himself, Malja arranged for Pressig's wife to look after him. This act would gain Pressig's trust more than any display — she had given him a hostage.

Pressig's wife took the boy's hand with a melancholy nod. The woman's eyes spoke of deep sadness, and Malja suspected she had lost a child awhile back. It was common enough. Tommy brought a slight smile to her face that surprised Pressig enough to stare slack-jawed for a moment.

Nearby a small group of Korstrians knelt in a circle. One chanted a prayer and the rest bowed until their heads touched. The Kryssta followers were, no doubt, off alone praying in a quiet corner.

As Malja prepped her horse, she listened to the droning chants. She failed to see how people could think a little singing would influence the world, but she did like the rumbling of the sound. It seemed to soothe her horse, too.

When the second bell rang, warm goodbyes turned into passionate cries. Weeping and arguing snaked through the town. She helped Pressig gather people up, forcing them from their families, reminding them of the reason for the battle. Malja had expected this — she'd seen it before. She did not expect, however, to see Tommy astride her horse.

"You're not coming," she said, gritting at the parental tone she heard coming from her mouth.

Tommy pointed to the amassing force.

"No."

He made a muscle and when that failed to impress, he pulled back his sleeve and pointed to the tattoo.

"Absolutely not," she said in a low growl. "You don't understand anything about this, and I don't want you to start. You will stay here, and I'll come back for you. Now get off that horse."

With a dirty look, he climbed down. He lifted a defiant chin and crossed his arms.

She drew upon all her will not to shout at the boy. "Stay here. If you disobey me this time, if you come after me—"

She didn't have to finish. Tommy rushed towards her and gave a short hug. She stiffened at the embrace but also warmed inside. Something told her she should kiss the top of his head, but she held back. Thankfully, he did not cry.

Later, astride her horse and moving with the small force, she hoped Tommy believed she would come back. She should have been gentler with him; however, things had been moving too fast. That was her life. Always too fast. Except if she wanted to be honest, she preferred the fast pace. The slow times, like marching hill after hill towards battle, these were the times she dreaded — stuck with only her thoughts and the faces of those she had killed.

Paying them their honor, Gregor had called it.

Ever since he found her alone and half-wild in the woods, he wanted her to slow down, to think about the lives she touched, to consider her place in the world. Most mornings he would wake early in their two-room shack, take a walk amongst the pines, and pick a choice vegetable from their small garden. He'd prepare breakfast while she set the table or played war with her doll (its left leg missing), and he would talk in his rich, booming voice. She didn't understand back then, but these morning talks were his way of sneaking in an education — a little history, a lot of agriculture, some math and reading, and endless discussions of philosophy.

"You're a tough girl," he said while cracking a korkor egg he had filched from a nearby nest. "You've already been through more than many seasoned soldiers experience in a lifetime." She could hear his concern, but also detected a touch of pride. "So I want you to learn something right now. You may not understand it all today, but you learn it, you remember it, and that'll be enough."

"Okay, Uncle Gregor," she said, setting her doll on the wood-plank floor.

"This is a dangerous world," Gregor said, chopping the onion he had picked and tossing it in with the eggs. "It's a violent world. With what those bastard magicians did to you, I don't think you can expect a quiet life. But that doesn't mean you've got to embrace it either. It doesn't mean you've got to find pleasure in killing. If you do that, you may well lose your soul. I don't want that to happen. So when you kill, I want you to remember to pay them their honor. Anything living that falls at your hand — good, evil, whatever — anything once living deserves at least a moment of thought — calm, peaceful, sincere thought. Pay them their honor, sweetheart, and you'll find the dead won't haunt your dreams."

But it wasn't her dreams that troubled her. It was the quiet moments with nothing to occupy her mind that brought back the ghosts. Thankfully, her most recent kill, the Bluesman, didn't trouble her. She could honor his skill and gracefulness without guilt. However, thinking of those she had failed to save — the Bluesman's victims who died because of her — these ghosts haunted her thoughts like stingbeetles swarming over their disturbed nest.

And then there was Tommy. She could still smell the brine that tainted every inch of that thief's ship. Brine and blood. She felt the storming sea roll her stomach one more time, and she heard the begging as she pressed her foot down, sending the ship's captain under. He had been an bestial man who had harmed Tommy for no other purpose than turning the boy into a battery. But no death could be worse than drowning. The slow helplessness of it.

At the front of the line, Pressig raised his hand and everyone halted. He gestured for Malja. Before them, a wide hill rose. "Other side of that," Pressig said, "is Terrgar. Any suggestions on the best way to do this?"

"You don't have a plan of attack?" Malja whispered so as not to worry the tired men and women — calling them *troops* did not feel right to her.

"To be honest, I didn't think it'd get this far. We're just a bunch of farmers. I knew people were mad, but this is more than I expected. I thought I'd stir up their anger and we'd, I don't know, protest. Maybe get a little something."

"And then what? They'd elect you to run the town? Give you a stupid title like Mayor or Duke? I once met a fool who called himself President. Is that what you want?"

At least Pressig had the brains to look ashamed. "Please believe me, I care about these people. I don't want them hurt. I was going to call the attack off. I was. Except you showed up, and then it all just, sort of, happened. I guess I thought with you, maybe we'd actually win."

With the disapproval of a parent forced to clean up her child's mess, she said, "Stay here. Order your people to rest.

I'll scout and when I get back, I'll have a plan."

"Oh, thank you. Thank you so much."

"Stop it. Act like you're in control or you'll lose them."

"Right," he said, regaining his composure.

"Does that thing work?" She pointed to the handgun.

"Not even if it had bullets." He turned away, and as Malja headed up the hill, she heard him barking out commands.

Near the crest, Malja tethered her horse to an oak and crawled on her belly to get a closer look. She pulled out her spyglass — a reward she had taken from a pompous fool in the Freelands. He had thought magicians conjured the object. She knew better. It bore the marks of being hand-made — the imperfections and artistic flourishes of a craftsman at work. However, since the spyglass came from the ruins of a pre-Devastation town, she would have to admit that, at the least, magic-powered tools may have played a part in its creation.

Peering through the cracked eyepiece, Malja gazed upon Terrgar — empty Terrgar. A few barricades had been erected at the obvious entry points and sniper nests had been set up in the two tallest buildings. But no people manned either location. Four main roads wound through the town to form a large square in the center. There she spied a crude throne atop a mountain of rubble. A man sat on the throne — presumably, Mayor Fawbry. Twelve griffle guards surrounded the rubble pile, each armed with a sword, pike, or an improvised weapon.

Griffles were once human. The Devastation had destroyed more than just the land. The mutations to the living were numerous. Those who survived often did so because their mutations provided advantages in such a harsh world. For the griffles, this meant strength and speed. They were short, muscular, and ugly — mottled skin, stringy hair, and flattened faces. Fawbry must have hired them cheap — griffles weren't known for their brains.

One griffle, though, looked oddly small. The runt of the litter. It had little tufts of white hair growing from its joints and it followed Fawbry's every step. She even watched it climb upon his back. He must have a serious hold on the griffles if they allow one of their own, even the runt, to be treated like a pet.

None of this posed a problem, though. The problem sat a few sword-lengths in front of the griffles and the Mayor. Two oxters. Large, brown beasts with four muscular legs — excellent for farm work except for the forked tail lined with poisonous barbs. Usually the poison glands were removed at birth. Malja suspected that was not the case with these two. Their faces were smudged, bumpy things like the patterns in a muddy footprint. Just to make matters more interesting these oxters were female — highly aggressive and armed with two sharp horns curving out of the snout. They struggled against thick chains.

By the time Malja returned to the group, the situation had worsened. Half of Pressig's mini-armed force had run off. Those remaining looked as if they just waited for an excuse to leave with a clear conscience. Two angry oxters could rip them apart with ease. She needed a better plan than relying on numbers.

With a resigned sigh, she nodded to herself. Deep within, she had known her real plan all along. The sight of the oxters made her wish for another route, but so be it.

"Look here," she said. She didn't need to. All eyes already watched her. "I am a true warrior, and a true warrior walks the path of death. When I set out for this Mayor, I did not expect you people. So, I have a plan, and I want you to do as I say. Follow me, and I might live another day. I assure you, though, you all will."

Pressig frowned. "I don't understand. What's your plan?"

"There are two oxters protecting the Mayor." Before the worried moans died down, she raised her voice. "I'll handle them alone."

Chapter 4

When it came to fighting, Malja preferred it this way — alone. She had hoped to convince Pressig's people to provide support, but after learning of the oxters, they just wanted to crawl home. Fine by her. They would've been a hindrance. It was better this way. No concerns but for her own skin. It felt good for a change.

A long time had passed since she traveled without another. Though she enjoyed Tommy's quiet companionship, she also worried about him whenever danger threatened. She told herself not to — after all, she had been two years younger than him when she had to survive on her own in the wild. And she couldn't defend him all the time. He had to learn to survive. That's why she left him back in town. Still, walking along Terrgar's empty streets, only having to care about herself — the corners of her lips raised a fraction.

As she came closer to the town's center, a strange tingling crossed her skin. At first, she thought of it as anticipation, but each dirt-crunching step dispelled this idea. It hit her like a sudden blast of air — the town was empty. Not just of people, she had expected that, but empty of all signs of life.

Terrgar had been built among the ruins of an ancient town, yet no sign of rebirth existed. Broken doorways rotted. Burned-out windows sagged. The remnants of grounders and flyers, transports that once ran on magical power, rusted under the elements. She had seen more evidence of life in the desolate Freelands. That thought resonated strong — this Mayor was little more than a failed Freelands warlord. He had no town here. He had no base of power. He only had his griffle guards and his oxters. He just wanted to bully the weak for easy food or women or whatever pleased him.

As she approached the town square, she heard an oxter bellow its deep, croaking moan. Malja unsheathed Viper and cleared her mind. She kept expecting an ambush from the empty buildings, kept expecting her assumptions to be wrong, but nothing challenged her progress. The shadows remained dark and empty. Nothing dared to pop out at her. She didn't even need to look for an escape route (not that she expected to use one) because every direction provided escape. Of course, that meant that every route could also be used to attack. Further proof that Mayor Fawbry had no tactical sense at all, that he was just a fool making a pompous stand.

She stopped at the square's edge. The animals' musty odors reminded her of mucking out Gregor's stables. A cool breeze blew by — a cue of the changing season, the passing time, the need to find Jarik and Callib.

From atop his throne, Mayor Fawbry said, "Are you serious? This is all they're sending? One little woman?"

"I'm not from Noogruff," Malja called back.

Fawbry sat forward and the runt griffle peeked over his shoulder. "Oh, really? Then what do you want?"

Attempting the most businesslike posture she could manage while still holding Viper, she said, "Ms. Nolan would like to speak with you at her residence."

Fawbry stroked his wiry, unkempt hair like a crazed teacher. He wore a tattered but colorful robe that rippled as he paced. "You hear that, Tufts? Ms. Nolan would like me to visit her? Well, Ms. Nolan can rot," he said and Tufts let out a high-pitched laugh. "I'm not leaving here."

At least he knows her. With a shrug, Malja said, "Then I'll have to come up and get you."

One griffle, stockier than the rest and wearing a breastplate (really a piece of metal with the faded words THE BEST DRINK painted sideways), broke ranks and whispered to Fawbry. Fawbry's face dropped as he shook his head. The griffle pushed Fawbry toward the ground. The other griffles stayed silent and Tufts scurried to hide amongst the ranks.

Fawbry protested once more, but the griffle growled and pointed off to a red-brick building. Fawbry nodded as if it hurt his heart. Satisfied, the griffle returned to his place in line as Fawbry stood and brushed off his robe.

"Go away. Tell Nolan I'm not interested," he said, and Malja swore she heard pleading in his voice.

"I can't go without you."

Fawbry's shoulders drooped as he let out a dismayed breath. Two griffles emerged from the red-brick building, leading two men and a woman — all three were bound and wore square cloths covering their faces, each secured with coarse twine. They were lowered to their knees.

A sickly quiet overtook the square. As if to shut out the world, Fawbry closed his eyes. The griffle who appeared to be in charge, Drink, stepped out once more and walked toward the condemned. The soft clicking of his armor echoed across the open square. He slid out his sword.

Too far away to strike, Malja could think of only one thing to do. She shouted. "Hey. Moron. Oh my, look. The squat griffle is going to be tough killing defenseless people."

Drink watched her. She couldn't be sure he understood her words, but he clearly comprehended her tone. "Poor baby. Did I make you feel sad?"

Some of those in line snickered. The stocky griffle snarled at them. They quieted down. With a snort as if to say, "Watch this," he broke into a full-on charge at Malja.

She stood ready with giddiness. Drink closed in and swung his sword. Malja met the clumsy attack, locking his blade in Viper's crescent. As he strained to free it, Malja kicked his kneecap. She heard the bone crunch. He fell to the street, his sword clattered next to him, and Malja sliced open his belly.

"Is that it?" she asked to the stunned enemy on the mound.

Tufts climbed Fawbry's robe and shivered on his back. Fawbry's eyes shared the same fear. One of Fawbry's griffle guards stepped forward. With a stoic face, he raised his blade and brought it down on the chains that kept the oxters at bay.

"No," Fawbry said, panic edging into his voice, but nobody listened.

It took the guard four sparking hits, but the chains broke. Like dogs let out of a kennel, the two beasts stampeded towards Malja.

She could never withstand such a blow, so holding her ground was not an option. Instead, she brandished Viper, let out a fierce battle cry, and charged. She had hoped to startle them. Such a move might have confused a human, but the raging animals stayed their course. As they neared Malja, they lowered their snouts, positioning their horns at deadly angles.

Malja sprinted on, the adrenaline rush boosting her speed. She could feel the thunderous vibrations of the beasts trampling the ground. She heard the griffles cheer and holler from the safety of their rubble mound. She focused on the oxters' legs. Timing would be crucial. She blocked out all distractions as she closed in. The moment had come.

Malja slid low.

One oxter had lifted its head, expecting her to vault upward. The other had barreled forward. Neither anticipated her sliding underneath.

Malja's assault suit eased the friction with the street, letting her slide as if on ice. She resisted the urge to cut the oxters open from below. She couldn't risk one of the enormous beasts collapsing and clipping her in the head as it fell. She popped to her feet behind them and dashed to the right.

The oxters spun, croaked their anger, regrouped, and observed her while hissing and displaying their yellow-black teeth. She moved fast, trying to keep one oxter between her and the other at all times. This way she only had a single opponent to deal with directly, and the other oxter had to work hard to get around its peer — exhausting work that Malja planned to take advantage of later. *If I make it that far.* The oxters, however, had other plans.

The one in the back, the one Malja now noticed had a red rash around its eyes, shot straight ahead, planted its forelegs on the other's haunches, and leapt over its head. It swiped at Malja as it landed, connected with her shoulder, and threw her into a pile of bricks.

Which hurt more — the beast's blow or the bricks — she couldn't tell. Both just hurt and made her angry. She scrambled back to her feet and rushed forward, swinging Viper with calculated fervor. Before she could take control of the fight, Red Rash flanked her. She stepped back, parrying horns and claws more than attacking. Each step she tried to reposition for a fairer fight. Frustration and rage played out on the oxters' ugly faces. They wanted to slow her enough for a poisonous tail strike.

From the corner of her eye, she saw Not Red go for a

wide swipe meant to finish her. Malja ducked and came up hard, thrusting Viper into its chest. The oxter yelped and yanked back, causing Viper's curved blade to cut more as it ripped out.

Without hesitation, Malja spun to face Red Rash, but the beast had already attacked. She met the blow full on, taking it on her side, and being thrust into more rubble. Not what she had planned, but in battle, improvisation ruled. At this point, Red Rash made a critical mistake — it should have struck with its tail, but first, it glanced at the other oxter. Malja did not want to miss such an opportunity. She rolled to the left, ignoring her bruised side, and positioned behind Red. It attempted to snap her with its tail. Malja sliced it off. Blood and cries erupted. Malja skewered the barbed slice onto Viper, and armed with the poisonous tail, she slammed it into each oxter. In seconds, they moved no more.

Panting as sweat dripped from her face, Malja straightened and tossed the bloody tail aside. Before she could face Fawbry, however, she heard him whimper and protest. Though he garbled his words, she understood — the griffle guards would no longer follow him. They would no longer wait.

They yelled as they charged into battle like a chorus of berserk madmen. Malja sneered, bracing for a tough fight. She did not dream of surviving. She never did in any fight. She thought only of inflicting damage.

They picked up speed and pointed their weapons at her. Malja readied Viper once more and took slow, controlled breaths. Channeling all her rage, she roared at her stampeding enemy.

With only a few steps to go before reaching the killing zone, the guards skidded to a halt. Surprise and perplexed fear covered their monstrous faces as they backed up and staggered away. Malja wanted to laugh. Her battle roar never had such a response before.

Then she heard the tidal wave break behind her. Pressig and his town flooded the square in pursuit of the guards. Pressig glanced over his shoulder and said, "They watched you fight. They wanted to help." He smiled in victory and pressed onward.

A few townspeople rushed over to free the three prisoners. The prisoners stood with the confused joy of those who had accepted the fate of Death — Malja had felt that way many times. She could not be sure if the newly freed people belonged to the town, but she could tell by their effusiveness that they would probably be joining soon.

Malja let her body relax for a few breaths. She looked at Fawbry, alone on his throne, yelling at his abandoning guards, reaching out as Tufts scurried away, and she thought of Jarik and Callib.

* * * *

The people of Noogruff couldn't hold back their excitement. Three riders galloped ahead to tell the town of their success. By the time Malja, Pressig, and the rest arrived, a full-blown celebration filled the main street.

Fire pits blazed and savory aromas of roasting meat touched every grumbling stomach. Warmed breads and hot vegetables were doled out to every plate. A handful of men and women brought out patched-together instruments and played one raucous tune after another. Couples danced under torchlight, their bodies shimmering with the flames.

Tommy showered Malja with hugs. She tried not to stiffen up under his affections, but she had no doubt he noticed her discomfort. He broke away and rubbed down her horse. Later, he played with her hair while she ate. This she handled better.

A little girl with straight, blond hair looked up at her with eager eyes and asked to hear the story of the battle. "You don't want to hear that," Malja teased before telling the story to the girl's rapt attention. By the time Malja finished, a crowd of children had formed around her.

"Tell it again!" they shouted, clapping their hands and banging the ground until Malja put down her plate and described the battle once more. She had never enjoyed trading stories with adults — it was just competition — but with children, the experience took on the purity of inspiration.

Tommy sat beside her, beaming with the pride of being her trusted ally. As she finished retelling the story, she decided to help Tommy's status a little more. Though they'd probably never see these people again, he deserved at least one night of fun playing the hero.

"You know Tommy helps me stay sharp, so I'm prepared for whatever threats might come our way," she said to the amazed faces. "We play a game I call The Reflex Game."

"Show us," the kids cried out.

Before Malja said another word, Tommy jumped to his feet and put his hands behind his back. Malja laughed and Tommy gave her a rare, genuine smile.

"Pair off," she said, and the kids rushed around to find their best friends. "Now one person do just like Tommy. The other do as I do." Malja faced Tommy and brought her hands together as if in prayer. The kids followed along. "Tommy's going to try to slap my hand. If he gets me, he keeps going, but if he misses, then we switch and it's my turn to slap his hands. But there are rules. I can only move my hands up or down, and they must stay together all the time. Tommy can try to fake an attack but if his hand comes around enough to be seen, he must follow through. And last, the most important rule — if he fakes a strike, but I react anyway, he gets a free slap. I can only try to evade a real attack. Understand?"

Some of the children launched right into the game. Others appeared to be afraid. Malja looked at them and said, "A warrior must learn to face down a threat and only react to true dangers. Play this game enough, and you'll be on your way to being a great warrior."

The little blonde girl had her hands out and concentrated on her partner's shoulders. "Then we can defend ourselves, right?" she said.

"That's right." Tommy and Malja played a few rounds and soon all the children were giggling, slapping, feigning, and smiling. With a nod, Malja sent Tommy off to play with the others. She returned to her meal, grinning at the playful sounds around her. She swore she even heard a giggle sneak out of Tommy's lips, but when she turned around he was silent. But smiling.

Later, parents broke up the game to send their children to bed. Though there were many complaints, most of the children were tired and some moved with sluggish steps. A few uttered words of thanks before heading home. With his eyes growing too heavy to stay awake, Tommy curled around Malja's knee. Pressig's wife, however, swooped in and carried him to her house.

A handsome, young man climbed onto a table. "Drinks for the victors," he said, raising two frothing jugs in the air.

Malja observed the eager townspeople line up to get drunk on fermented whatever, and she let a new smile drift across her face. She rarely got to see this side of battle. Often while others celebrated, she traveled onward. This time, however, she had little choice. With Tommy asleep in the house and Fawbry locked away, she would have to wait for things to settle down before she could say goodbye.

Besides, she thought, eyeing the young man doling out drinks, *I don't want to leave just yet.*

A rapid-fire giggle soared over the general party noise, and Malja's eyes spotted a young gal being wooed by one of the rescued prisoners. She searched for the others and spotted them standing near the musicians. That suited her fine. It was interesting, maybe even pleasant, to see everyone so happy, but she didn't want to be forced into an awkward bout of praise from those individuals.

"We certainly owe you a big thanks," Pressig said as he approached Malja. He offered her a cup of the drink which she took without a word. It tasted sour, but the alcohol kick more than made up for its lack of flavor. "Oh, and don't worry about the ex-Mayor Fawbry," he went on. "He's tied to a chair in the Wilk's house. He won't go anywhere."

"I'm just glad nobody died."

"A couple broken bones and plenty of bruises is all. Thank you for everything."

Malja took another swig of her drink and put her mouth to Pressig's ear. Quiet and cold, she spoke. "You were lucky. You ever send these people into a fight like that again, you'll have nothing but corpses to celebrate with." Pressig tried to pull away, but Malja clamped down on his hand. "And if I ever hear that you let such a thing happen, especially because we both know you did this for politics, I'll hunt you down."

She released his hand but locked eyes with him until she saw the shock fade into resignation. She had no delusions that her threat would protect Noogruff from Pressig's ambitions for too long, but he would be cautious for a while. He left his cup behind when he made his exit.

Malja looked about for the handsome man who had supplied the alcohol. Before she could find him, a loud warbling emitted from the trees coupled with a buzzing, electric crackle. The music stopped as all eyes turned toward the forest.

From the shadows emerged a dirt-spackled, flatbed flyer loaded with salvaged items and things brought from far away. Each corner of the roofless vehicle had a cylinder blazing electric energy that kept it floating on air. At the front sat the magician who supplied the electricity and a filigoto driving.

The filigoto waved his stumpy hand as he brought the vehicle to the ground. He was short, wide, and bald with no neck to speak of. Another mutated version of humans, the filigoto had no homeland other than whatever they traveled in. They became traders by necessity.

"Good evening, all. I'm Weyargo. Here to trade," he said with his melodic, lilting voice.

Many townspeople encircled his flatbed to see what he had brought. Malja knew a few filigoto. They were fine enough creatures. Never bothered her much. And they often brought tales from other countries.

"Corlin," most would say, "is the only place to be. The others are empty of everything. Towns are so far apart, and there are so few people."

Indeed, Malja heard Weyargo speaking a similar line to his new customers. He probably praised whatever country he was in. "It's what I've always told those from other lands. You must come to Corlin. It seems most of the people in the world live in this wonderful country. Now, ma'am, doesn't that look lovely? I'll make a fair deal with you."

While Weyargo made one fair deal after another, his magician rested. Malja watched that one closely. Just in case. He twitched a few times and seemed unsure of his surroundings, but all went well.

The townspeople were so high on their success that they bought more than they should — fabrics and spices from Penmorvia to the north, shovels and hoes from Corlin towns to the east, and more alcohol from wherever (no one cared). When the last purchase had been made, Weyargo blew kisses to the people as he climbed into the driver's seat. "Thank you all," he said. "Enjoy your new things, and I promise to stop by when I come back this way later in the year. May Korstra and Kryssta smile upon you all."

The magician concentrated on his tattoo. With a bang, the flyer's engines ignited. The people stepped back, making a commotion of startled laughter as it lifted into the air and flew away.

To see a working flyer like that had been quite an event. Most people went their entire lives without ever seeing anything move that wasn't hitched up to horses. For these townspeople, this day had become far more memorable than any battle victory in the past.

Once the trader left, the musicians started up again, and the party resumed with even greater enthusiasm than before thanks to the extra alcohol. Malja surveyed the townspeople, searching for the handsome man. She found him dancing with a plump gal, twirling and laughing and flashing a charming smile. Malja didn't dance which was exactly why he caught her eye and waved her over.

When she stood, her alcohol-soaked head spun. She played it up and begged off the dancing. To her surprise, and the plump girl's ire, the man left the dance floor and walked over to her.

"You didn't have to stop dancing for me," she said.

"Well, you are the guest of honor," he said. Then in a mock-conspiratorial whisper, he added, "Besides, Nalli is a nice girl, but she talks a lot and steps on my feet."

Malja finished her drink in two gulps. "I'm not much of

a dancer. Your feet might be safer with Nalli."

"You trying to say I should be nicer to her?"

Malja laced her fingers behind her head and stretched back. She didn't miss his eyes snatching a peek at her breasts. "I've seen a few towns and I'll tell you this much — most are far less friendly."

"Well, we like being friendly," he said as he stroked her knee.

"That's a bit bold."

"You don't get anywhere waiting for things to just happen."

Malja licked her lips. Traveling such an empty land meant she often went without human contact for long periods, and though she couldn't picture settling down in one town for any length of time, she wondered if a girl like Nalli had it better. Safer, certainly, but safer didn't mean much. She felt far more alive during the dangerous times in her life than the calm ones. Except for sex, nothing quite matched.

But sex often did. And with the life she led, that kind of contact rarely found her. No way would she miss a good opportunity — especially a good-looking good opportunity. "Let's go," she said, pulling on his wrist.

"What?"

"Will we be bothered in the stables?"

As Malja led the way, the man's face shifted from confusion to excitement. "By the way," he said, "my name is —"

"Don't care."

The closer they came to the stables, the hotter Malja's blood burned. The second they stepped inside, she wrenched him around and pressed her lips against his. They stood and kissed while music played in the distance. But her mind refused to shut off its game of remembering horrors.

She saw the bleeding head of Duke Brotta as she tossed it into a swarm of hungry konapols.

"Something wrong?" the man asked.

"Harder," she said, smushing her mouth into his. She grasped his body, squeezing and rubbing. She leaned back, letting him lick her neck. But she saw the emaciated magician Lexip as she burned him alive.

She ripped open her lover's shirt and fumbled off his pants. She heard the wet slush of the Bluesman's sliced body. With a push, she sent her man to the ground. The scent of seawater and bile attacked her nose. She slipped out of her assault suit, straddled her partner, took hold of him and thrilled to his startled gasps as she guided him inside.

For a few minutes, her drunken mind shut down. The flashes of her violent past went dark and only the rough pleasure between her legs remained. She lifted slow and dropped hard, grinding her pelvis toward the ground, trying to think only of her technique and the sheer delight of skin on skin.

She had no illusions of a grand climax. For all his bravado, she could tell her lover lacked experience. The man tried to say something, but she ignored him. She simply took what he could offer and collapsed when he had nothing left

With her head on his chest, she listened to his heavy breathing and pounding heartbeat. Those memories itched to return, but she refused to give in. She rolled onto her back, pulled her man on top, and pressed down on his head until he got the message. She would not let him come up for air until she had her release.

* * * *

Malja woke to the sound of a horse being saddled. The rider shushed and cursed and snapped at the horse. With her head throbbing, Malja sat up, careful not to disturb the man next to her, and investigated the noise.

Fawbry.

She sneered as she pulled Viper from her clothes pile. She walked straight into view, letting Viper lead as her threat. Fawbry startled at her approach. His face dropped in disbelief.

"You're naked," he said.

"And you're trying to escape. Question is — will you sit down and let me tie you up or are you going to do something stupid and let me kill you?"

Chapter 5

The first cool day of the Postkryssta season had arrived. It wouldn't be long before the mornings began with a light frost and the chilly Korstraprime rains would follow soon after. Tommy nestled in front of Malja as she guided the horse back to Ms. Nolan's mansion. A second horse trailed behind with Fawbry bound in rope. She had intended for Fawbry to walk but the people of Noograff wanted to give her the bay in thanks. She still considered making Fawbry walk — especially after his attempted escape; however, she succumbed to the lure of faster travel. Especially with colder weather coming.

"I ought to thank you," Fawbry said. He had a north-country voice now that he wasn't playing Mayor — a slight accent as if educated from an early year. "Really," he continued. "I wasn't very good at that Mayor-leader thing, but I couldn't get out of it. I thought my incompetent leadership would've ended it, but those griffles refused to go and I didn't want them angry with me. They would've torn me apart. Literally. But they're loyal, I guess. Anyway, they probably think I'm dead now. By Kryssta, I would've been dead, if not for you."

Tommy pressed against Malja, trying to sleep despite Fawbry's ramblings. She rested a hand on the boy's thin shoulder.

"Anyway, thanks," Fawbry said. "And I'm sorry about this morning. I'm sure you understand. I've got to take the opportunities as they come. Nothing personal. So tell me about Ms. Nolan. You work for her long? What's she like?"

"Fawbry."

"Yes?"

"Stop talking."

As they traveled on, Malja fought against her mounting excitement. She had explored too much of the Corlin countryside, battled too many of its inhabitants, and suffered too greatly at its callous hand — all just to find Jarik and Callib. She had never felt closer. Yet she had grown accustomed to her best leads drifting into the air like dust. Fawbry, though, seemed to be the right kind of coward — the kind that worried about an immediate threat more than one far away. She expected her pressure on him to bring results.

Then she'll have Jarik and Callib. She'll track them down. Confront them. And before she sinks Viper down their throats, she'll get answers.

Tommy startled awake and looked at Malja with concern. She must have tensed her muscles without realizing. Patting his shoulder, she eased him back into slumber. It wasn't so easy to calm her thoughts.

That night they camped against a burnt-out home — only two stone walls remained. Fawbry tried to engage her in conversation, but she ignored him. No point in talking when she would be rid of him soon enough. Tommy, perhaps still high from the party, approached Fawbry with his hands together.

"What?" Fawbry asked. "You want to pray? You know about Kryssta?"

Malja snorted. "He wants to play The Reflex Game." To Tommy, she said, "It's okay. You can untie him."

Tommy did so and eagerly pantomimed how to play. Malja pulled out her eight-page book and read a little, but mostly she watched Fawbry. She had no fear of untying him. She recognized weakness and knew he wouldn't dare use Tommy as an escape. Still, she watched.

Though not as fun as the night before, she could see that Tommy enjoyed playing with Fawbry. And, to her surprise, Fawbry appeared equally amused. The sight of her cowardly prisoner slapping hands with her sweet boy made her feel odd because it seemed so normal. The boy amazed her. After all he had been through, he could still be a kid. She wished she could know his secret.

"Want to play?" Fawbry asked, while rubbing his red hands.

She was about to say *No* when Tommy pulled her over by the arm. They played the game, teasing and striking and feigning, until Tommy went to sleep. Without a word, Malja tied Fawbry up — a coward like him would run when she fell asleep. She returned to her book.

Fawbry shook his head. "I got no place to go, y'know." She didn't answer. "Right. I'll just be over here if you need me." He managed a few more sarcastic comments but eventually quieted down.

For awhile, Malja just soaked in the silence.

* * * *

Late the next day, they reached Ms. Nolan's mansion. Malja's heart sank. The main gate had been smashed open and bullet holes marred the concrete pillars. The number of bullet holes spoke to a large group attacking with great purpose — one doesn't waste bullets on a small target. Ms. Nolan was important, yet Malja couldn't help but wonder — *maybe they had expected me to be there.*

The gate guard lay dead on the ground, his white sash spattered in crimson. The four northern konapols never made it out of their cages. Their lifeless eyes stared at Malja, mocking her.

She dismounted, and with Tommy's help, untied Fawbry.

"You're letting me go?" he asked, rubbing his arms.

Malja checked the guard's body for weapons or anything useful, but found nothing. He'd already been searched. "You can go, but you won't."

"Really now? Why's that?"

"Because Ms. Nolan is probably dead. Somebody's working hard to kill off anybody who can help me with information. Who do you suppose is next?"

"Who? Me?" Fawbry hugged himself, looking smaller than ever before. "I don't know anything."

"You do, and you'll help me."

"But—"

"Do you think you're safer alone or by my side?" Malja asked and trudged into the mansion. She said nothing when she heard Fawbry follow.

The interior faired worse than the exterior. The intruders had run out of ammunition or working guns and resorted to melee weapons. Fires burned low in the corners offering enough light to see. Five people hung from the foyer beams — the staff.

"Perhaps the boy and I should wait outside," Fawbry said, but Tommy sped up, passing them all for the large room where they had first met Ms. Nolan.

The statue of Prophet Galot lay in three large pieces and thousands of tiny marble shards as if the Devastation had happened again. Furniture had been piled into meager barriers working toward the back hall. Ms. Nolan had mounted a noble defense though outnumbered and inexperienced.

Stepping over the cracked waterways, Malja saw a dark spot on the floor. Though she knew the answer, she leaned in to be sure — blood. Fawbry interrupted her thoughts.

"You think anybody lived through this?"

Glass shattered down the hall followed by an anguished cry. The sound echoed throughout the mansion. The cry of a burning soul.

"Never mind," Fawbry said. "I don't want to know."

Tommy settled against a wall, pouting at Malja's body language. She needed him out of the way and safe. Though he clearly wanted to come with her, she was pleased that he knew what times called for what actions. Fawbry would have to learn.

"Stay here," she said. Fawbry opened his mouth, probably to protest any plan other than leaving right away, but Malja glowered at him.

With a nervous nod, he raised a finger as if making an intellectual point. "I'll stay here."

Malja slunk down the hall, wielding Viper and watching every flickering shadow. The intricately carved door to the Dry Room had been blasted outward as if a giant fist had punched through it. Inside, she found Ms. Nolan, a guard, and another man — their bodies stacked in the corner like a cord of wood. The cage that held Ms. Nolan's sister, Audrex, no longer held anyone. The bars had been torn apart. Splintered wood and twisted metal littered the expensive floor.

Malja examined the corpses. Ms. Nolan's face had locked in a final expression of agony. Or *maybe betrayal,* Malja considered while glancing at the empty cage. Bruises covered the guard's body and his clothes were soaked. Drowned or beaten to death. Malja hoped for beaten — drowning ... no, she couldn't think about the thief's ship. Not now.

The third corpse caused Malja's stomach to squeeze tight. He wore a suit — all black, trim cut, black shirt, gold buttons. She looked closer at the wood scattered on the floor. Not too far away she found it — little pieces of guitar. One chunk had the letters BLU carved in it. The rest of the word lay elsewhere on the floor, but Malja knew it well.

"Ms. Nolan, looks like you were right. They did come for you," she said with a bitter chuckle. The evidence troubled her, though. She could see well enough that these Bluesmen attacked (she didn't want to get stuck on the fact that the Bluesmen had shifted from a lone assassin to an organized group) and that Ms. Nolan's people defended hard. In the end, the Bluesmen won out. The most troubling part — Audrex's cage. If Ms. Nolan had let the madwoman loose as some last desperate weapon, she would have opened it without destroying it. Besides which, Malja could not see Ms. Nolan using her sister like that. Not if her story was true. The Bluesmen, however, would be idiots to rip open the cage. They would have unleashed an insane magician upon themselves. Judging from the Bluesman she had killed in the woods, they were not idiots. The only other explanation she could see involved a stray gunshot. But such a blast would have pushed the bars inward not outward.

Unless ...

Malja's heart raced as she envisioned a deadly possibility — a trap. The Bluesmen kill Nolan. They know Malja will be returning. They want to kill her, but they don't want to be around for it. Why? Because they're not supposed to kill her. But she killed one of theirs, and they're mad. They set some kind of explosive device to Audrex's cage, or perhaps they have a magician who can do such a spell. They leave. The explosion blasts the door, rips up the bodies, and frees an insane magician. Audrex is a trap.

Before Malja heard the scream, she dashed toward the main room. She flew in and saw Fawbry curled in a ball, hiding in his multi-colored robe, blubbering for help. A column of water stood over him, its body shifting from basic shapes to hideous faces to tortuous blades. Malja slashed through the water, and the twisting column fell like a deluge of rain.

"Are you hurt?" she asked while looking for Tommy. She found him where she had left him — against the wall.

Fawbry stood on teetering legs. "I'm fine. There was this crazy woman—"

"I know."

A tendril of water shot out from the waterways, a monstrous mouth drooling water at its tip. Malja cut it down but another rose farther on. As she cut through the new threat, another appeared. She spun toward the latest tendril but one more snuck from the side and slammed her head with water. The force hit like solid ice, knocking her down and rattling her skull. The water continued to shower her. It wouldn't let up. She struggled for air. Her lungs strained. Her chest burned.

Without enough air for her full strength, she still struck out at the tendril drowning her. She didn't slice through it but hit it hard enough to break off its assault. When it stopped, she gasped and coughed and spit up water.

Audrex entered at the far end of the room. Her bloodshot eyes refused to blink. She stepped into the waterway. If she had any sanity while in the cage, it too had escaped. She looked like an abstract drawing — every feature askew, every detail off-kilter. In a high-pitched cackle that pricked their skin, she said, "This is my home."

She stared at the tattoo on her arm and the water trembled. Her previous conjuring had taken its toll. Malja had a small window to act. Still coughing and off-balance, she used a smashed chair to help get on her feet. Her brain thrummed as if someone had wrapped her head in a blanket and smacked it.

"They're almost ready," Audrex said. The lustful yearning in her voice told Malja who *they* were — Jarik and Callib. "Soon the brothers will have the power to fix this blighted world. They'll emerge from hiding and save us all." Four dragonfly wings issued from her back and fanned out as if preparing to fly. "But no matter what — this is my home."

As Malja reoriented herself, she caught Fawbry watching like a spectator, his mouth as wide as his eyes. She had moved too slowly. She could read it on Fawbry's face. She braced for a fierce blow when she spotted Tommy — *Oh no,* she thought.

A crackling bolt of lightning arced from the air near Tommy and struck the water. A screech poured out of Audrex like a foul wind filling the room with its revolting presence. Malja spun — her head dipped and weaved. A column of water, jagged like knives, froze in place. Electricity coursed through it and reached out for Audrex. Her body jittered as if performing a possessed dance. Her eyes rolled back. Smoke rose from her arms and wings.

"Tommy, stop!" Malja said, but the boy continued. She could see the determination on his face — he meant to kill.

Summoning her remaining strength, Malja sprinted across the room, pulled back Viper, and swung through the madwoman's neck. Her head splashed in the water, the jagged column collapsed, and her screeching silenced. Tommy let out a breath and clambered to his feet. The smell of burnt air mixed with burnt skin. He swaggered toward Malja and offered a proud smile. Without pause, she slapped it away.

Catching her breath and forcing herself not to yell, she said, "You are not a killer."

An enraged grimace formed on his tight lips, and he

bolted outside but not fast enough. Malja saw his tears. She waited a moment to compose herself. The boy needed time to calm — they both did. Besides, she still had things to do. While cleaning Viper before sheathing the blade, she said, "Okay, Fawbry, time to speak."

"What?" he said, still shaken by all that had happened.

"The late Ms. Nolan said you had information that would help me find Jarik and Callib. I didn't go through all this to come out with nothing."

Fawbry tugged at his hair. "No, no, no. That's not fair. You can't do this to me."

"I am doing this."

"Go find someone else."

"Sorry. You've got the information."

"Is this how you deal with everything in your life — threats, coercion? You should try being nice to people. Didn't your mother ever teach you to be nice?"

Malja punched Fawbry in the gut. "Watch what you say."

"Sure," Fawbry groaned. "The hell with nice. This is much better."

"I'm not interested in anything else about you except what you know."

"Right. Jarik and Callib. Do you know what those lunatics will do to me if I help you? Have you any clue what their capable of?"

"More than you know."

"Then why ask me? You should know I can't."

"Stay by me, and you'll be safe."

"Like I was safe here?" he said, ending in a squealing scream. "No, and no again." He froze at the sight of blood on his hand. Not his, but Malja suspected that only made matters worse. He plunged his hands into the waterway without Audrex's body and scrubbed. "You," he said, snapping out his words, "are not safe."

Malja resisted the urge to throttle the man. Instead, she spread her hands and said, "Then tell me. What do you need to feel safe?"

"To feel safe enough to tattle out Jarik and Callib? You're joking, right?" Malja glared at him, and he shrunk back. He muttered to himself, and his chest sagged. "You don't really want me. Trust me. I know only one thing, one person who might know where they are. That's it. That's all I know. Hardly worth all this effort."

"If it's so meaningless, then give me the name."

Fawbry's face contorted as he strained for an escape. He looked from one side to the other. No answer appeared. His wild hair made him look cornered, and for a moment, Malja thought he might strike out like one of his oxters.

But he brightened a fraction. Then a bit more. An idea had formed. "Fine, fine. You want me to talk? Take me to Barris Mont. He can keep me safe. You get me to him, and I'll tell you the name."

"Thought I wasn't safe."

"I'm not stupid," Fawbry shouted. "You're better than nothing. And I'm marked now. Right? So, you take me to Barris, okay? That's the deal."

Malja nodded. "So where is this guy?"

"He's not a guy. He's a ... well, he owes me. He lives near Lyngrovet. At Dead Lake."

Wonderful.

Chapter 6

The rich campfire aroma did little to soothe Malja. Though Tommy and Fawbry had been snoring loudly since sundown, Malja couldn't quiet her tired head long enough to fall asleep. They had been riding west for several days, but not making good time. The horses needed extra rest. They had been pushed hard, and the Postkryssta coolness had given way to a surprising, late blast of heat. Malja figured it would be better to go slowly, if it meant still having the horses in the long run. Besides, if she rode the horses into the grave, Tommy would be even angrier with her. For a boy who didn't talk, he had become even quieter since their fight.

She stood, stepped to the side, and faced away from the fire before stretching her sore body. She didn't think about the motions, designed to keep her night vision clear and her awareness toward possible danger, she just moved. Her popping joints blended with the snapping fire. Stifling a yawn, she walked to a wide stream nearby. The conjured assault suit she wore never needed cleaning, but she did. She removed her clothes and stepped into the cold water. Her over-heated body relished the sensation, and she carefully undid the braids in her long hair, letting the water seep in all the way to her scalp. If only everything in knots could be undone so easily.

As she washed off dirt and sweat, her hands felt the ridges and valleys of her numerous scars. *They're my tattoos.* Except these didn't turn a person into an object of power. These didn't drive a person mad. It was so unfair — an innocent boy like Tommy doomed for nothing. Nobody asked him if he wanted to be a magician. He had no choice.

Nobody gave me a choice either.

Gregor had tried to build a normal life for her. He had given her dolls and dresses. Took her flower-picking. Built her a dollhouse, even. But the magicians had done their damage. She ignored the dollhouse and played with the kitchen knives. She dirtied the dresses with mud and blood. She sliced through hordes of pansies and violets. *When those bastards are dead,* she thought, *then I'll have a choice. And Tommy will, too.*

She remembered reaching out to Tommy's cowering form, offering to rescue him — *No, I can't allow myself to rewrite the past.* The night she found him should remain a night she paid honor.

Bending backward so her head cooled in the water but her ears stayed just above and always aware, Malja opened the gates on this one particular memory. Not to pay any honor, she decided, but simply to be honest with herself.

She remembered waking to urgent banging on the cabin door. She remembered the churning sea rolling her stomach like a thoughtless mother rocking her baby too hard. She remembered the young crewman standing in the corridor.

He wore blue, threadbare trousers, a filthy, torn shirt, and a round, white cap — what passed for a uniform on a thief's ship. He took her to see Captain Wuchev, and when they stepped into the narrow corridor, she saw blood decorated the metallic walls in long slashes. Through one cabin door, a crewman slumped over dead, his hair matted and gooey. Mage-rats, the crewman explained, had conjured the storm and raided the ship.

She had chosen to take the boat to avoid this very thing. She thought she could cut across the water to save time and lives in her effort to find Jarik and Callib. But the violent world always followed her like a foul dog.

Captain Wuchev stated it all clearly. The salvaged-metal ship had a rounded back like a half-shell and a wide main deck thrusting forward with three makeshift masts cut into the rusting deck. In a heavy storm they were useless, but before leaving shore, he had a magician conjure electric power and stored it in batteries.

"Up there," he said nodding to the front of the ship, "you'll find the battery station. I've got one left. There's a lever to switch over to the full battery."

"No problem. I'll cut through the cargo hold and —"

"If it were that simple, I'd have this weasel do it." He pointed to the young crewman. "The hold is armed with spells I had installed for this trip. It even held off those thieving pirates. They got everything else, but they didn't get my prize. So, no, you can't go in there. You got to go outside."

Crossing the main deck had been brutal. Powerful winds screamed in her ears and shoved her around. The rain bounced off her assault suit like impatient fingers beating a random rhythm. Icy water found its way down her neck and underneath the suit. It drenched her in seconds. Lightning flashed and thunder cracked. The smell of salty, ocean water blended with her nausea.

She worked her way from one key point to the next. A stack of containers lashed to the deck. A door level with the deck. The first mast. When it came time to run for the second, the ship lurched upward and she fell.

On the rain-soaked deck, Malja swooshed down and gained too much momentum. She slid right by the second mast and rolled on her back only to see the third mast coming upon her like an immovable wall hungry to break her bones. *Viper!* She spun onto her stomach, snatched

Viper from her back, and slammed the blade into the deck. With a trail of sparks and the shriek of metal grinding metal, Viper dug in and slowed Malja's descent.

The ship crested. Malja jumped to her feet and stumbled for the door. Every muscle moved, but with maddening sloth. She pried it open, and once inside, heat enveloped her. She leaned back against the door and took a moment to shiver in the darkness.

The room smelled foul like rotting food and feces. Even with no light, she felt cramped. Soon her body would move again. As her heart calmed and her breathing slowed, she heard breaths she had not taken. They were quick and shallow — fearful. Someone hid here.

She listened close, building a mental picture of what she heard — breathing in the corner, scuffing feet as the person tried to melt into the wall, metal rattling. Malja stepped forward, holding Viper back, ready to attack. A spark popped from the corner followed by a ball of sizzling electricity. A magician. Though blinded by the sudden light, Malja swung Viper in front of her.

Often in battle, time slowed. This moment, it slowed enough to see that her enemy was not an enemy. It slowed enough for her to pull Viper back before beheading a child.

All went dark again as the spell dissipated. Malja took a few steps back, staring at the black space where a little boy cowered.

"It's okay," she said. "I won't hurt you. I thought you were a pirate. I'm sorry. I promise I won't hurt you."

With another pop, a small electric ball ignited in the air near the boy. He wore remnants of clothing and had been chained to a large pipe passing through the room. To her left, Malja saw a light switch. She flicked on the dim bulbs so the boy didn't have to maintain his spell. A gentle humming came from Malja's right. Looking that way, she saw two batteries, each towering over her. At eye level, a meter read full on one and three-quarters on the other. Her forehead wrinkled as she turned to the boy.

"He uses you for electricity?"

The boy said nothing.

"He said we were running out of power." Malja thought over the treacherous crossing of the main deck. *Wuchev expected me to die out there.* "Is Captain Wuchev working with the mage-pirates?"

The boy said nothing.

Magician or not, Malja refused to let a little boy be treated like property. "Close your eyes," she said, and flipped Viper so it would strike on the outer-crescent. With careful aim, she swung onto the chains. After three solid hits, the metal gave way, falling to the floor with a freeing clatter.

Rubbing his sore hands, the boy gazed up at Malja and offered a grateful nod.

"I'm Malja."

A smile crept onto the boy's face.

"You got a name?"

The boy returned to his sullen silence.

"No? How about ... Tommy? It's a bit unusual, but then again, so are you."

Again, the boy smiled, and Malja found a glimmer of pleasure warm her.

Listening to Fawbry and Tommy snore as she dried off, Malja felt that same glimmer inside. She just hoped she hadn't snuffed out the matching one in Tommy. He did his jobs — took care of the horses, collected firewood, helped find water — but he barely glanced in her direction.

"I'm sorry," she whispered before settling in to sleep. "But I hope you'll understand. Someday."

＊ ＊ ＊ ＊

Morning arrived with the appetizing aroma of eggs cooking in sweet milk and onions. Malja kept her eyes closed, letting the flavors in the air tempt her tongue. For a moment, she thought she would hear Gregor's deep melodies telling her about planting seasons or Corlin history or why evil must be fought by good people. When she opened her eyes, she found Tommy, and while she missed Gregor terribly, the boy was a welcome sight. He pulled a skillet from the fire and offered her a plate. He then took his own plate and sat facing away.

"Where did all this come from?" she asked, hoping the tears welling inside her did not fall.

Fawbry appeared from behind a tree, buttoning his fly, and said, "I figured Ms. Nolan wouldn't miss a few items. You know, your boy is quite handy with a skillet."

Sitting up, Malja said, "He's not my boy."

"Oh. Sorry."

"I can't have children. I don't menstruate."

The shock on Fawbry's face matched her own. Maybe she had not fully awakened, maybe the weight of the last few days had finally hit her, but the words just blurted out.

Fawbry stood, plate in hand, unable to speak.

"I think Jarik and Callib did it to me. Makes me a better warrior, I guess." She dug into her breakfast and Fawbry followed. "Parents do that kind of thing sometimes. They can be harsh to try to make you better." Tommy didn't react, so she focused on her food. It warmed her belly and calmed her body. Afterwards, she acted as if she had not said anything so personal. Fawbry played along.

"We'll get there today," Fawbry said while saddling his horse.

"Good."

"We just have to cross the Yad."

She knew this would be required, but she hated it regardless. The Yad River cut through the Corlin countryside like an old bone fracture. Its waters ran deep and fast. There were no bridges but plenty of bridge remains. Officially (not that there were any officials), nobody knew why the bridges always failed along the Yad. Some thought the fish used their natural connection with magic to fight what they perceived as an invasion. Some thought the warring brother gods, Korstra and Kryssta, caused the destruction. Most, however, believed every attempt to bridge the river failed because of sabotage.

The Muyaza magicians controlled all crossings of the Yad. They had their lives tied to it. As long as they existed, no bridges would last. They had established villages at all the key points and sent teams up and down the riverbank looking for anybody stupid enough to start constructing a bridge. They never left enough proof that they were responsible for the accidents that followed.

Long before reaching the Muyaza village, Malja smelled them. They did not bathe out of contempt for water. It was something to be controlled and dominated — nothing more. The other smell cutting through the air balanced out the rank odor — cooking meats. Soon the trees thinned out, and Malja saw the village forming a half-circle facing the river.

The Yad stretched off into the distance. Its waters sped along, creating a dull rumble. The massive amount of moving water cooled the air with its fishy odor. One look vanquished any hope of crossing without the Muyaza.

A small line of people formed outside the village. Two boys sat up front. They collected the toll. They had rich, golden-brown skin and striking, dark eyes. Muscular arms and chiseled chests found unlikely pairings with ripples of fat around the neck and round potbellies. Waddles of loose skin hung below wide lips. Along their sides grew thick bumps that moved like the stumps of amputated limbs.

They wore dark, heavy animal skins which, Malja admitted, looked better than some of the ad hoc creations people muddled together. Each also wore a carved piece of wood in the hair. Some wore cubes. Some wore a swooping curve. Others wore a jagged bolt.

"I'd hate to give up a horse," Malja whispered as they took their place in line, "but what else do we have?" This type of negotiation never worked well for her. She knew how to bargain when holding Viper at somebody's throat. The finesse required for a less threatening situation often eluded her.

Fawbry puffed up. "Don't worry. I know these creatures."

The line moved slowly while the boys inspected each offering with care. Most customers were quiet, humble, and knew what to bring. Food held the most value. Using magic to cross the river burned a lot of energy. Offering a chicken, a dazku, or such got fast, respectful service. Items that could be traded for food at a later date were met with grumbling and negotiating.

One man offered his services as a cook. The boys said no. He argued and pleaded. "We got cooks," they said and pointed for him to leave. The man got angry and yelled obscenities. In no time, three adults walked from the village, each carrying a club adorned with rusty nails and flexing their oversized arms. Before they reached the line, the man had slinked away.

"You sure about this?" Malja asked Fawbry. She didn't want to end up having to kill those three men because Fawbry wanted to take responsibility and screwed up.

"I'm not a brave man," Fawbry said. "Trust me. I want

to get across the river without any trouble."

Malja couldn't argue — partially because of his brazen honesty and partially because their turn in line came up.

The two boys looked bored and petulant. "How many?" one said with a thick, guttural accent.

Like a traveling merchant, Fawbry raised his hands to punctuate his words. His multi-colored robe fanned out, mesmerizing the boys for an instant. "The three of us, plus the two horses."

"What you pay?" one boy said, fighting his urge to smile at Fawbry's entertaining form.

Fawbry moved closer to the boys while checking over his shoulder. "Look here," he said. The boys peered into his hand and exchanged an unsure look. One boy motioned to the other. The other jogged off to confer with one of the adults. The way the adult scowled gave Malja an itch to grab Viper and prepare for slaughter. Though she could control her hands, her eyes still sought out battle information. The longer the boy and the man talked, the more she saw the fight coming.

She noted how flat the land lay. The hill they came down was too far back for any initial advantage. She observed those in line, gauging if any posed a serious threat. The boy trotted back and whispered to his cohort. Malja focused on the adult watching from a distance. Any sign of an attack and she would take out the boys first. She hated the idea but the shock might gain her enough time to save Tommy and herself. Maybe even Fawbry.

The boy giving orders swiped the object from Fawbry's hand and said, "We see you again, food or no cross."

"Of course, of course. Thank you," Fawbry said. He even added a slight bow and waved to the adult glaring at them. "Thank you," he yelled.

As they walked toward the village proper, Malja asked,

"What did you give them?"

"Nolan's coin."

Malja let a grin escape and swore she heard Tommy snigger.

A young Muyaza woman stood by a small hut. She asked how many were crossing and if the horses would go, too. With an unreadable face, she led them into the inner-yard. The constant activity exhausted Malja just to watch.

The tribe worked hard all day. Each member had a specific task, all designed to get people across the river. In front of the small huts, the women cooked non-stop, using large cauldrons and whatever food came there way. Some plucked feathers, some butchered a carcass, while some stirred and stirred. Mangy correts and squeaking pheng-mice scampered for bones and gristle amongst the waste piles. A long table stretched toward the shore. Sitting on the gravelly sand, the men surrounded the table and shoveled in food like starving orphans. Meats and vegetables piled high in bowls kept arriving. The older ones received deference while eating, but the extra food did not help. All the elderly men were skeletal, wasting away. They looked lost and confused.

Malja missed the signal, but somehow three men were assigned to them — two young, one old. This was always the combination. The two men lifted a wooden litter from a tall stack. They placed it next to the old man and waited with patience as the young woman guided him to the center. With the grace and expertise of people who have done this for a lifetime, they lifted the litter and rested its arms on their fat-padded shoulders. The young woman gestured for Malja and her group to follow the men to the river.

Malja started at the sight before her. She heard Tommy gasp. All across the river, dotting the waters from shore to shore, Malja saw these three-man teams, each surrounded in a shimmering bubble of air. The Muyaza magicians practiced only this one spell, and they did it well. The old ones sat on the litters, focused on their tattooed legs, and created the protective bubble so the others could walk across.

"Come on," Fawbry said, for their team already had walked to the shore. As impatient as Fawbry sounded, Malja caught him running his forefinger across his forehead — a sign of prayer to Kryssta.

Why not? They were stepping into a river, a rushing body of water, something which under other circumstances she avoided. To make it worse, the only thing protecting them was an old man's magic.

Magic ability varied from magician to magician. Part of it was training. Part of it was innate. Some could glance at their tattoos and have a solid spell in a few seconds. Others worked harder. And others strained the whole time. Likewise some spells required more effort even from the best magicians.

The Muyaza tried to use only the best among them — drownings were bad for business — but Malja didn't know this magic well enough to judge the quality of their assigned magician. Her mouth dried as she neared the water. She tried not to think about magicians, magic, or madness. *Just keep walking.*

Water rose around them, as did Malja's tension, but the field did not puncture. The Muyaza had lined this section of the riverbed with wood planks so they could walk without stumbling over slippery rocks and uneven terrain. Spotted fish swam up, stared at the people and horses, mouthed a few O's, and swam away.

Malja tentatively ran her fingers across where she expected the field to be. Her fingers vibrated and the sensation rushed up her arm, shaking her bones. She snatched back her hand and rubbed it on her leg. It didn't hurt, but it was not something she wanted to experience again.

The farther they walked, the higher the water rose. Despite her assault suit's attempt to regulate her temperature, Malja shivered and sweat prickled a line down her neck. She worried about the bubble having enough air. She worried about the old man dying suddenly. She thought about the pain of drowning.

And she thought of the thief's ship and the way she had killed Captain Wuchev. *Tommy better appreciate this.*

About halfway across, the river became shallow, and the Muyaza halted for the old magician to rest a moment. Water passed over their feet and splashed on their ankles. Malja glanced back to see the village had become tiny. That's when she saw the Bluesman.

She whipped out her spyglass to check — another dark-skinned, dark suited fellow with a guitar. This one had a gray beard and one eye clouded over. He argued with the Muyaza. Probably wanted them to hurry.

"Something wrong?" Fawbry asked.

"No," she said, closing the spyglass. "Not yet."

When they reached the opposite shore, they thanked the Muyaza. The men nodded. The village on this side mirrored the one they had left as if the river had cut one village in half. The two litter-carriers set the old magician down with great care as a young woman arrived to guide him to the food table.

Malja mounted her horse, invigorated to be on an animal on solid ground again. "Let's get moving."

Chapter 7

The hours that followed threatened to bring about the ghosts of Malja's memory, but she managed to deflect such thought by focusing on Dead Lake. Fawbry called it a reminder of how the Devastation had changed the world. Before, the area had been composed of hills and forests, roads and towns, houses and families. Children played in their yards, climbing trees and throwing balls. Mothers and fathers worked to better their families and society. Magicians strolled the streets like holy leaders of peace and prosperity.

In the instant of the Devastation, the town vanished. A giant hole engulfed the land and rains filled it in. Those unfortunate enough not to disappear with the land and roads and homes floated in the new lake, adding their blood to the water.

All these years later, little life had returned. The innocent blood poisoned the shores. Nothing grew. Gray rocks littered the ground and the occasional bone washed up in the limp tides. It reminded Malja of the Freelands — a dark, wet version.

Hazy fog rolled off the waters bringing on night a few hours early. Tommy shifted in the saddle, and Malja tried to comfort him with a firm hold, but he shirked off her arm. The horses' various sounds — hoof against stone, air forced through nostrils, headshakes jingling reins — amplified in the narrowing visibility. Malja's eyes never ceased searching for threats.

"Almost there," Fawbry said, his eagerness

unmistakable.

All of what counted for civilization lay so far back that Malja understood why Fawbry might feel safe here. Desolate and destroyed, the area would be lonely, but alone and alive sounded better than surrounded by others and dead. A figure appeared in the haze causing Malja to reconsider the "alone" part.

"It's okay," Fawbry said. "They're just the Chi-Chun."

"I thought they were a story."

"No, the Chi-Chun have existed for a long time. I'm not saying they really have the magic to ward off the dead. Frankly, I don't really believe the dead are going to rise. But they believe."

As they rode by, Tommy's hand trembled. Malja fought off the urge to respond. The Chi-Chun presented a frightening figure. He stood six feet tall, but seemed bigger, framed by bony trees and thin foliage. He wore a frayed, black robe — tattered cloth that draped him like seaweed. He stood motionless with his hooded head hung low and his arms outstretched. Malja imagined the pain his arms would radiate after only a few minutes. If the stories were true, he would stand like that for several hours.

Fawbry explained that the Chi-Chun were a sect of Korstrians that had few but highly devoted followers. They believed Dead Lake was the epicenter of the Devastation and if not constantly kept in check, a second blast would occur, strong enough to ensure extinction for every living thing. "According to their texts, the first sign of this blast will be the return of all the dead at Dead Lake," Fawbry said with a derisive snort.

"Wait, wait," Malja said. "You can read?"

"No, of course not," he said with a fumbling cough. "And if I could, I wouldn't waste my time with Chi-Chun nonsense. I mean, they spend hours like that for what?

Another will come along to relieve them. Then they go to their little commune, pray, eat, sleep, start all over. Nothing else. What kind of life is that?"

Malja settled back in the saddle. She didn't care about the Chi-Chun, but to find another who could read thrilled her. He could deny it all he wanted, but she had heard the education in his voice earlier, and now he let slip that he could read.

Gregor had taught her and if for nothing else, she loved him for that infinite gift. Jarik and Callib had taught her much as well but only what served them — never what would solely benefit her. Teaching a child should be an act of love in many ways. For Jarik and Callib, it was an act of control.

Over the next hour, they saw three more Chi-Chun. One stood unsteady, his arms shaking. Fawbry said that one must be new. Malja thought they looked like creepy scarecrows. They existed, after all, to scare away the dead.

"We're here," Fawbry said, but to Malja, this patch of gray looked much the same as any other they had traveled across.

Tommy nudged her and pointed to the one difference. A decrepit, wooden dock poked out into the water like a splinter. The lake lapped against it with a steady, dull clap. A Chi-Chun stood her outstretched vigil at the tip of the dock like a ghost forever waiting a lover's return.

After dismounting and tethering the horses, Malja and Tommy stood back while Fawbry approached the lake. For a coward, he seemed to be quite gutsy. Fawbry squatted and slapped the water three times, paused, slapped three times, paused, and continued the pattern for a full minute. The Chi-Chun stiffened at the disruption but did not break her pose.

Fawbry straightened, cupped his mouth, and called out,

"Barris! Barris Mont!"

Malja kept close watch on the motionless Chi-Chun and readied for an attack. Fawbry called out again, his voice fading in the fog but still crossing the water. The Chi-Chun lowered her arms, turned around, and removed her hood.

Her night-black skin hid most of her features like the dark lake hid its depths. Only her deep-set eyes — a bold, sickly yellow — and her matted hair — knotted with weeks of grime — revealed the dangerous mind beneath. She looked like the dead returned. Malja thought these Chi-Chun had taken the idea of studying the enemy a bit too far.

The woman advanced towards Fawbry, her agile and speedy feet surprising all. Malja started to retaliate but Fawbry put out his hand, motioning for her to wait. When the Chi-Chun reached him, she widened her eyes, pointed at him, and said, "Do not call upon the damned."

"Barris is not damned."

"Blasphemy! Do not speak such names or I shall call the power of Korstra, and with His might I shall lay a curse upon your head."

"Fine, fine. Just do it and get out of here, so I can call Barris Mont in peace."

The Chi-Chun woman sucked in air as if she might explode should she hear anything more. "You vile heathen."

"No, ma'am. You are the heathen. I follow the right and just Kryssta, the greater brother god, the true leader of all mankind."

"Blasphemy!" The woman pressed her thumb against Fawbry's chin. He did not move away, though he rolled his eyes and huffed disdain. "I curse thee," she said, her words seething hatred. "I curse thee in the name of Korstra, the wise and powerful brother god. Change your path, heathen, or this curse shall follow you always." She put her hood back on and kneeled at the edge of the shore. In seconds, her body swayed as she mumbled words Malja could not make out.

Fawbry waved Malja and Tommy over. "Don't worry," he said. "I've been cursed before by the Chi-Chun. If they have any real power, curses aren't it. Now that I say that, I can't think of anybody ever suffering from a curse. Must not be real."

"She's dangerous," Malja said, her wary eyes hawking the woman.

"Do you really think I'd stand up to her if she were?"

"Good point."

"Come. Onto the dock."

Malja waited. "I'm fine here." Having just crossed the Yad, even standing on a rickety dock overlooking a large lake felt too close to water.

Fawbry shook his head as if mocking a child but wisely left it at that. He walked out on the dock and tapped the water once more. Malja noticed that Tommy had left her side. He hovered near the Chi-Chun. *Facing his fears. Good.* Before she could say anything, a low groan bubbled up from the lake. Fawbry hurried back to the shore.

"He's here. He's here," he said, giddy and impatient.

The Chi-Chun woman inched back but continued her praying.

From the water, a dark object emerged. Malja thought, at first, she saw the head of a man, but as it moved closer, as it rose higher, she saw nothing that resembled a human form. The head-like shape became an eye, one of many, and its large size hinted at the creature coming.

To say Barris Mont was enormous was to say a grain of sand was small. The word failed to convey any real sense of proportion and power. Barris was massive. Taller than the trees and wider than a house, he moved with slow yet powerful grace. A monstrous, lumpy shape — soft and wet and malleable. Good for underwater living. Waves of fish odor pulsed off him. His purplish-black skin looked like an enormous bruise, and his eyes popped open at random points like blemishes. Worse were his legs. More than a tentacle but not as sturdy as a foot, Barris had so many he looked like a mound of dark meat atop thick, never-ending noodles.

The Chi-Chun let out a cry and pressed her head to the stony ground. Tommy watched in gasping disbelief. Fawbry danced about like a child expecting a new toy.

"Barris," he said when he finally regained a little control, "this is the warrior Malja and her companion, Tommy."

A gray appendage wormed out of Barris. Its prehensile tip settled on Fawbry's head. Fawbry closed his eyes and, with a relieved grin, grew rigid like a corpse shortly after a battle. Two similar appendages emerged and took hold of Tommy and the Chi-Chun. It had not happened quickly, yet Malja did not react. The sheer size of Barris had stunned her. But when she saw another gray snake coming for her, she snapped free from her awe.

She brandished Viper and took on a fighting stance. "Let go of them," she said.

In a deep, indecipherable voice, Barris spoke. His tones shook the ground. Leaves fell off trees. Two birds darted into the sky, cawing a frightened warning to others. Malja dropped to her knees and clutched her ears. Her bones radiated pain from the marrow outward as they vibrated against her muscles.

"Stop! Stop talking!" Her words sounded muffled, and she feared she might go deaf. He spoke no more. For now. Wiping at the tears in her eyes, she looked up at the sky and saw no end to Barris. She wobbled back to her feet.

Weaving like a drunkard, she swung Viper toward the gray appendage attached to Tommy. Another splashed from the lake and slapped her down. As she hit the ground, a sharp rock poked the small of her back.

The gray tube, for she could think of nothing nicer to call it, still waited for her, its tip motioning for her to join. She stumbled to her feet, her body complaining at each movement. If Barris chose to speak again, Malja knew her ears would bleed and her body would fail. Death would come swiftly. But still that disgusting tube beckoned.

She wanted to check on Tommy, but her heart told her not to bother. She had failed the boy. Alive or dead, she had failed the boy.

No. I only fail if I do nothing.

She grabbed that gray tube so hard Barris let out a startled complaint — loud enough for Malja's legs to buckle, but she managed to stay upright. She pulled the tube closer. Another tube tried to strike her, but she wouldn't fall again. She dodged the attack with one step and with a second step, she planted her legs solidly.

"I don't want to hurt you," she said, knowing how absurd her words sounded, "and since Fawbry wanted to be here, I think you don't want to hurt us. So, you just let go of the boy, and I'll let go of you. We'll leave you in peace. Okay?"

Nothing happened.

"Fine. I'll go first," she said and let go of the gray tube.

Barris spoke. The ground shook as vibrations radiated outward with explosive force. A dying tree splintered and fell. Distant animals screeched and fled.

Malja collapsed as blood dribbled from her nose and ears. The pressure on her head brought spots to her eyes. She felt like the brother gods had each taken a side of her skull and pushed.

She rolled on the ground, clutching her head, trying to focus. She saw Tommy. Despite the vibrations shooting endless jolts straight through to her bones, she reached for the boy. Her breathing labored and her vision clouded. She rolled onto her back, fighting for air. She found Viper and tried to think of a way to strike back. But part of her mind began wondering what form Death would take.

Barris finally stopped. All fell into silence. Malja couldn't even hear her own heartbeat. She felt the gray tube slither across her leg. She held Viper now but could not find the strength to left her weapon. The tube entered her field of vision.

Barris did not hesitate. The tube lowered onto Malja's head.

Chapter 8

Malja, come here now," a voice called from behind. She knew that thin timbre — Callib. A terrified yelp surged up Malja's throat, but she clamped her mouth against it. Brutal lashings waited for her should she turn around. "Malja," Callib said, exasperated and harsh, "did you kill my dolyan birds?"

"Yes, sir," a little girl answered through her bawling.

Malja whirled around to see a four-year-old girl clad in a black assault suit. The dead lake, the barren trees, the overcast sky — gone. Tommy, Fawbry, the Chi-Chun, Barris — gone. Before she could say a word, little Malja vanished.

Another Malja appeared in the distance. Eight-years-old. The younger version of her practiced with a new sword she had been given for her birthday. Malja remembered the day well. Lunges, parries, sweeps, and slices. Over and over she went through her forms — each choreographed step a tutorial for battle. No windows to distract her. No warmth to lull her. Just cold, echoing stone and damp, musty odors. Warm tears stung in her eyes, but she kept practicing.

Then she was ten, crouched at the door to her room listening to her fathers argue in the hall. "She's a complete failure," Callib said. "There's not a bit of magical ability in her. Nothing."

"Failure?" Jarik said, his deeper tones always more striking than Callib's shrill rants. "It's a success she's survived this long."

"Obviously, but—"

"You continue to think you can change her, but look at what she is. Look at what she can do."

"What? The fighting?"

"Yes, the fighting. She's by far the most talented warrior this world has ever seen. We did that. That's success."

"That's your success. It has nothing to do with finding safe passage, and quite frankly, it's a waste of our valuable time and resources. She's nothing but a failure to me."

She stared at the door. Burning tears streamed down her face, but she wiped them back.

Again the world dissolved. Malja gasped as her vision flooded with memory after memory. She saw her days training, her days being yelled at, her days being beaten. She saw the morning they tossed her in a sack and abandoned her in a forest.

She felt the fear and the loss and the betrayal. Yet she also had the context of an adult looking back to aid her. She admired little Malja's pluck. That girl refused to give in.

She saw the week she had struggled to survive, scavenging for the mere basics — eating grubs, enduring freezing rain, fighting off hungry konapols. She saw the day she thought she would die of starvation, the same day Gregor found her on his morning walk and decided to take her in.

The years with Gregor were pleasant but never secure. She listened closely and tried to obey his rules. But no matter how often he professed his love for her, she kept an eye out for any change to come. At some point, she expected, he would grow tired of her burden and dump her.

With a jolt like riding in a wagon run by a spooked horse, she saw a seventeen-year-old Malja returning from a three-day hunt. She had a load of meat to store for Korstraprime. She called Gregor to give her a hand. She really just wanted to show him how well she had done. He always praised her accomplishments, and she never tired of hearing him.

When he didn't answer, she cupped her mouth and said, "Wake up, Lazy-head. I'm home." The concern on her face lacked any humor. Both Maljas — old and young — tensed as the seventeen-year-old approached their tiny shack.

The older Malja closed her eyes, knowing what awaited the younger. Gregor — ripped to pieces. Blood and tissue strewn about like sloppy decorations. Burn marks on the walls and a sour stench marring the air — sure signs of magic.

Only two magicians would have cared about an old man and his daughter living alone in peace. Jarik and Callib. The younger Malja, her eyes cold and dry, tripped on her way outside to throw-up. The older knew what happened next. She could never forget about the man hiding in the second room. She braced herself for the coming confrontation, for the moment that changed so much, but the vision skipped ahead, cheating her from watching her truly discover her strength and saving her from having to deal with it. Now, she saw herself standing before the shack as she burned it and Gregor's remains to the ground. And she made her oath. She would find her fathers. She would unleash the beast for Gregor's sake.

More years soared by her — all the dark, dreadful places she had seen. The barbarians of the Freelands, the criminal magicians holding towns hostage, the constant battle against roving groups of killers and cretins — all of it washed her in the blood of memory.

But then she stood in a gleaming, white room. Not a memory. She had never seen such a room before. A window encompassed an entire wall letting the sun glitter off the white marble floor. A white desk and chair occupied one side of the wide room. Far across on the other, Malja saw a white couch. She had seen furniture before but never in such pristine condition. Two white birds chased each other around the ceiling.

"I'm sorry it took so long to settle on a meeting location," said a man in a gray suit with a brilliant green tie. He touched his desk and the birds vanished. "Usually I can find a memory that's happy, warm, and above all else, safe. I could not find such a place in you. Admittedly, I'm pressed for time, but still, you've lived a bitter life."

Malja thought hard on what she had seen and heard. She offered the most intelligent reply she could muster. "Huh?"

The man smiled, revealing just how handsome he could be — and clean. His skin, his hair, his clothes — everything smelled as clean and clear as the spotless room. "I apologize again. This can be a bit disorienting the first time." He raised a finger. "Let's begin with introductions. I'm Barris Mont." He offered his hand.

As Malja shook, she said, "But you were that huge thing."

Barris laughed. "Yes, I was. Still am. All this is going on in my head."

"Your head?"

"Well, it was meant to be yours, but as I said, your life has been rather dark. So I brought you into my mind instead."

"Then this is your memory?"

"Back when I was human. Before the Devastation."

With timid steps, Malja approached the window. Never had she felt so shy, so unsure of what she would do with what she would see. Before she felt ready, the world opened up.

The office she stood in must have been miles in the air, for she could see the city spread out to the horizon. Far below people scurried about and grounders zipped along the road. Other offices floated in the air while some buildings simply stacked upon each other, reaching for the clouds. Lights of every shape and color winked and flashed and dazzled.

A scarlet bird with white-tipped wings slid along the air and settled on the window ledge. It seemed nonplused by this amazing, breathing city. It seemed at peace.

Malja saw that the city was at peace, too. Despite the speeding grounders and bustling people, despite the airborne offices and the numerous advertisements, despite it all, the city moved with a quiet, peaceful grace. The engines, the food, the lights — all powered by magicians, silently doing their job from the shadows.

"It had elegance, don't you think?" Barris said.

Malja could not hide her wonder. "It was beautiful."

"This is the city of Winsal, one of the great cities of the Southern Countries."

Though she wanted to see more — indeed, she could have stared at it for hours as if she were a magician casting a massive spell — she pulled away and put on a thoughtful look. "So, Mr. Mont, what is all this for? What do you want?"

"You, of course. But I need you to be honest, and honesty often requires comfort. So, I suppose you could say that all this—" Barris pointed to the world around them. "—is about your comfort." With a smile that suggested a surprise, he pressed another button on his desk.

A young man entered with a stiff walk. He wore black pants, a white shirt and jacket, and had a funny, little tie. He carried a silver, covered tray. When he approached Malja, he bent towards her as if in solemn reverie.

"A little gift," Barris said.

The man lifted the tray cover to reveal one firm, red apple. Malja thanked the young man as she took the apple.

Before the young man had left, she bit the fruit.

Delicious. Exquisite. Perfect.

For an instant, she could believe in the world outside the window — she did not stand at the edge of a putrid lake, and the sun gleamed off life like the bursting juice in her apple.

"Good," Barris said as he settled on the couch and patted a spot at his side. She sat, marveling at how the cushion felt softer than a moss bed. He placed his hand on her shoulder and said, "We have much to discuss."

Malja pressed him back like a young girl fending off a kiss yet not wanting to hurt the boy's feelings. "What are you talking about? 'Much to discuss.' I brought you Fawbry. He's the one who wanted to be with you. Though you sure are cute." *What did I just say?* Malja's head felt fuzzy. "Did you ... do something to this apple?"

"No," Barris said, his face filled with worry. "You're reacting to being in my mind. You're not supposed to be here. The experience can be euphoric — and sometimes disrupting. So, listen. I need you to focus. This is important."

"Sure. No trouble. Stay focused. But just know I'm good at a lot more than fighting." Malja lurched forward and whispered quite loudly, "I'm talking about sex."

Barris held Malja's chin and said, "I want ..."

With a drunken slur, Malja said, "You want ..."

"I want you to ..."

"You want me to ..."

"I want you to kill the brothers, Jarik and Callib."

No words, no magic, no concoction of any kind could have snapped her sober faster. "What?" she said, all traces of euphoria flushed from her system. Her skin wriggled like someone had plucked out her dirtiest desire and spoke it out loud just so she could feel its slime dribble down her chest. Maybe that's exactly what happened. Maybe he plucked it right from her head.

She put some distance between them. She couldn't understand how he had made her feel violated. She never had kept quiet about her hatred for Jarik and Callib. Ms. Nolan had known. The Bluesmen knew. Yet she couldn't shake the feeling that she had been severely wronged.

Barris reclined, crossed his legs, and said, "Good, you're clear-headed again. It won't last long though, so focus. Now I know you want to kill them. I want it, too. For different reasons, of course."

"What reasons?"

"No time for that. What matters is that you complete your task. That's why you're here. I have to know with absolute certainty you won't back off at the end. I have to be sure you won't afford them any sliver of compassion."

"You think I won't do it?"

"I think part of you is still a little girl who wants her daddies to love her."

"Gregor loved me."

"But Gregor is not Jarik. Gregor is not Callib. Gregor can't tell you about your mother."

Malja threw her apple at Barris. He ducked and the apple exploded against the wall, leaving behind a wet spot and splatters of fruit. "I'll kill them. It's that simple. I certainly don't need you to motivate me."

"Okay," Barris said, cautiously sliding to the far end of the couch. "Let's move on, then. The boy, Tommy, you must leave him with me."

Malja let a laugh burst out of her, but she had no idea if it was the effect of this place or her honest astonishment. "You were just in my head, you idiot. You should know I won't let him go."

"And yet, you must. If you truly care for him, then you

know he is not safe with you. Not with the task you have ahead. He is a liability to you. Jarik and Callib may feel some sense of caring towards you — in fact, I'm counting on it — but they won't care about the boy. They'll use him against you. And that cannot be allowed to happen."

"You're wasting my time. Tommy stays with me."

"You don't understand. The boy is growing, and he'll be vulnerable."

Malja wrinkled her eyebrows. "He's young. He's supposed to grow."

"He's a magician, too," Barris said. Malja's stomach twisted. "And I have given him a second spell."

"You've *given?*"

"In the old days, before the Devastation, before I mutated into the lumbering thing I am, I was a Sotnol. There were many back then. We're not really magicians, yet we're not really just people either. We're the spell givers. More accurately, we unlock spells. I enter a magician's mind and help him or her unlock the potential that resides there."

"And you did this to Tommy."

"He did it to himself. I merely showed him the doorway."

Malja kicked the desk, careening it into the wall with a screech. "If any of this were real, I'd kill you right now."

Barris shrugged. "Lucky for me, then, that I'm big enough to squash you." Barris stood, brushed his pants, and once more rested his arms on Malja's shoulders. She giggled at the thought of dancing with him. "Stay focused," he said.

She snapped back her attention. "I'm not leaving him. I've protected him this long. I'll continue to protect him."

"I expected this. Hoped for otherwise, but expected it nonetheless. So, I'm sending the Chi-Chun woman with you. Her name is Tumus. She'll know how to care for the boy as he adjusts to his new ability."

Malja wanted to argue, but she felt the drunken state just on the edges of her control. "Anything else?"

"Cole Watts will tell you where Jarik and Callib are. Watts is your key." Barris placed a finger on her open lips. "Shh. Patience. Fawbry knows how to find Watts. I do not, and I don't want to know."

"This is ridiculous. Why should I listen to any of this?"

The walls rippled as if seen through a waterfall. Barris lowered his head. "I'm sorry. If we stay any longer, your brain may be damaged."

"Then answer quickly. Why should I listen? And what exactly did you do to Tommy? And why do I need your Chi-Chun? And —"

Barris became transparent even as he sighed all too real. "You'll have to answer it for yourself. Goodbye, Malja."

"Wait. Tell me something. Anything. Why are the Bluesmen trying to stop me?"

The jolt of fear and surprise that hit Barris spread across the fading office. He said something, but only an odd childlike voice — several steps out of synch and speaking in a language that sounded made-up — followed his moving lips. When he disappeared completely, Malja felt a giant force shove her through darkness. Another force grabbed her inside the chest and yanked hard enough to cause an unheroic squeal.

Malja opened her eyes. Fawbry, Tommy, and Tumus were all lying by the dock. Malja sat up and scanned the hazy lake. Barris was gone.

Chapter 9

Nobody was happy. Tommy crouched on the rocks clutching his arm as if it had been broken. Tumus, the Chi-Chun woman, stood near the dock watching the lake — her mouth open, her face stoic, her mind lost in disbelief. Knee-high in the water, his worn but flashy robe soaking, Fawbry kicked and splashed and screamed.

"You bastard! Come back here. You can't do this to me. This isn't right. Come back here."

Malja didn't care about Fawbry, and she didn't care about Tumus. At that moment, she wanted only to hold Tommy and ease any suffering Barris had caused him. Yet she could not move. She watched Tommy rubbing his arm and wondered if this marked the beginning, if the magician in him would now take over, if the little boy she had rescued would cease to exist, if madness waited to consume him. She tried not to look across his skin for the new tattoo. She snuck a peek anyway — not a brave approach but she couldn't bear to let Tommy see her face if he, indeed, had a new marking. A wave of relief crashed over when she did not see it. But if he lacked the tattoo, then Barris had done something else to him. Perhaps something worse.

"I won't do it," Fawbry said, now sobbing into the lake. "I don't care about what you want."

The sun rose. Malja wondered how long they had been unconscious and how long they had been in communion with Barris. A new day awoke around them, and for her part she wanted to make it worthwhile. Cole Watts. Find him to find Jarik and Callib. Find them and put an end to the constant gnawing, constricting, worrying tension in the middle of her chest that even thoughts of Gregor could not ease.

"I refuse," Fawbry went on. "You hear that, you big bastard? I refuse!"

With a tinge of pleasure, Malja turned toward Fawbry. This she could handle. "Fawbry, get out of the water."

Her voice cut through his panic. He stopped screaming at the lake and looked over his shoulder. Dripping with confusion and fear like an abused pet, he shook his head. "He was supposed to keep me safe. Not send me off with you."

"Where do I find Cole Watts?"

Fawbry pouted at the lake. "I don't want to go there. I don't want to go to the Freelands."

"You don't have to. Tell me where in the Freelands, and I'll go by myself. You can stay here. All of you can. Just stay here where it's safe."

Everyone stopped their personal mourning and stared at Malja. Fawbry even stumbled a few steps away from her. Nobody said a word.

Tommy broke the silence first. Pushing himself to his feet, he let out a single, puppyish whimper. He walked to her side, cold determination set in his eyes, and huffed as if to say *Don't even think about arguing.* Malja had no such intention. She had expected Tommy to come. No matter how angry he might be, he wouldn't leave her. Not yet. But she needed Fawbry for information — not just Cole Watts's location, but his connections, his importance. Everything Fawbry could provide, she wanted.

Tumus's dark face twisted in a tug-of-war. Her lips quivered, and for a moment, Malja feared she would have two blubbering fools to contend with. But with a garbled shout and a rude gesture to the lake, Tumus stomped over to Tommy.

One more.

Fawbry still shook his head. "I'm not a fighter. I'm not brave. I'm not smart. I'm just trying to survive."

"You're more than that," Malja said. "You're the one who got us across the river. You're the one who fed us so well that morning. And as for brave, the only reason we're here at this lake is because you stood up to me. Now, you know where Cole Watts is, and you know Barris wants you to help me."

He crossed his arms. "Okay. I'll tell you. Then you can go off and take care of it all and it doesn't matter to me. I'll be here."

"Except Barris wants you with me. Can you guarantee he'll protect you when you go against his wishes? I don't know. I don't think you'll be as safe with him as you think. Come with me, and you know I'll protect you. And it's what he wants. Really, your situation hasn't changed that much. I'm still your safest bet."

Fawbry thought this over for a second and slapped the water hard. While wiping his eyes, he trudged out of the lake. "I hate you."

* * * *

As they approached the last hill before reaching the Muyaza village, Malja's concern for Tommy's welfare grew. Illness had set in fast. His face burned with fever while his body shuddered against her. Holding the horse's reins in one hand and clutching Tommy to her breast with the other, Malja made the silent promise that should anything happen to Tommy, she would kill Barris Mont.

Fawbry and Tumus shared the other horse a few feet behind. Neither said much except for the occasional complaint against the placement of one's hand or the smell of the other's body.

Cresting the hill, Malja saw the Muyaza village already buzzing in the morning's work. A short line formed outside the village where the requisite two boys sought payment for the crossing. One spied the horses and their riders. Recognition ignited astonishment. With frantic gestures, he pointed them out to the adult males standing in the distance.

"Guess word's gotten out about us," Fawbry said — his first words since they had left the lake.

Malja reached over, flipped open the saddlebag, and produced a dead rabbit. She had caught it when the little thing made the mistake of crossing the dirt road they rode on. It wasn't much, but she hoped it would be enough. If it wasn't, then she knew other ways to get what she wanted.

Before the fierce Muyaza male had stopped his approach, he waved them off. "No," he said. "No welcome here."

Malja tossed the dead rabbit onto the ground.

The Muyaza scoffed at the offering, the stumps on his sides bristling. "No good."

"The horse," Fawbry said.

Malja looked over her shoulder in shock as Fawbry dismounted and pulled Tumus off. He walked the horse up to the Muyaza and handed him the reins. The Muyaza looked at the reins in his hand with even greater shock than Malja.

Fawbry glanced up to Malja. "We can always get another horse." For a fleeting moment, the words unnerved her — people rarely thought the way she did, let alone actually acted upon such thoughts.

The Muyaza looked back at the village and then at Malja. He inspected the horse, licking his lips as he ran a hand over the meaty rump. Something at the village made him hesitate, though. With an incredulous shake of the head, he bent down, picked up the dead rabbit, and walked the horse back to the village. The others followed.

They entered the main circle of homes, and the village stopped. The cooking stopped. The talking stopped. Even the ceaseless eating stopped. Only the sizzle of meat and the rumble of boiling stew disrupted the uneasy silence. At length, a woman assigned a Muyaza team to Malja and her friends. Nobody seemed eager to move, but the woman spat out a few words and business returned to its usual pace.

With the old Muyaza upon his litter and the protective bubble formed, Malja's group entered the river. The villagers snuck glances but refused to meet Malja's eyes. The air felt colder than the previous crossing, the water less welcoming, the bubble less secure. The litter carriers exchanged worried looks. Malja gripped Tommy tighter and tried to ignore the rising water. After a few minutes, Malja noticed Tumus had edged her way to the right side of the horse and placed her hand on Tommy's foot. Fawbry walked ahead near the litter.

Something was wrong.

Malja felt it vibrating deep within like the coming of an earthquake. More than just fear of drowning — this was her warrior instincts shooting off. When the river had risen to the point that only her head and that of the old Muyaza on the litter broke the surface, she saw it. There were no other litters in the water. Despite people bustling and cooking and trading, nobody else had entered the river.

She looked back at the shore. Searching. The tall Bluesman stood out clearly against the little Muyaza village

— gray beard and clouded eye. The Muyaza stayed far behind him. They fretted about, but none would challenge the strange man. He raised a lengthy pipe — no, not a pipe — a rifle. Before Malja could warn anybody, the muzzle flared and a crack rolled across the air. The bullet splashed a few feet upriver.

"Faster," Malja said but she didn't need to — the carriers had picked up the pace. She checked the shore. The Bluesman went through the reloading process with the careful and efficient motions of a trained soldier. When he lifted the rifle to aim, Malja leaned over Tommy, pushing him lower to the horse's neck. The shot snapped out and the head of the old man on the litter exploded.

The bubble surrounding them tore apart like strands of saliva pulled away by water. Anguished cries erupted from the Muyaza on the shore. And the river reclaimed its territory with a powerful thrust. It swept Malja from her horse. It ripped Tommy from her grasp. Water spun her, flipped her, tossed her aside. She couldn't tell which way was up, and each time she thought she had it right, the river spun her into disorientation again.

She smacked into a rock, her back scrapping against the jagged surface, the force of the blow knocking out what little air she had in her lungs. And then — light. A glint of sunlight from above. Pushing off the rock, she swam hard for the surface. Her lungs burned, and a dark thought crossed her mind — *I'm not going to make it.* The surface didn't seem to be getting closer. She was going to drown. Each stroke felt as if a giant pressed its enormous fist against her ribs. But when she burst into the air, gasping for every lungful she could manage, her surprise cost her. She missed grabbing hold of a log.

Striving to stay above water, she swam hard with little to show for it. The river fought her, its unmerciful hands pushing her chest and pulling at her legs. She searched for Tommy but only saw Fawbry. He had found purchase on a large boulder and hugged it like a crying child to his mother's breast.

The river yanked Malja into its muddy jaw, filling her vision with browns and greens, grit and sand. Sounds mutated into bubbled nonsense. Three strong strokes brought her back to the surface. She spun around, seeing water and the shore and Fawbry falling away from view. Something else, too. A small, dark shape limp in the water. *Tommy.*

Swimming away from the shore, Malja battled the waters for every stroke. The boy's body bumped against some rocks but did not react. *Don't think about that. Just get him.* Water crept down her throat — a dirty trick of the river, but as she coughed and spit, she swam. She saw Tommy on that thief's ship, his cautious eyes, his small hand in hers as she made her promise. So she swam. Deeper into the river's angry flow.

Bracing on a nearby rock, she grabbed the body. Blood drenched it as much as water. She turned him over. Not Tommy. The Muyaza litter carrier — cracked open his skull on the rocks.

As she dropped the Muyaza back into the current, she saw the shattered litter within reach. It took several tries, but she snagged it and floated her way downriver.

Soon the waters began to ease, and the river's grip relaxed. She paddled toward shore — it took a hard effort, but the river put up less of a fight.

A dark stone formed in her belly. As she stepped out of the river, her assault suit dotted with beads of water, her body dry, her long hair sopping wet, she bit back against the urge to cry. Still no Tommy.

Her eyes scanned the river once more. She saw the small

figure of Fawbry leaping from his mama boulder to the river's edge. One foot landed in the water and he scrambled the rest of the way to safety. Nothing else. Nobody. Not even the horse.

"Over here," a breathless voice called out.

Malja looked behind her. About twenty feet inland, Tumus waved for help as she bent over a small body. Despite her exhaustion, Malja sprinted across the grass. The stone in her belly lifted to her chest where fear and hope tugged at each other like two wild animals ravaging the same piece of meat.

Tommy lay underneath Tumus. She slapped his face, trying to bring normal color back to his bluish skin. Pushing Tumus aside, Malja sat Tommy up and reached around him from behind. She squeezed hard just below his ribs, hoping to force out anything. Brackish water vomited from him with each squeeze. By the time Fawbry had joined them, Tommy had coughed the last out and began to breathe.

"What the hell happened?" Fawbry said.

Malja ignored him. She hugged Tommy and asked, "You okay?"

Tommy nodded. Normal color returned to his face. "He's okay," she said and let a few tears fall. She hugged him tighter, as if the river could jump the bank and take him away. "I'm here for you. You understand? Forget about Nolan's place and all that. I'm sorry about it. Okay? I'm always here for you."

Tommy squirmed from her tight grasp and verbal bombardment. He reached out to Tumus and held her hand. Tumus snatched her hand back and moved a short distance away. As she wiped water from her face, she said, "He'll be fine. Cold water probably helped with the fever."

Malja knew she should say thanks, that she should

sound a little grateful — after all, Tommy was alive. But, though she loathed the idea, a new pain plucked in her chest when Tommy had reached for Tumus. She should have been the one to save him, not this Chi-Chun crazy. Worse still, Tumus had the nerve to pull away her hand.

Malja walked a few steps from the group and tried to cool off. However, seeing the smoke of cooking food from the distant Muyaza village only fueled her fire. And that target she could focus on with less confusion.

Once Tommy could walk, Malja led them back to the Muyaza. Nobody argued with her. Tumus probably didn't care. Fawbry took one look at her seething anger and kept quiet. And Tommy always trusted her. That's all she really needed.

She trudged on, each step strengthening her as she felt the warm coat of the warrior enfold her. If she had the time and knowledge, she would have built a bridge crossing the Yad, and she would've done it right next to the Muyaza village. They would try to stop her, and she would cut them down. But she lacked that much time. She would have to be content with getting across the river and putting the villagers in their place.

The Bluesman had run off. No surprise there. And the Muyaza seemed eager to return to their normal lives. They were not ones for open confrontation. They would mourn their losses at night, in private. At the sight of Malja and her party, one woman cried out and the tribe froze.

They watched her as if she were a ghost — unsure if they could believe their eyes. With Viper in her hand, Malja pointed at the nearest old man and at two younger men. She gestured toward the litters. They needed nothing more. In a few tense seconds, the old man sat atop the litter and attempted to calm himself enough to form the protective bubble. The tribe watched. A few men squinted in impotent rage. Many looked down in shame.

They crossed the river with speed, not even stopping at the halfway point. The two men carrying the litter rushed along as if Malja had poked them with Viper. When they reached the other side, the Muyaza at that village halted everything — even the babies were hushed. Five horses were tied to a post, awaiting their turn at becoming dinner stew. Malja pointed to three, and under her watchful eyes, Fawbry and Tumus untied and saddled them.

"No," snapped a male sitting at the dining table. Three horses represented a lot of hard work. He stood, revealing his chiseled, muscular body and white scar across his chest. He stormed toward them, throwing a konapol bone to the side. A woman motioned towards him only to collapse in tears at his stern, determined face. He opened his mouth, displaying long, sharp teeth, and again said, "No."

Malja no longer bothered with words. She grabbed the man's wrist, twisted it, ducked underneath his arm, and pulled up, pinning his arm behind his back. With two swift kicks, she popped his knees forward, sending him to the ground. She raised Viper, cutting the air with a low whoosh, and swung down with every intention of watching that blade sink into the man's chest. But the blade never made it.

Tommy blocked her arm with his. They locked eyes. It took only a few seconds, but for Malja, those eyes spoke for years. Years of abuse, of strain and hurt, and of betrayal. She had no idea whose years she saw — his or her own.

She released the male. He walked off, trying to regain face in his angry steps. The woman who had wept for him approached, and he spit out harsh words and raised his hand but did not strike. Malja mounted a dappled gray and pulled Tommy into her arms. She cradled him, and like a child, he settled into his familiar position. Fawbry and

Tumus each took a horse and followed Malja's lead out of the village. Nobody dared even to look at them.

Soon, she would need Fawbry to lead the way, but for now, she knew where to go. The Freelands. A barbaric dead land she had hoped never to return to. A place that made the Muyaza look like the friendliest of neighbors.

"I hate the water," she said.

Chapter 10

During her youngest years, while under the magical protection of Jarik and Callib, Malja never suffered from sickness — not a cold, not a fever, not a rash, not a bellyache, nothing. Health surrounded her like a golden aura. When they tossed her away, she slogged through the next few years contracting every possible bug Corlin had to offer. Gregor did his best to comfort her during times of sickness, but he also explained that fighting her way to health would train her body to defeat the bugs in the future.

"Sometimes," he said, "a good fight is the best lesson." Watching Tommy sweat and shiver in her arms, she wondered how Gregor ever had the strength to let sickness run its course.

She held Tommy, wiped his brow, talked to him — anything she could think of. She told him about Gregor's tiny shack and how she loved the place. She talked of the way Gregor played *Find the Apple* and in doing so, helped her discover the endless nooks of the small, two-room home. He made it feel bigger. She described Gregor's laugh, his stern voice, and even the way his belches chirped out instead of a loud boom.

Tommy mustered a weak grin. She wanted to read for him, but they lost *Astronomical Wonders* in the Yad. Instead, she described the solar system as best she could recall. He listened well, but she thought it all sounded made up.

Malja talked on for he seemed to like it. But she was no doctor, and this illness she did not understand. She tried to warm him and make him feel safe.

Fawbry and Tumus fumbled through constructing camp. Though slow and inefficient, they did get the job done. Soon the warmth of the campfire helped calm Tommy. He closed his eyes and slept to the rich aroma of burning pine.

Malja watched his shallow breathing, his weakened body, his trembling lips. *Make it better,* she commanded but nothing changed. She longed to do something active — kill something, defeat someone, run somewhere. Anything would be better than sitting here watching Tommy burn away.

"Let me hold him," Tumus said.

Malja started and cursed under her breath — she should never let anybody sneak up on her. "Go away," she said.

"Barris ordered me—"

"Barris isn't here."

Tumus's yellow eyes narrowed. Tossing her hands up, she said, "Stupid." To Malja's relief, Tumus stormed away. To her disappointment, Fawbry slipped in place.

"You should be nicer to her," he said, squatting near the campfire. "It's not her fault. Besides, imagine what she's going through. Raised her whole life to think she's saving the world as some magic protector against the dead, that Korstra has it all planned out. Then Barris comes along and suddenly nothing she believed in is true. It's sad."

Tumus flew back with a fury Malja wished to see in most warriors. "You be quiet, you Kryssta-loving fool. You know nothing of my people but the lies your pathetic priests tell you."

Fawbry put some distance between them but laughed. "Oh, really. So what are you doing here? Did Korstra tell you to convert us or something?"

"Shut your filthy mouth. Don't you speak the Lord's name."

"The Lord is not Korstra."

"Blasphemy!"

Malja snapped in a harsh whisper. "Both of you, stop it. You'll wake Tommy."

"My apologies," Fawbry said, adding a silly bow. "I can't educate such a heathen when she so excitable."

"You're the heathen," Tumus said, pacing as she spoke, flexing her fingers, rolling her head — all actions Malja recognized. If Fawbry kept pushing, she expected Tumus to strike out. "You have brought the curse of blasphemy upon us," Tumus continued. "You should go away."

"I didn't want any part of this. But I trust Barris, and I trust Kryssta. And Kryssta help me, I might be starting to trust Malja. So I'm staying. Besides, if I'm cursed, you're the one who put it on me. Remember?"

Tumus's head pulled back like a cat smelling rancid meat. "Are you saying this is my fault? Do you really want—"

Malja cringed as they geared up for more arguing. Tommy didn't stir, so she figured she should let them get it out. However, she suspected these two could keep fighting all night and most of the next day.

But then Tommy began to shake.

Just a short spasm in the arm. Then the leg. Then his body bucked in a wild display. He moaned and flailed. With surprising force, he belted Malja off of him. She scrambled back, trying to hold yet not hurt him. She called his name.

"This can't be," Fawbry said. "Barris can't be right."

Malja had never seen anything like this. White, foamy spittle pooled in Tommy's mouth. Her heart pounded. She tried to hold down his limbs but couldn't keep him still. Her mind blanked. She struggled to hold him. No other part of her could move. *Is this panic?* Tommy was dying before her eyes and she had frozen. *Is this how people feel when*

I attack with Viper?

From her dazed fog, she heard a voice — an authoritative voice. "Pull her off."

"I'm trying," Fawbry said. Malja felt hands on her shoulders, and she let them lead her back a few paces. Like snow dropping down her back, shocking her with its cold, the situation became clear and chilling again. She started for Tommy but Fawbry blocked her path. "No, Malja. If you want Tommy to live, let Tumus help. Barris warned me that when the time came, Tommy might need her."

Standing at Tommy's feet, Tumus spread her robed arms like black wings while Tommy thrashed about below her. Malja broke Fawbry's grip with ease and stormed ahead. Tommy kicked out and stiffened like he had been petrified. She let out a sharp cry. *He's dead,* she thought.

The boy arched, his belly lifting to the sky, and a hot blast of energy shot out of him. It exploded in all directions, lighting up the night like a golden funeral pyre. But the energy curved — literally shifted directions as if an invisible wall had formed amongst the trees and rocks. The energy turned in on itself until it found the one open release — Tumus.

Like a sword thrust straight through an opponent, the energy pierced into the Chi-Chun woman. She staggered but remained standing. It poured in, and she cried out. When the last of it had entered her, the forest darkened into night. Nothing radiated out of her. She had absorbed it all.

She lowered her head and rubbed her belly like a newly pregnant woman. Malja crawled to Tommy who sat, awake and looking healthy but tired. He pointed to his mouth. *I'm hungry.*

Bursting into joyous laughter, Malja wiped her eyes. She gazed up at Tumus. "Thank you."

Tumus let out a satisfied breath. "This was only the first. There will be more."

"More? What's the matter with him?"

"Nothing. He's just becoming a magician."

As Malja handed Tommy some nuts, she looked at his right wrist. Three swirling lines that had not been there before now marred his skin. She felt nausea. They were faint lines, could've been mistaken for dirt, but clear to her — the beginnings of a tattoo.

She wanted to shout but said nothing. She remained by Tommy's side while he inhaled his food. Tumus also sat next to Tommy, observing every motion, every breath. When he winced before belching, Malja witnessed the anticipation in Tumus. Whatever her exact part in all this, the Chi-Chun woman wanted it to happen again.

* * * *

Later that night, Tommy slept with a full belly, and Fawbry snored nearby. Malja stood watch. The closer they came to the Freelands, the more vigilant they would have to be. Luxuries like a full night's sleep would have to wait until this ended.

Malja hated guard duty. Not enough to occupy her mind. Too much time for her memories to return. After her experience with Barris Mont, she knew her memories would overwhelm her if given the chance. Too many walls she had built up, Barris had knocked down.

As if it had only just happened, she could feel the ground as she threw up outside the shack — Gregor's mutilated body just out of her sight. Taking a long, raking breath, she rolled to the side and screamed. When her voice died out, she heard the whine of the wooden floor. Somebody was still inside the shack. Jarik or Callib, it didn't matter. Malja intended to make them pay.

She didn't have Viper back then, but the short sword she wielded had been with her for many years. She knew its weight well. Coupled with the over-confidence of a seventeen-year-old, she found no problems with her plan of bursting into the shack and slicing apart anything living she saw. The man hiding inside, however, thought fighting back to be a better idea.

Tommy moaned and kicked out in his sleep. Malja watched him for several minutes, her eyes glistening in the firelight, and she waited. One more moan or whimper or cry, any sign of distress, and she would wake him. She knew the nightmare he suffered. She had seen it in his eyes when she rescued him.

She remembered the cold rain rattling the tiny battery room Tommy had been locked in. She had cut his chains, and he had smiled. But she picked up the chains and examined them. They were old and rusty like the ship. She looked at the boy's wrists and saw where prolonged binding had left its marks.

"Well, Tommy," she said, trying to figure out what still troubled her. "The Captain doesn't appear to be a friend to either of us. He tried to drown me and he keeps you locked up here." Malja bolted up as her thoughts connected. "Why didn't the mage-pirates kill you? Or, at least, take you with them? And Wuchev must've seen me make it across the deck. He knows now that I know something's going on. He'll be coming. He has to. But he doesn't want to cross outside, and his precious cargo ... there is no cargo."

With a scowl and a grunt, Tommy snatched the chains and threw them across the tiny room. He stepped in the opposite direction and, pushing a box out of the way, revealed an access hatch in the floor. He opened it, a rusty whine echoed around them like an aged alarm, and descended on a ladder.

Malja hesitated. Though he appeared to be little more than an abused boy, Tommy was a magician. However, being stuck on a ship in a raging storm left her with few alternatives. She sheathed Viper and climbed down.

The ladder ended in a narrow corridor. She caught sight of Tommy at the far end, opening a doorway. By the time she reached the door, he had stepped inside and stood on a wide platform overlooking the empty, cavernous cargo hold. Empty, except for a simple box at the center of the hold floor.

"What's in there?" she asked.

Tommy stared at it, his eyes blazing hatred.

"Is that what the mage-pirates wanted?" Malja shook her head. "No. Because there were no mage-rats."

A loud bang echoed in the hold and the entire ship groaned to the side. Tommy pointed to the rusting hull. Malja climbed down to the cargo hold's floor and inspected the hull. She knew nothing about ships, but even her untrained eye could see the ancient metal dying. The bang repeated and the metal whined as the storm battered the hull.

Squatting to Tommy's level, Malja looked him over and said, "Wuchev killed his crew, didn't he? He drugged us and killed them. That's why I slept through everything."

Tommy nodded. Not a moment's hesitation. He knew the answer. She wondered how he could be so clear when he was chained in the battery station — unless by some magical means he could spy on the world outside. But that sounded paranoid to her. Magic didn't work like that. At least, not any magic she had ever come across.

She stepped back from the boy, her heart pounding against her ribs as if Callib had rebuked her for some minor infraction, reminding her that this little boy would grow up to be a ruthless magician. From the corner of her eye, she saw the box. Something about the box had bothered the boy.

Moving closer, her stomach rolled as the ship took another trip along a steep wave. With her hand resting on the rough wooden lid, she gazed back at the boy. If he proved to be more magician than boy, then she would have to defend herself. *Can I really kill a child?* She wanted to say *no* without hesitation, but she didn't know. She understood that deep within her the capability to perform such a vile act existed if it turned out to be necessary. She just didn't know if the rest of her would protest.

She lifted the lid and gazed in the box. A robe. A ripped, dusty robe.

Malja looked back at Tommy. His face gave nothing away. Before she could say a word, Captain Wuchev stepped out of the shadows. He held a single-shot handgun. From the dented barrel to the chipped wood body, Malja figured he would be lucky if the gun fired without exploding, luckier if it came near its target.

"You're not being very cooperative," Wuchev said.

"Not really trying."

To Tommy, he gestured with the gun. "Come join us, little maggot." Tommy rushed to Malja's side. Wuchev glanced at the box. "Do you know how much that's worth?"

"Don't care," Malja said.

"People would give me everything they had just to look at it. I could stop running this ship. I could build a mansion, pay for guards and a few magicians to power the place. I could live like our great ancestors once did. All because a bunch of backwards Korstra zealots think that has spiritual powers. They really believe Korstra wore that. As if a brother god had need for mortal clothing. Kryssta forgive me for dealing with such heretics, but it's worth it."

In Wuchev's eyes, Malja saw more than sheer greed. "When I approached you, you couldn't turn me down without causing suspicions amongst the crew."

Wuchev sneered. "They already were on edge because I wouldn't allow them in here. If I turned away easy money like you ... well, I'll tell you something, though — I never thought you'd make it across the deck in this storm. You're reputation is well earned."

"The storm," Malja said, another point clicking in her brain. "No mage-rats. You conjured it."

"Remarkable, isn't it?" he said and lifted his shirt with his free hand. A design like seven blades spinning in the wind tattooed his stomach. "Spent my whole life working on only the one spell. Takes a lot out of me, that's why I kept the one crewman alive. I needed a partner."

"So, what now?"

Wuchev sauntered back and forth in front of the box, waving the gun in lazy motions. His pleasure at holding somebody in his power filled the air with an arrogant stench. His eyes twitched and searched with paranoid fervor — mad from magic. "Now, my pretty dear, I'm going to—"

The hull screamed as a long crack formed near the floor. Water spewed into the air like a fountain gone berserk. Wuchev jumped, and Malja took full advantage of the precious seconds afforded her. She hurdled the box and blocked Wuchev's arm as he tried to aim. The gun fired into the air, flame licking out of the damaged barrel, and the burnt smell swirled around them. He spun away from Malja and attempted a few jabs, but she far exceeded his limited skills. She feinted to the side and punched him hard on the temple. His eyes rolled back and he dropped to the floor.

To Malja's surprise, Tommy also had taken advantage of Wuchev's initial distraction. While she had been disarming the foolish Captain, Tommy had snatched the robe. He stood on the edge of the shadowed hold as water blanketed the floor.

"Wait," she called, and despite his worried expression, he did not run away.

Malja bent down and shouldered Wuchev. As the frigid water rushed around her feet, she stood and groaned like the old ship. He was lighter than she had expected but still a burden. She looked at Tommy's questioning face and said, "If I don't have to kill, I won't." *I'm glad I don't have to kill you.*

Tommy led the way through the hold and into the narrow corridors. Wuchev's head dragged on the walls, but Malja had enough trouble lugging the fool to worry about his forehead getting cut up. Water followed them, and when they reached the first set of stairs, Malja could feel the little heat left being sucked away by the ravenous sea.

Stepping out onto the main deck, sheets of rain covered them. The waves had become mere foothills in the sea, and the wind had eased back to a strong breeze, but the storm had not abated. Wuchev could get the thing going but he couldn't control it.

Malja placed Wuchev on the deck, resting against the door frame. With reverence, Tommy approached the port railing. He held the robe over the side. He dropped it into the sea. Walking back, he wore a solemn grin. Behind him, light blue painted the horizon as dawn approached, promising a warm sun and a pleasant day.

The ship took a long time to sink. There was no rush. With Tommy's help, Malja lowered a lifeboat into the water after laying Captain Wuchev inside. She searched the cabins for the young crewman, called out for him, but she never found him and he never answered.

Later, when the storm had vanished into the distant horizon and the ship had disappeared into the sea's darkness, Malja rowed under the soothing morning light. Tommy stood in the boat for a while, displaying excellent balance.

That's when Wuchev let out an enraged roar and swiped Tommy's legs. The boy splashed into the ocean as Wuchev lunged for Malja. Malja fell back, posted her foot in the air, and caught Wuchev in the gut. His eyes bulged as the air in his lungs forcibly shot out of his mouth. She tossed him overboard.

Tommy scratched and clawed at the edge of the lifeboat. Malja rushed over and reached for him — his skin paling and his body shivering in the cold water. As she pulled him up, Wuchev splashed to the surface and latched onto the boy. He punched the boy's ribs. He grabbed at the boy's hair. Madness painted his face as he tried anything to break that boy's grip.

"I'll drown you, maggot!"

Malja swung her leg over the side and pressed her foot against Wuchev's head. She looked straight at Tommy and said, "I promise you, I won't let go." Pulling on Tommy and pushing on Wuchev, she started to separate the two.

Wuchev screamed, but Malja did not stop. "I'm sorry," he blubbered. "I'm sorry. Don't let me die. I'll take it all back. I didn't mean to hurt anybody. I wasn't going to drown the boy."

Malja raised her foot and for a second, Wuchev smiled as if he had won. With her teeth clenched and her top lip lifted in a snarl, she slammed her heel into his nose, breaking it with a gush of blood, and sending him into the water. His muted screams were strong enough to come through the water for longer than she had expected. She yanked Tommy aboard, and without pause, returned to the oars.

Tommy looked at her, his eyes shimmering with such a blend of emotion, Malja couldn't tell what he thought. She stared right back at him, unwavering, not giving him an alternative but to deal with his thoughts. She saw fear in those eyes. And anger. And newborn freedom. She thought she saw tremors of the magician within him. And she knew he saw the monster within her.

But he stepped over to her. He sat at her knees. And he rested his head against her leg.

Tumus joined her, snapping Malja from her memories. Malja couldn't decide if that was any better. They were quiet at first. Malja wished she would leave and chose to scan the trees rather than risk inviting conversation. She tried to clear her mind, but Tommy's eyes would not leave her. She even tried to think about Gregor's attacker, but doing so with Tumus right there left Malja feeling wrong as if she had defiled his memory a little. She hoped Tumus would give up, but such hopes were dashed as Tumus cleared her throat.

She began with some dull talk about Fawbry, the cooling weather, and horses. Malja answered in as few words as possible. She knew Tumus was building up the courage to say something and just had to wait it out.

At length, Tumus said, "What do you know about the Chi-Chun? Other than the superstitious nonsense Fawbry spouts."

"Not much."

"Well, let me teach you some things."

"No, thanks. Don't mean to be offensive, but I don't really care what you believe. Korstra, Kryssta — all that religious stuff never served me well."

"Then I feel sadness for you," Tumus said with honest

pity in her voice. "Listen, though, please. I'm not seeking a convert. I do think what I have to say is important for you and our task — it's about Cole Watts."

Though Malja did not look away from the woods, her skin prickled. "I'm listening."

"Thank you," Tumus said. "First, you must see that those who follow Korstra and those who follow Kryssta were not always enemies. Long ago, the brother gods ruled as one, and the world lived in glorious peace. All existed in perfect balance. All was as it should be. Trouble came along with Elatria — an exquisite princess. Some say a goddess as well. The brothers each fell in love with her and each sought to win her over the other. But they are gods and immortal. The world suffered under their endless battle. Until one day, Korstra made a bold and gracious gesture. To save the world, he would give up Elatria and dominion over half the people, and in exchange he called upon Kryssta to do the same."

"Split control of the world and nobody gets the girl. Nobody's happy, but their pain is equal."

"Exactly. But Kryssta betrayed Korstra and stole Elatria away. What neither god knew was that they had formed Elatria themselves. And so she required both of their love to exist. Without Korstra, she perished. Now, Fawbry will no doubt tell you this was all Korstra's fault, but —"

"What does any of this have to do with Cole Watts?"

Tumus smiled as if pitying a naïve child. "Elatria's death brought about the Devastation."

Malja shook her head. "I don't believe that."

"It doesn't matter if you believe or not. It is true. Elatria died, and the Devastation came, erasing most of the world and reshaping the rest. Korstra wept at this loss, but he still had control over half the remaining souls. That included the magicians. Korstra looked down and saw a man drowning in Dead Lake. He pulled together all the matter he could grab quickly and transformed that man into a conduit — a godlike creature, but a damned one, who would someday aid in Korstra's return to power, yet never enjoy peaceful bliss."

"Barris Mont?"

"Yes."

"Are you saying that through Barris Mont a brother god has sent us on a mission to find Cole Watts?"

"Patience. I'm almost finished. Korstra promised there would be signs to tell his followers if the brother god taking control was him or Kryssta. One of these signs, one that tells us Kryssta is coming, is called the Rising of the Dead. Don't listen to Fawbry. We don't think corpses will come back to life. That is nonsense. We circle Dead Lake so that Korstra can speak to us through Barris Mont at any time. But as for the dead — well, what do you know of science?"

"Almost as much as I know about religion."

"Before the Devastation, mankind created many wondrous things. Buildings that could fly, ways to communicate across oceans, and machines that could think and work and talk. It took a tremendous amount of magical energy, but they succeeded. These are the dead we worry about. The machines. If they rise again, Korstra will have lost. So, Korstra made us, the Chi-Chun. We absorb the energy, we redirect it if needed, we keep the dead dead, and help prevent Kryssta from victory."

"Sounds like more superstition."

"Except that Cole Watts, the one we seek, builds these machines."

Chapter 11

Of all the land in Corlin, the Freelands had been hit hardest by the Devastation. Though it had never been good land for farming, it had flourished with rugged trees and dangerous wildlife. After the Devastation, it transformed into barren rocks. Those creatures that survived did so by the most ruthless means. No day passed without the death of something. And oftentimes death was preferred. By the time trees grew again and more animals returned, those that dwelled in the Freelands had grown accustomed to the area. They understood and accepted its rules. Many saw no other way to live.

Malja led her team along the remains of an ancient road. Every so often they came across a sign marking the way. The signs varied in size. Some were like a shield posted on a metal rod. Some were enormous, mounted on metal framework, spanning the distance across the pocked pavement and beyond.

"The road used to fill up the whole space," Fawbry said "I've seen a few up North still intact. I can't imagine what the world must've been like to need a road this wide. I mean, look there." The skeleton of a grounder long ago stripped of anything valuable rusted off to the side. "These grounders weren't big. A road this wide — you could've fit five, six, maybe seven or more across. Can you even begin to picture the numbers of people a world like that had?"

Malja didn't have to. Thanks to Barris Mont, she had seen it. That world had been breathing and vibrant. It overflowed with exuberance for human life that literally floated amongst the clouds. Surely a world like that would never allow monsters like Jarik and Callib. She didn't lie to herself — evil must have existed. But in her world, especially in the Freelands, people tolerated evil. People tried to strike bargains with evil just to be left alone, to survive.

In the Freelands, evil thrived. Here, such things held a twisted logic. But in that glistening, peaceful world she had witnessed, it made no sense. Evil lived off want. There was no want in that world. *Don't be an idiot. People always want what they don't have.*

The road hugged the sides at each hill and found every crevice as a detour. Half the time chewed-up pavement disappeared leaving only a dirt path to follow. Sometimes the road vanished completely. In fact, Malja realized they could have picked up a different road by mistake. According to the sun, though, they still headed in the right direction. That would have to suffice.

"You're pushing my tolerance," Tumus said.

Fawbry had been making little comments all day — praising Kryssta for fresh air or cursing Korstra for a sore muscle. Malja wondered what offense had brought Tumus to the point of threats. The answer forced her to suppress a laugh. Sitting in his saddle, scrunching his features with studious concentration, Fawbry silently read from a tiny book.

"Put away that vile affront or I'll be forced to put it away for you," Tumus said.

Feigning confusion, Fawbry looked up from his text. "This? The Book of Kryssta? It's hardly an affront. The fact that Kryssta's guiding hand kept this book safe when I nearly drowned in the Yad should tell you that much. Besides which, even if you don't follow its wisdom, the poetry in these pages is beautiful." Fawbry held the book out. "Here, try it."

Before Malja even saw Tumus's frustrated, hurt features, she knew Fawbry had done a nasty thing. Odds were that Tumus could not read. No shame there — most people couldn't read. But for Fawbry to flaunt his education, to literally shove it at her, that lacked any sense of respectability.

Perhaps he recognized his error because, in a solemn voice, he said, "I know you don't believe, but let me share with you one thing from this —

> *My brother, my earth, my home, my world —*
> *The endless angles of ourselves —*
> *We inhale what others exhale —*
> *We are formed from others' dust.*

— Do you see? We are all one to the brother gods. After all, even Korstrians believe the goddess Elatria was formed by the brother gods together. We are all one."

Tumus led her horse ahead, but her hostility lessened for awhile.

As the day wore on, Tommy's fever returned. Malja dismissed her concerns at first, but when dusk approached, there could be no denying. He had begun the day bright and joyful — sitting upright in the saddle, pointing at trees and birds, smiling. Now, he curled in Malja's arms, shivering and sweating, pale and pained.

Tumus had noticed, too. She never stopped watching him, and every little groan or shift or sigh he made elicited an overbearing response. In seconds, her horse would ride alongside and she bombarded Malja with questions about the boy that had no answers. She touched the boy's brow with the back of her hand, touched his shoulder to readjust his shirt, and touched her own lips mumbling prayers. Malja bit back her desire to knock Tumus off her horse.

The sun lowered turning the gray rocks milky blue. The air grew colder. Ahead, they saw a dilapidated structure — a welcome sight amongst the endless rocks.

The one-story building had a wide roof that jutted out several feet creating a covering for the horses. *Probably meant for grounders,* Malja thought. Shaped like two cylinders smashed together, the building appeared to have been a way station. Old batteries were piled against the wall, each one so empty of magically-created electricity that its power gauge lacked enough power to give a reading. No surprise, of course. Those things hadn't been charged in over a generation. For that matter, the only thing keeping Nature from reclaiming the space was the barren remoteness of the area — that and the occasional travelers fixing it up for a night or two.

"We'll stay here tonight," Malja said. Tumus dismounted and hurried to help Tommy down. Malja turned the dappled gray away and said, "See if you can find some firewood." Before Tumus's confused pout found a voice, Malja spied Fawbry near the doorless doorway. "Be careful."

Fawbry stepped away. "Don't worry. I'm not going in there until you do."

Once Tumus left on her futile errand (Malja would be shocked if she found more than a sapling or two), Malja eased Tommy off the horse and handed Fawbry the reins. Tommy stood by one of the dented posts holding up the overhang. Any minute he might collapse. She pulled out Viper and approached the doorway. Something smelled horrible like urine-soaked rags.

Inside, Malja saw a dusty, marble-topped counter with holes smashed through it. Behind the counter, an archway opened up to another room. Rubble lined the paint-peeled walls. In the center, a circle of stones marked the spot many had used for a campfire. Malja peered at the domed ceiling — black with soot. She couldn't see an air vent, but there had to be one, otherwise a campfire would choke the room.

Just in front of the campfire, she found the source of the stench — four rabbits and a hawk, blood drying on the floor. Her thought — blood sacrifice of one of the smaller religions. When she turned to leave, however, she saw that her thought was severely incorrect.

"What in Kryssta is that?" Fawbry asked. "It sure stinks."

"I told you to stay outside," Malja said.

Tumus entered with Tommy. "It started pouring out there and the overhang is full of leaks. Cold rain is the last thing Tommy needs."

"Go back outside. I'll take care of this," Malja said with a glance at the undulating, brown mass pasted high on the wall.

Tumus stepped closer. "Is that an egg sac?"

"Cocoon. Now get out before anything breaks free of that."

Fawbry raised an eyebrow. "Looks like someone threw a crap at the wall."

Tumus pointed at the dead animals. "Those are for the baby when it gets out."

"It's a snake-cutter," Malja said, "and when it leaves that cocoon, it'll eat everything in sight."

Fawbry scratched his head. "So can't you kill it now while it's stuck in there? We'll get a fire going and have baby snake-cutter for dinner."

"I told you to wait outside. When I strike, if it survives the first blow, I don't want it coming after any of you."

"I don't want that, either. You've convinced me. We'll wait outside."

"It's too wet, too cold," Tumus said. "Tommy can't take that."

"It'll be just a moment," Fawbry said. "Just pray to your Korstra to protect the boy."

"I do. All the time."

Malja pointed to the doorway. "Go. Let me get this done." Tumus scowled, but she followed as Fawbry headed out. Tommy, however, stepped forward. He placed his hand on top of Malja's — the one gripping Viper. His hand felt clammy and ill, but his eyes cut into her with icy clarity. She tried to pull away, but he held fast. "I don't like killing," she said, unsure of why she spoke, hating the little girl she heard. "And I've killed more things in my life than I ever wish on anybody. Everyday I live with it. Everyday I know I've got more killing ahead. Right or wrong doesn't matter. Justified or not doesn't matter. I do it because it's all I know. And it kills me."

Tommy released her hand and collapsed. Tumus hurry to his side. Malja wiped her face — tears glistened off her cheeks.

Breaking the silence, Fawbry said, "Um, I think it's hatching."

Malja did not move. She searched Tommy's unconscious face for an answer as to what had just happened. Behind her, she heard the cracking cocoon. He had touched her and she could not stop her talking. She heard the kittenish cry of the baby snake-cutter. He had pierced her with his eyes, and she revealed so much of herself. She heard an odd crinkling as the baby snake-cutter ate its cocoon. The only answer she saw — Tommy had used magic on her.

"Malja," Fawbry said as he clambered on top of the counter, "it's almost out."

She spun around to face the baby beast. White like snow

and covered in mucus, the four-foot snake-cutter flopped to the cracked, tile floor. Its tubular body and hundreds of tiny, slithering legs gave it the snake illusion. Its head, however, lacked any such image. It didn't even have a face. Instead, its front end closed tight like a sphincter. Eyes on either side and a long-hair mane made this one of the ugliest creatures Malja had ever seen.

Righting itself, the baby shook off the fall, eyed one dead rabbit, and launched into it with abandon. It slurped and groaned and mewed. Each sound flipped Malja's stomach. She clenched her teeth and snarled. The snake-cutter's eyesight may have been poor, but its hearing worked just fine. Its head shot up, searching for a threat.

Malja looked back at Tommy. He had used magic. On her.

With a raw, primal scream unlike any war cry she had ever made before, Malja swung Viper. The tip hooked the snake-cutter. It cried out like a child strangling its tears and jerked away causing its skin to tear. Malja kicked it to the wall, shredding its skin as it ripped free from Viper. Wriggling against the wall, it moaned and screeched as its blood pooled. Malja moved forward. It cringed at her approach.

Again she struck hard with Viper, launching the baby into a new frenzy of cries.

Again she struck hard. Holding his ears, Fawbry yelled, "Just finish it." But she didn't want to. She wanted it to fight back.

Again she struck. Blood sprayed against the wall. Tumus cried out at each blow, her shocked voice melding with the dying creature's.

Again. Malja's arm shook as Viper cut straight through to the floor.

The cries weakened. The blood flow lessened. Still,

Malja struck.

When she finally stopped, she let Viper clatter on the tile floor. She stumbled backward. Rain and thunder played a double rhythm. Her frenzied fury still echoed along her skin, pulsing with her heartbeat. Lightning flashed. She looked at Tommy — the magician. He gazed up, shivering next to Tumus.

"Don't ever use magic on me again," Malja said and walked into the rain.

Chapter 12

As night edged in, Malja worked on the horses. Under fluttering torchlight, she slid her hands along the withers, kneading when required. She scooped the rib cage and massaged the chest, working the rubdown all the way to the legs. She cleaned out a metal container and collected rainwater so the horses could drink. She talked to them and combed their manes. By the time she had finished, most of her anger had dissipated.

Fawbry spent this time clearing out the mess she had made. He built a pile of rabbit, hawk, and smoke-cutter bits and covered it with stones and mud to keep scavengers away. He built a fire using the charred remains in the campfire circle — not enough for a good blaze, but it would keep them warm.

Malja had watched this as she worked. Now, she stood by her dappled gray, stared out at the rain, and listened to its drum rattle on the overhang. She heard Fawbry behind her — sounded like he made extra noise so as not to startle her into a swift attack.

"You okay?" he asked.

She shrugged.

"You can come back in, you know."

She glanced at the doorway. "I don't think that's a good idea."

"Don't be stupid. We're your friends." Malja raised an eyebrow and Fawbry laughed. "I am, at least. I'm trying. Tommy is, you know that. Tumus probably not. The point is, we'll listen to you. We understand."

"I doubt you could ever understand."

"Oh, really? Just because I know when to run, doesn't mean I don't know anything about anger, about rage so powerful it takes over all of your thoughts."

"This was more than just being really mad."

"I know. I do. You think of me as I am, but even a coward will fight if there's no other choice."

Lightning flashed against the wet, rocky landscape. Fawbry rested a hand on his black mare. Malja watched as he tried to rub out a harsh memory swimming just below the surface of his words. An authentic smile crept upon her lips. Any more anger and these horses won't want to be touched again.

Fawbry said, "Years ago, when I was a young man, I lived up north with my parents. I worked our farm in the mornings and went to school the rest of the day. Things up there are a little better, a little more stable, and my father thought some kind of education would set me up for a good life.

"I did enjoy school. I miss it. It was simpler. You just had to show up and learn. At least, that's how it was until I started noticing girls."

"We do have a way of complicating each other's lives."

Fawbry grinned. "Yes, we do. I've often thought men and women would be better off living in separate colonies that only get together once in a while to procreate."

"I can think of a lot of men and quite a few women who'd hate that idea."

"Well, they never went after the wrong girl. It sounds silly now, but back then I would've done anything for Yolen. She possessed me with a fire I've never felt for another woman. But she was not a good person. I put up with her using me and tolerated her infidelity. I was a real idiot. My parents saw through her, and they tried to make me see, but I ignored them. What kid is going to listen to his parents when they're telling him to give up on someone he wants?

"Things changed when I met Pung Kirkle. Big guy. Always had two big friends with him. Yolen left me for Pung, and I couldn't do anything about it. As hurt and sad and betrayed as I was, I would've just gone off and cried and maybe, someday, moved on. But Yolen was cruel, and Pung was her new dog. It began with simple teasing, then they started hitting me in passing, and then ... well, then we get to the whole point of this."

Thunder rumbled. "I take it you fought back," Malja said, "and you felt bad about it. This is different."

"I didn't just fight back. I lured them. I waited until Pung and his two thug friends were alone. And then I called them names — I knew that's all it would take to get them to chase me. I ran down a dead-end alley. They slowed down, knowing I couldn't escape, thinking they had all the time. But I had planted a metal pipe with jagged scrap attached.

"My first two swings caught them by surprise. Both of Pung's buddies fell. One lost his nose. The other took it in the side and was bleeding bad. Pung — I saw him become afraid. That made me feel good. Really good. Like I had exposed him in front of the world. Like I was powerful. Euphoria and—"

"I know it well."

"I suppose you do. Anyway, he swung at me. The problem for him was that I had been hit by him many times. What was one more? I didn't flinch, and I didn't turn away. I took the fist."

"And then you were in range."

"Exactly. I smashed out his kneecaps. He curled up and cried — may have even wet himself. But I didn't stop. I couldn't. All my hatred and anger and jealousy and everything poured out with each strike. I just kept hitting. I screamed and kicked and I couldn't find a way to stop. He almost died. Had I been stronger, he would be dead.

"I ran away that day. Headed South. Trouble for me was that the South was more barbaric than I could handle. Brains got me far, but in the end, people down here solve everything with a sword."

"Is this meant to make me feel better?"

Fawbry patted his horse and headed toward the door. "No. Just wanted you to know you're not alone."

The rain picked up, and the wind shifted. Malja backed up, but the storm reached her no matter where she stood. From the doorway, Fawbry said, "Come back inside."

"Maybe later."

With an angry howl, the wind shifted again taking the rain with it. The sudden drop in noise filled up with Malja's laughter. It came out in short bursts, initially, but when Fawbry joined in, the floodgates released. She laughed hard, not even sure why, but letting the wondrous sensation run its course. Tears formed and her chest ached, but each time she thought she had control the laughter exploded again. It seemed like it would never end. Until she heard Tommy cry in pain.

A bright light flashed through the doorway. Malja dashed over to Fawbry. Inside, Tumus sat against the wall holding Tommy in her arms. Both were covered in sweat. Tommy's eyes were closed.

"He's okay," Tumus said. "This one was rough, but he's fine now."

Seeing Tommy secure in the Chi-Chun's embrace twisted a hot spear through Malja's chest. With a sharp motion, she waved Tumus outside. Easing away from Tommy took some maneuvering, but Tumus managed not to wake him. As she stepped outside, Malja said, "How much more of this does he have to go through?"

"I don't know. If he were back at the lake, Barris could guide him. Alone like this — he has to find his own path to each spell."

Malja stepped back as if slapped. "How many spells does he have?"

"I don't know. Barris didn't tell me. But the power I've been absorbing from him is more than anything I've ever experienced."

She watched Tommy curl up. Her heart pounded unlike anything she ever felt before battle. When he woke, she hoped he would understand and not think she had broken her promise. She clasped her hands so she could feel the tight grip that she imagined kept Tommy safe. With a curt nod, she said, "Then we can't wait. Fawbry, saddle up our horses. Tumus, you stay here with Tommy. You'll be safe enough inside. The smell of that dead snake-cutter should keep most things away. We'll leave what food we have, but ration it. And when we get back, I expect him to be in good shape. You let anything happen to him, you better run. Understand?"

Tumus nodded. Malja suppressed a grin — good to see her authority voice still held its power.

"Where are you going?" Tumus twisted the black shreds of her robe. "In case Tommy asks."

"To find Cole Watts, of course."

Chapter 13

B y the time the rainstorm had passed and the morning sun breached the sky, Malja and Fawbry had crossed nearly ten desolate miles. The horses were exhausted. Two long treks with little rest in between left them sore and irritable. Malja shared the sentiment.

She pictured Tommy waking up to find her gone. She knew she had made the right choice — he needed close care right now. Care which, it galled her to admit, she could not provide. But even if Tumus could help him with his magic, he would also miss her. He had to. When she returned, he'll sprint towards her, his arms open wide, ready to wrap around her legs. Maybe then she'll get him to listen to orders more often.

They stopped for an early-morning break and let the horses wander free for a bit. Not too far, though. Malja kept eyeing them like a worried parent watched a toddler. This was the Freelands, after all. Not a place to be caught without a horse.

Later, when her bladder demanded attention, she asked Fawbry to watch the horses. She found a boulder to get behind and relieved herself. Afterward, she didn't move. She remained squatting as her mind flashed through the memories Barris Mont had churned up.

I'll kill that damned thing for what it's done to me. She'd rather have Gregor's voice pestering her about paying the dead their honor. She considered those thoughts for a moment. Perhaps it was as simple as that. If Gregor had been right, and he often was right, then by paying them their honor, she had been able to bury her memories safely. Barris Mont dug them all up again. If she paid the honor once more, she hoped that might be enough to stop these flashes.

Except Barris didn't unearth the horrors of her years as a warrior. He dug into her formative years. There weren't any deaths to pay honor to. In fact, he pulled her into his head after seeing her at seventeen on the day Gregor ...

She stood fast and nearly toppled from the head rush. With one hand against the boulder, she took several deep breaths.

Gregor.

That day had started out so well. After three days hunting, she had accumulated enough meat to last them through the first quarter of the Korstraprime season. Not only had she caught and butchered the meat, she even smoked it herself. Usually Gregor insisted she return with her catches so he could smoke it in the little smokehouse he had built out back. But this time, she had done it all on her own.

She constructed a sled from fallen logs and loaded it with all the meat. Lugging all these pounds had not been easy, but as she neared home, the energy within her rose to the occasion.

"Gregor," she called out. "Come give me a hand."

She couldn't wait to see his face when he laid eyes on all this food. When he didn't come out, she cupped her mouth and bellowed, "Wake up, Lazyhead. I'm home."

Nothing. Her body tensed as she approached the shack. *He's probably asleep,* she tried to assure herself, but her innate warrior's sense, something she had yet to really understand at seventeen, warned her that the situation felt wrong.

She opened the front door and let out a sharp gasp. Blood covered the walls and floor and furniture. An animal had forced its way in and attacked and shredded Gregor.

No. On the walls, Malja saw burn marks, and the air smelled sour. Magic.

Her stomach flipped and she rushed outside to vomit. She heaved until nothing more would come. Rolling on her back, clutching her stomach, she fought for a breath that didn't shake with tears. *Gregor. It's not fair.*

She heard something — a sound of movement from the shack. Malja got to her feet and lowered her stance. Caution, hatred, anger, and sorrow swirled around her heart. She pulled out her short sword. *Just like hunting dinner.*

Moving slowly, carefully, she stepped into the shack. The bedroom door was closed. She positioned in front of it with her sword ready to thrust forward should anybody attempt to open the door and bolt out.

Again she heard movement. Her prey hid in the bedroom. No doubt in her mind.

Her nerves jangled and her hand shook. It was one thing to spar an opponent where there were set rules of conduct. To fight for real — she had never experienced such a thing. But one glance at the bloody mess on the floor ignited her rage.

"For Gregor," she yelled and kicked the door in. She rushed forward, looking for anyone or anything to slaughter.

A man jumped from the side. Without thought, she lunged at him, thrusting her sword into his gut and twisting the blade for maximum damage. His face froze in astonishment as blood dribbled from his mouth. She stared back, her own mind stunned by the act of her first kill.

But the door slammed behind her and a blow to her back thrust her against the opposite wall. In the surprise, she dropped her sword, leaving the dead man skewered on the floor.

A man pushed his fist in the exact spot he had struck

her, forcing her to arch away from the pain. He grabbed her arm and wrenched back and upward. With his other hand, he kept her face shoved into the wood. She could hear his heavy breath in her ear and felt his bristled cheek against her head. He smelled of fish and alcohol.

"You're not supposed to be back yet," he said.

"I'm going to kill you," she said, trying to fight back. He raised her arm and the pain stopped all struggle.

"Now, now. You just calm down, and we'll get out of this fine. See, you shouldn't be here. We were told only to kill the old man. Not the girl. Specifically not the girl."

"What? Somebody hired you to do this?"

The man chuckled, and it sounded like alley sex with a whore. "Oh, stupid girl, see that? You got far worse things to worry about than me. I mean, you don't want to be on the bad side of the brothers. And if they're killing off somebody you care about but letting you live to stew in it, well, you must've done something pretty bad to them."

Malja stomped on the man's toe. He screamed out but held on to her arm. With his free hand, he punched her in the side.

"Don't do that again," he said. "There's no need. I just want to get out of here alive. I've told you who's responsible, so there's no need to bother with me. Think of me as just the messenger. I'm sorry the news was so bad, but I got my own problems and now that I've done this, I'm hoping a lot of my problems will go away."

"You killed Uncle Gregor."

"And you killed my friend."

"I'm going to find you. You understand? I'll find you."

"Shut up, now," he said.

Only then did Malja realize the man had hardly moved since putting her against the wall. She thought of the burn marks and the sour stench. She felt his hands grow warm, the smell grew worse, and she felt a blow to her head that knocked her unconscious.

Hours later, she woke and gathered her things. She made a funeral pyre out of the shack, and over Gregor's burning body, she vowed to kill Jarik and Callib for this and all the misery they had brought to her life.

"Malja?" Fawbry called. "You okay?"

"I'm fine," she said and leaned her head against the cool boulder. Whenever she thought about that day, the day that started everything, she rarely considered the man she killed. Her first. She always thought of Gregor and the vow and the man that got away. But her first kill had also been that day. That's the honor she had failed to ever pay.

She took a moment to remember his face — hook nose, small eyes, and a dark hatred on his brow. She knew nothing more about him than that frozen look, but it sufficed. She could feel the memory easing down inside her to a place where it would not plague her thoughts.

"How much farther?" she asked Fawbry as she walked around the boulder.

"A couple miles, I think, and we'll see the cabin."

Fawbry stretched out on the ground, and Malja sat next to him. Playing with a few rocks in the dirt, she knew her mind needed to refocus. She said, "The other night Tumus mentioned something about machines. That Cole Watts makes machines."

"Yeah, she did."

"She? I thought Cole Watts was a man."

"Not in the least," Fawbry said with a snicker.

"Oh? Did you have a relationship with her? Is that how you know her?"

"Absolutely. She's an incredible woman. I met her when I first came down here. She helped get me on my feet, helped me work through all my guilt over Pung."

"You're not together now. What happened?"

Fawbry's eyes darkened. "She's ambitious. I tried to be, too, but you know what? Nolan was right. Some parts of us can't be changed. I don't have the ruthless instinct required. By Kryssta, I couldn't even keep a gang of griffles together."

Neither spoke for a while. At length, Malja left to retrieve the horses. When she returned, she said, "So what about the machines? Is it true? Cole Watts is making machines."

Fawbry swung up onto his horse. "Probably."

* * * *

The ride was short. The afternoon sun barely began its descent. Fawbry pointed to the last hill, and when they crossed over, Malja saw the cabin.

The base had been built of gray and white stone. The rest used wood and a flimsy metal not often found this far from a city — Cole Watts would have had to carry it in on horseback. A gated, metal fence formed a perimeter. One floor, a porch, some windows, even a chimney. In a town or countryside, a cabin like this would be enviable even with the rust, the dirt, and the dents. Out here, such a thing was unfathomable. If Malja had not seen it, she would never have believed it.

They walked the horses a short way back and tied them to a tree out of eyesight. Then they approached on foot. Malja had Viper out and ready. She heard the wind, saw the shadow of a little creature darting under a rock, smelled the Freelands' usual odors of mold and decay. A patch of tilled soil made a rough square in front of the home, but nothing grew and nothing rotted. Just empty soil.

"Don't touch the fence," Fawbry said as they

approached the gate. He picked up a rock and tossed it at the fence. The entire gate brightened as if reflecting the sun. A second later, when it had returned to normal, only a pile of dust remained of the rock.

"She's a magician," Malja grumbled.

"No. But she's always been fascinated by magic, and she's always tried to find ways for regular people to make use of it."

"So how do we get in?"

"As long as the password's the same, that'll be no problem." Fawbry winked as he pulled out his small copy of the Book of Kryssta. He searched for the correct page, leaned towards a meshed, circular object next to the gate, and said, "Password start —

> *We are fragile —*
> *Without wonder, we languish —*
> *Without knowledge, we suffer —*
> *Without purpose, we perish."*

The gate clicked open. Fawbry flashed a smile and led the way onward. They walked the yard without incident, but the fence and gate had heightened Malja's alertness. She would have pounced upon a bird if it had flown near her.

As they stepped on to the creaking porch, Malja listened for any signal of attack. She stopped at the front door and motioned for Fawbry to stay still. She listened. She scanned. She sniffed.

"I don't think anyone's here," she said.

"Of course not. That would've let me out of this mess." Fawbry banged on the door. "Cole? You in there?"

Malja shoved Fawbry to the side. "Just 'cause nobody's here doesn't mean you can't be heard."

"I'm going to assume you're referring to either hungry

animals or Kryssta himself, both of which don't matter in this case. Let's just try the door."

The door opened without trouble, and after feigning shock, Fawbry entered. Malja scanned the outside one last time before following.

Inside, the cabin was sparse but tasteful. It reminded Malja a little bit of the shack she had lived in with Gregor. Though far more roomy, the place felt comfortable like a true home. It also felt wrong — the comfort did not exist for them. They were trespassers.

"This is Cole Watts's place?"

"I know it doesn't seem like it, but this is it." Fawbry pointed to a torn, yellow couch. "I slept there for almost three months. And that fireplace hated me — it always sent sparks flying in my direction. I swear it used magic. Didn't matter where I stood in here, a spark always found its way to me."

"How sweet. Where's Cole Watts?"

"Not here, apparently."

"I can see that much. Where would she go?"

"Could be anywhere."

Malja heard a clicking — a steady sound like a bird repeatedly poking between rocks in search of food. *Click. Click. Click.* Slow and silent, Malja edged around the room listening for the source. *Click. Click.* Fawbry heard it, too. He moved just behind Malja as she neared a closet door. Making as little noise as possible, she tried to lift the door latch. It popped up with surprising ease.

As she opened the door, the clicking grew louder. Old wood-plank stairs led into a dark basement. "We'll need torches, if we're going down there," she said.

Fawbry peeked over her shoulder. "Then let's not go down there."

"Just get some wood."

"Wait. She probably has something rigged for light." Taking tentative steps, Fawbry climbed down the stairs, all the while feeling along the walls with his hands. "Here we are." He pushed a button and the basement flooded with the pale light of magical electricity.

Malja went downstairs. The basement reminded her of being in Barris's mind — stark white room, stark white couch, stark white tables. This was no office, though. The tables overflowed with metal parts, colored wires, and strange equipment. All showed various levels of decay — some just tarnished, some rusting away. The air was cooler than above and smelled oily.

From a back corner, Fawbry called out. "Found that noise."

Malja walked over, careful not to disturb any of the metal contraptions. At Fawbry's feet Malja saw what looked like a metal arm ending in a sphere, the whole thing mounted on a wide, flat stand. The clicking noise appeared to correspond with the arm moving in a circle.

"What is that?" Malja asked.

"Don't know. Just another of Cole's machines."

"I'm glad Tumus isn't here. She'd think this is the end of everything."

Fawbry chuckled.

Browsing amongst the tables, Malja came across a doll's head. Wires poured from the neck and connected to a metal box with several buttons. Like water raging over a levee, a memory of Jarik and Callib splashed into her.

She had thought it no more than a toy. At seven-years-old she couldn't be expected to understand. Besides, her fathers presented it as such.

"See here, little Malja? See this button? This brings the machine to life," Jarik said, pushing a green button, and indeed, the machine sprang into motion.

It looked like a stick man with a doll's head on top. Over the coming years, she would learn its true purpose. It stood firm on its platform, but it could thrust attack, side parry, and weave its torso with amazing agility.

"Every day," Callib said, standing at her doorway, "you are to practice with this machine. This is in addition to the rest of your training."

"Cole Watts," Malja said, and Fawbry looked up. "She made all this?"

"She's very bright. But she thinks she can save the world. Bring us back to before the Devastation. I told her that there aren't enough people anymore. Cities like those of before — they need people to operate them. Lots of people. I doubt we have enough left in the world to man even one city."

"Is that why you left her?"

"She started trying to contact Jarik and Callib. Said she worked for them before, that they understood her, that they would help her change everything. It was pretty clear she didn't need me anymore."

"Doesn't look like she's been gone long."

"She might've gone to stock up on supplies. Maybe we should wait. See if she returns."

"Maybe," Malja said, wondering first if the doll head would sound like the one she practiced on long ago, and then if she wanted to hear that sound ever again.

"Look at this." Fawbry lifted a rusty frame from a pile of rusty frames.

"Looks likc scrap."

"That's why it isn't. Cole likes to hide her work in plain sight. The shiny, impressive machines usually do the least. Something like this, though — it could be great. Maybe some super weapon for you."

"Or maybe just a frame for a painting."

"Who paints anymore?"

"Somebody must, otherwise, where do the paintings come from?"

"Very true. But in this case, very wrong. See here? There's a button on this frame."

"Don't —"

Too late. Fawbry pushed it. A high-pitched whine emitted from the frame. Fawbry placed it on the table like a father handling his baby and backed away. A clipped beeping began.

"That doesn't sound good," Fawbry said. The beeping quickened. "I think maybe we should —"

"Run!"

They raced up the stairs. As they reached the top, a loud whomp reverberated the floor and hot air pressed against their backs. Fawbry fell hard while Malja stumbled but regained her footing. Dust filled the air. Crackling like a healthy campfire seeped up through the floorboards along with thick smoke and intense heat.

Malja helped Fawbry to his feet and shoved him towards the door. He pushed back in the opposite direction. The smoke thickened fast. She saw only a hazy outline of the cabin. She tried to turn Fawbry around, but he swatted her hands away. He tried to speak and merely coughed into a hacking fit. But even as he coughed, he managed to point and Malja finally understood. She had been the one going in the wrong direction.

As they staggered outside, flames climbed the walls. She forced Fawbry to keep walking until she thought they had reached a safe distance, several feet beyond the fence. There they both collapsed — coughing, gasping, wheezing, and eventually breathing.

Fawbry sat up first. Malja watched as his face broke into the smile of someone relieved to be alive. She had seen that look many times; probably had it cross her own face, too. Often, the next expression became serious — either a heartfelt gratitude or a sober recognition of mortality. Neither came to Fawbry's face, though. Instead, he looked into the distance with dismay. And he raised his hands.

She knew it was too late but instinct propelled her to her feet. Five Bluesmen covered them with three handguns, a shotgun, and a guitar.

"Care for a song?" the guitarist said.

Chapter 14

They rode in on horseback. Malja and Fawbry's hands tied behind their backs. The shotgun-wielding Bluesman towed them along, holding both of their horses' reins in one hand. Their captors made no effort to hide their destination. That troubled Malja more than anything.

From afar, the place appeared like an oasis — an extra-large farmhouse surrounded by acres of working farmland nestled amongst barren mountains. Two men handled livestock in a small but sufficient pasture. Farm hands tilled land, harvested food, fixed fences. A well-maintained stable stood near a wide barn. In every direction beyond — gray rocks, straining trees, dust and death.

The closer they came the more Malja smelled the fragrant farm aromas — most pleasant, a few rank. Even as she noted numbers of men and women, exit windows and doors, easy to climb terrain and dangerous spots to avoid, the smells lifted memories of Gregor into her mind. He knew a farmer nearby and would trade for manure to fertilize their garden. He would take their food scraps and dump them around their apple tree. If she wrinkled her nose at the odor, Gregor would look askance and say, "Just wait 'til you taste an apple from here. You'll want to toss everything onto the pile." Gregor said he had picked the spot for the shack because of the tree. Wide and gnarled, wrinkled with age, unlike any apple tree Malja had ever seen. And he had been right. It created the most delicious fruit.

One outbuilding they passed harbored three men working amongst a mountain of sawdust. Guitars in various stages of construction hung from every available wall, post, and rafter. Next, a row of well-kept but cheaply-made buildings lined the way. Each appeared to be packed with people sleeping.

They rounded a corner and approached the stables. One squat building on the right Malja took for an outhouse, but when she peeked inside, she saw a man in a black suit standing on a stool before a cracked and smudged mirror. Another man circled his legs, making marks on his clothes with a white stone while nearby two women used needles and thread on some cut cloth. Malja had seen Gregor mend his shirts and pants before, but never had she seen such fine threads and delicate work.

Three stable boys hurried forward and walked all seven horses away, leaving Malja and Fawbry heading with the men toward the house. A chubby fellow rocked on a wooden chair and smoked a pipe. His pale skin stood out amongst all his darker brethren.

"Get out of my chair, Suzu," the guitarist said.

Suzu bounced out and lowered his head. "Sorry, Willie."

Willie took his seat and strummed a few chords. "Go tell her we're back. Tell her I got two birds. Ask her what she wants with them."

"You got it, Willie. I'll be right back." Suzu hurried inside while the group listened to Willie play — nothing fancy, but a pleasant tune with a steady rhythm like a trotting horse.

A sweating laborer walked by with a basket of potatoes on his shoulder. "Hey, Willie," he said with a booming voice.

"Hey, Rev. We gonna have a feast tonight?"

"You know it. Might even gut a knonol in honor of our

guests."

"Oh, that'd be great. I love what Cook can do with a knonol."

"That's the truth."

The men laughed, and Rev rounded the house with a joyous step. Malja had seen towns filled with people who found peace and happiness in a special harmony they built between each other and working the land — rare but she had seen them. She had also seen towns ruled by madmen and followers who thrived on abducting the unfortunate and carving up their bodies and souls for survival. But never had she seen both co-exist. How Willie could be an assassin, a Bluesman, and also carry on with Rev like a happy farmer baffled her.

Suzu returned with a glass of some gold-brown drink. Little clear cubes bobbed in the glass, making odd chiming clinks. He leaned his bulk over and whispered to Willie. Eyeing Malja with both fascination and trepidation, Suzu went back inside.

With a nod at Shotgun, Willie said, "She wants them locked up. Don't take any guff, but keep them alive."

Malja didn't know the word *guff,* but she got the idea. She stayed silent and Fawbry only grunted as they were roughly handled. Shotgun guided them to the stables — ten stalls, five on each side, and a wide path down the middle. Shotgun opened a stall and tied them to the barred door. As he backed out, he tipped his head with a contrite but firm expression. He pulled a stool over and lowered with a relieved exhale.

"I don't play guitar as good as Willie, but if you want, I'll play awhile for you."

Malja turned away. She had worried that Fawbry's cowardly streak would cause her trouble, but looking at him, she saw rage. She nodded at him — *I feel the same.*

"I hate you," he said. Her surprise must have shown because he continued. "I may not have been doing great, but my life was a lot better before I met you."

"I didn't ask for you to come along here. I wanted to leave you at Dead Lake."

"Well, don't worry. When we get out of here, I'm leaving you and all your stupidity."

"I'm not the one who blew up that house."

Fawbry rattled the gate and kicked at the hay floor. "Hey, can I be put in another stall? Please. I can't stand to be with her."

Shotgun raised his hands and shrugged.

With another kick at the door, Fawbry said to Malja, "Y'know, if you would just let this all go, so many people would be alive right now. Death is all over you like perfume, and you don't care. Poor, little Malja is mad at her daddies so everybody must suffer. Have you ever stopped long enough to think about what a mess you've made of all this?" While he barked out all his frustration, Malja wanted to defend herself but felt as if Gregor, not Fawbry, criticized her actions. She stood like a scolded schoolgirl. She could see his disapproving frown and wanted to hug him. *This is for you, Uncle Gregor. I do this for what they did to you.* But as the figure before her pounded the stable door, she saw Fawbry once again.

His voice rose as he continued his rant. "Jarik and Callib — clearly they don't want you finding them. They don't love you. And for most of us scattered around the world, Jarik and Callib don't matter. They're just names."

"You're wrong 'bout that," Shotgun said. "Those magicians are nothing good, but they're far more than just names."

"Great. Thanks. Now I can't even argue without somebody interfering."

Malja took a sharp look at Shotgun. "What do you know about Jarik and Callib?"

"Kryssta help me," Fawbry said. "Have you heard nothing I've said? Let it go or we'll all be killed. You want Tommy dead?"

Malja shoved Fawbry aside. Swiping her hair away from her eyes, she returned to Shotgun. "You were going to say something about the magicians."

"Me? I got nothing to say." Shotgun stood and scratched his chin. He sauntered out of view for a moment, every step infused with a cockiness that under different circumstances Malja would find attractive. When he returned, he held Viper. He practiced a few swipes, inspected the blade, and even ran his thumb on the edge. "This is a fine weapon."

"I know," she said, gritting her teeth.

"Lots of chinks in it, though. Must've tasted a lot of action."

"Keep playing with it, and I'll see it gets a taste of you."

His confidence faltered, but he brought it back quickly. He did place Viper gently on the ground, though. Refusing to meet Malja's eyes, he settled on his stool and crossed his arms. Malja called to him and banged the gate, but he refused to answer. He cast his gaze outside.

I couldn't have scared him that much. But something had shifted. Fawbry crouched as far from her as his bonds would allow. Malja leaned back against the gate. *Wait, listen, and observe.* The more information she had about her opponents, the more chances she'll have at success — Gregor taught her that.

Hours later, after the sun had set, Suzu appeared. He whispered to Shotgun, who stretched his legs. "Time to go," he said. As Fawbry rose, Shotgun shook his head. "Just her. You stay with me for now."

"Of course," Fawbry said and slumped down.

Suzu led Malja along the dirt path to the house. Little bags with candles lined the path. Two armed men guarded the porch. Even from halfway down, Malja could hear the party. Giddy yelps, explosive laughter, shouted names — all riding the crest of a thundering music wave.

Off to the side, a group of people formed a large circle. Two dogs were let loose, growling and barking and fighting. People cheered and laughed.

At the porch, however, Suzu turned away from the door, leading her around the side. A rusting ladder connected to metal stairs that jutted from the wall ended at a platform and door high above. "Go," Suzu said, pointing upward.

"Can't climb with my hands tied behind my back." Suzu pursed his lips and searched for someone to help him decide what to do. Though Malja enjoyed watching him wiggle in discomfort, she had more important matters at hand. "Relax. I want to go up there to meet your boss."

"She ain't my boss. She's just—"

"Shut up, Suzu," Willie called as he turned the corner. He had taken off his suit coat, and his fine shirt stuck to his chest with sweat. "I'll take her up." Suzu relinquished Malja with grateful relief and scurried away.

Willie escorted her into a small, sumptuous apartment. The pounding party downstairs reverberated in the floor and walls. Willie directed her to an overstuffed chair and waited by the door. Low candlelight and deep-red paint closed the room in. All the furniture had been carved with intricate patterns and several portraits of guitarists hung on the walls. In the distance, Malja heard a dog yelp followed by a huge cheer erupting from the circle of onlookers.

A woman entered from a dark hall. At first, Malja only saw the dress — a slinky, red cloth that hung loose and low.

It sparkled off the candles. As the woman closed in, her dark skin finally contrasted enough to be seen. She was exquisite. Malja rarely found women appealing, but this time she thought she saw what men found so interesting. Though flat-chested and more straight than curvy, sexuality slid off this woman like lava burning down a mountainside.

She flowed into a chair opposite Malja and with a rich, silken drawl said, "My. Look at you. All grown up."

"You're Cole Watts?" Malja knew the answer, felt it the second she saw the woman, but she had to ask anyway. Gregor had many sayings on the subject of assumptions.

"I am," Cole said. "And you're a very special young lady."

"Is that why your people have been trying to kill me? Because I'm so special?"

If Malja's abrasiveness rattled Cole, she never showed it. In fact, the more tension Malja felt, the smoother Cole seemed to become. Crossing her legs, showing off her strong, tone calf, Cole said, "Sweetie, think about it. I've had you under guard for quite awhile. If I'd been trying to kill you, why would you still be alive?"

"You've certainly been trying to stop me from finding Jarik and Callib."

"That I have been doing. But not for any reasons you might think of."

"Then why don't you tell me."

"Mmm, yes, we'll get to that. But first, Willie, please excuse us."

Willie leveled his hard eyes on Cole. "I think it best I stay. To protect you."

"That's very thoughtful," Cole said, her voice harder than his eyes. "However, it's entirely unnecessary. Malja's a seasoned fighter. She won't harm me until she knows such an action will help her. She's not rash. Willie dear, you could learn quite a bit from a woman like this."

"Maybe so, but —"

"Willie. This office don't belong to you, yet. So leave now." As an afterthought, she flashed a faux smile. "Please."

Clenching his hands, Willie said, "Of course. My apologies."

Cole watched him until he turned and walked out, closing the door with a loud bang. Returning her seductive smile, she faced Malja. "It's never easy being a leader, is it? Something we have in common, I imagine, considering Fawbry."

"He can be trying."

"Why that's an understatement."

Raucous laughter pushed up from party. Malja asked, "What's the celebration?"

Cole rose and poured a drink at a small counter. Her hands moved smooth and sure, but they were calloused and scarred. "Dear sweet Malja, you ain't ready for that party. No, ma'am, not just yet."

"Okay. Since you won't answer my questions, I guess your pal Willie might help me out."

"A little patience, please. This is our 'getting friendly' phase. Or if you prefer, this is foreplay. We'll get to the hard action soon enough. And as for Willie — well, I suppose that's part of what this is about. That is to say, just who is it you're going to support?"

"I have no interest in your games."

"'Course you do. You want Jarik and Callib, don't you? Well then, you'll have to help me out."

"Fawbry warned me you were ambitious."

"Oh, I'm a lot of things."

"So what is it you want? How do I help you?"

Cole returned to her chair like a spider that knows its

prey is caught. "Right now, patience. I've got a party to attend or I'll lose some support. Next time we meet, you'll understand, and then we'll see if you'll help me." Cole finished her drink. "I'm off now. Willie's waiting outside to take you back. Goodnight."

Walking back down the candlelit path with Willie just behind her, Malja tried to digest her brief meeting with Cole. The woman certainly intrigued her, but Cole's strangeness worried her more — in this case, strange meant unpredictable. If Malja wanted to get free but also obtain the whereabouts of her fathers, she'd have to find a way to make Cole predictable. Or get real lucky. When Willie placed a firm hand on her shoulder and guided her away from the stables, she knew luck had abandoned her.

He took her into the middle of the fields where only the moonlight revealed them. Two men joined up — he called one Robert and the other Lonnie. More oddball names — and she thought Tommy was a funny name.

"Is he ready?" Willie asked.

Lonnie kept his eyes on the house. "He's the best he's gonna be. I don't promise anything beyond that."

"I know. Thanks for doing what you could."

Robert kicked a clump of dirt. "C'mon, let's get this done before anybody wonders where we gone to."

Grabbing Malja's arm, Willie led the group toward a rundown shack on the far end of the field. Next to the shack, the necessary equipment for making alcohol sat. Heat radiated outward and with it a sour odor — the machine rarely got rest, Malja guessed. They didn't stop there, however. They walked for several minutes — well beyond the tilled land and into the harsh world just outside the oasis. They came upon two men seated before a rock face. One of the men strummed a sad tune on a beaten guitar while the other blew a soft accompaniment into a mouth harp. Neither stopped playing as Willie approached, but the guitarist did acknowledge him with a nod.

Willie shoved Malja to the steep rocks. Lonnie rushed ahead and walked right through the stone — just disappeared. As they led Malja through the false wall, she tried to determine which of her captors was the magician.

A cool, stone passageway led to a round room — probably had been an old cave. Years of usage showed many improvements including cots, table and chairs, a metal stove made from old cars, and even an aluminum chimney that bored into the stone ceiling.

Robert pushed Malja into a chair. Willie opened his hands and said, "I'm going to be honest with you — as best I can. But in the end, you're going to have to choose which of us to support."

"If this is all you've got," Malja said, surveying the cave, "then Cole's already won."

"Oh, we've got more. We've got Old McKinley for one. Lonnie, bring him out."

Lonnie went deeper into the cave. He returned pushing a chair on wheels. A bony, old man sat in the rickety chair with a stained, blue and white blanket covering his legs. His curly white hair made a drastic contrast to his dark skin. The left side of his body drooped — eye, mouth, shoulder, arm. His right eye quivered and drool slid from his mouth.

They brought Old McKinley beside her. He lifted his right arm and touched her face like a blind man. His hand traced her throat and shoulder, then settled on her breast.

Malja slapped him away. "No way," she said and stood.

An invisible force yanked her back into the seat. She growled as she tried to move, but her body had become locked to the chair. The old man's hand fondled her again. This time she saw the tattoo on his palm — *he's the magician.* And considering how fast he pulled off that spell and how destroyed he looked, he had to be quite talented.

"Now," Willie said, "you may not want to help us, but I can't have you helping Cole Watts."

"Don't you think you've jumped ahead a bit? I mean, I never said I wouldn't help you."

"I tend to do that. Jump ahead. 'Specially when I know the outcome. See, I can read it on your face. You won't help me. At least, not yet. So why waste the time yapping?"

Old McKinley groaned and slobbered.

Malja wriggled but couldn't move enough to avoid the old man. "Look, Cole didn't tell me anything. Maybe you can explain to me what's going on and then I can—"

"No, you won't believe if I tell you. Understand this is about a lot more than just who runs this farm. This is about real power. Big power. You got to see the party to get it."

"Then what am I here for? Just giving the old man a thrill? Take me to the party."

Willie motioned to Lonnie who wheeled Old McKinley back into the dark. Malja felt the pressure holding her to the chair release, but she made no attempt to get up — not with Willie and Robert holding the advantage.

Willie said, "That old man is more than a magician. He's seen things — and now he sees things. This wasn't about him getting a thrill. By Korstra, he's so old, I doubt anything works down there. No, this meeting was so he could touch into you, gauge what I should expect from you."

"You sure? Because his hand seemed very happy."

"He ain't no joke. He's a great, powerful man. He sees you now. He knows you won't help me. He tells me so, but I still find it hard to believe he's never wrong. I mean, we're all wrong once in a while."

"I don't understand what you people want but—"

"I know." Willie backed away. "Don't worry.

Tomorrow. We'll try again."

Without another word, Robert escorted Malja back to the stables.

Chapter 15

Fawbry grumbled as he tried to find a comfortable position for sleep. With his hands secured to the door and fresh manure clogging the air, he failed. Malja stood as far from him as her bindings allowed. Since her return, Fawbry hadn't said a word to her. He hadn't even shown the slightest bit of curiosity as to what had happened when they took her away.

Not that she could tell him much if he did ask. Clearly, some kind of struggle for rule had become quite serious. Cole Watts and Willie had followers, bases of operations, and mounting pressure. Why they wanted her and what went on at those parties troubled her, but for the moment, she saw little recourse other than to wait and gather more information.

Waiting, however, would be torture.

More than any other, two thoughts plagued her mind. First, she kept picturing Old McKinley — his dead left side, his drooling mouth, his eager bony hand. He smelled like a rotten fruit — a sharp, sour odor of sickness. Every time Malja saw his visage in her head, she thought of Tommy.

Her overactive mind leapt ahead and formed a hideous image — Tommy as a withered man. Crazed by magic, palsied and helpless. Old McKinley's brother in insanity.

Whenever she managed to obliterate this line of thinking, a second powerful thought hit her. Shotgun snored from his stool. Good. She didn't want an eavesdropper.

"Fawbry," she said, her voice soft. Fawbry leaned

against one wood wall and closed his eyes. "That's okay. You don't need to talk. But, please listen." She paused, her trepidation like new food in her mouth. "I-I'm sorry."

Fawbry raised an eyebrow. "Excuse me?"

"You're right. I've dragged every one of you into this, and now you're stuck here because of me. For that, I apologize."

Looking away, he said, "Doesn't really do me much good now, does it?"

"I just thought I should say that. When you told me about Pung and Yolen, I understood more than you realize. You did what you did out of the need to satisfy the Black Beast."

"What's that?"

"Something Gregor, my guardian growing up, once told me about. I talked often to him about what I would do if I ever found Jarik and Callib — how I wanted them to suffer for all they had done to me. 'Vengeance,' he said to me, 'is the Black Beast that never lets you free.' He pointed to the charred wood in the fireplace. He told me the Black Beast was like that wood. On the surface, it's cold and harsh. But its desire burns quietly inside, waiting for the opportunity to reignite. Then it'll fiercely consume itself and all around it until nothing remains but ash. 'Let go of all your hatred,' he said to me. 'Be careful,' he said. He warned me."

"So why don't you listen to him?"

"I did. I tried. But the Black Beast never lets go. When I was seventeen, Jarik and Callib had my Uncle Gregor murdered. That's when I made my vow to the Beast. That's when my search really began. So, I'm sorry that you got caught in this."

"You really think that's enough?" Fawbry said. He kept his gaze on the dark ground. "Saying you're sorry is just words. You should've listened to Gregor. The man sounds smart. Had you listened to him, we'd have never met, and I'd be a lot happier. So I don't really care that you feel bad about any of it."

Malja could think of nothing else to say that would make things better, so she let silence cover them. It didn't last long. A minute later, Fawbry turned a challenging look at her and said, "If you're truly sorry, then change. If not for yourself, then do so for Tommy. Change your ways of doing things. Otherwise, you ought to shut up."

"You mean I should put away Viper and become a farmer or something? No. I'll always be a warrior."

"True. But *why* you kill is more important than just being a warrior. Change that and you change everything."

The next morning, they took Fawbry away. They came in, gave Malja a bowl of oatmeal, and left with Fawbry. All throughout the day, she waited but he never returned and no explanation came. She thought of Tommy often and of Fawbry's words, and she wished she believed in one of the brother gods so she'd have somebody to pray to. Instead, she waited. Alone.

When night arrived, so did Suzu. The walk up to Cole's office was quieter. No party this time. No candles lining the path. No drunken dog fights. All appeared calm and sleepy.

Entering the office, Malja came upon Cole and Willie — anything but calm and sleepy. They glared at each other like enemies on the battlefield. One raised an eyebrow. One clenched teeth. An entire argument occurred without a word spoken. At length, Willie let out an exasperated sigh and stomped out, rattling the windows with the slam of the door. Cole dismissed the tension with a wave and poured Malja a drink.

"I'm sorry about him. He's a fool. He's got his friends and his magician, but he's a fool. Yes, I know about Old McKinley. I'm sorry you had to meet that lecherous scum, but as a result, you've already helped me."

"Oh?"

"Until last night, I only had rumors and deductions to figure out Willie's strength."

"You followed us. Then the whole meeting between you and me was just a way to flush out Willie's hiding place?"

"I did want to meet you, and I do still want your help. But bless your heart if you think each step I take revolves around you. You've come here at a complex time, and I must capitalize on any opening my opponents leave me."

"*That* I can understand."

"I thought a fighting metaphor might help." Cole tapped her painted nails on the arm of her chair. "Do you know how magic works?"

"You're born to it."

"But that doesn't mean you can't understand how it works, even if you can't do it."

"Then I guess, no, I don't know how it works."

Cole tapped her nails faster. "It works by vibrations. Some of it does, anyway. Little, rapid movements that grow together, feed off each other, until you have a reaction. It's called sympathetic vibration. Magicians and many animals can create these initial vibrations. But it also occurs all around us. Music, say for example the kind created from a guitar, also creates sympathetic vibrations — not nearly to the magnitude needed for magic nor the right frequency for that matter. Unless, of course, you brought together a lot of musicians, built a device that could increase the power of their total vibrations, and knew what frequencies to emit. Why, then you might be able to create your own magic."

"Are you saying you've done this? Created your own magic?"

While Malja sipped her drink — something fruity with a hint of alcohol and amazingly cold — Cole slipped out of her chair and sauntered toward a stout cabinet. She pulled out a metal contraption that looked like a crab with its legs wrapped around a ball. She set the thing on the little, wood table before Malja.

"Creating magic is easy," Cole said. "The real challenge is creating machines that can work with or even enhance magic."

"So what does this machine do?"

"That one can tell if you're lying. It can read your body signals at a mere touch and then interpret those signals as to whether or not you've been a naughty girl and lied to me."

"I take it you want to use it on me."

"When you're ready to pledge your aid to me, then we'll use it. After that, you'll get all you want and more."

"More?"

"My sweet little Malja, oh, yes more. After all, it's not enough to find Jarik and Callib, is it? That would be nothing, but for blood. Don't you want to know why you are so special? Don't you want to know where you come from? Who you really are? Or is it all just about killing them?"

Malja sprang to her feet and put out her arm. "Fine. Hook up your machine. I'll take your pledge."

"Dear me, no. Not like this. Why that would be extortion — well, it would if there were any law in this world. Besides, I can't show you tonight anyway. But there'll be another party tomorrow night. If you really want to pledge yourself to me, we'll do it then."

"Pledge *myself?* You said it was just my help."

"See that. You're not ready. You don't get it yet. But you will." Cole headed down the dark hall. "Be sure to tell Willie I give him my fondest."

When Malja left the room, more confused than when

she had arrived, Willie grabbed hold of her. She didn't resist. She wanted to go this time. Without a word, he guided her into the fields.

Robert and Lonnie were less agitated this time, and all three escorted her to the magic wall that camouflaged their cave. The two men guarding the way smiled and gave Malja a casual salute before starting up a new song. Once inside, they sat her down and Lonnie rushed off to fetch Old McKinley.

The old man started with her legs this time. He inched close to her, sniffing her thighs through his mucous-filled nose. As he worked toward her face, his white stubble poked at her neck. He leaned back, his head at an awkward angle, spittle dancing on his lips, and whispered to Willie.

"You're lucky you didn't make that pledge," Willie said. "If you'd been lying, the magic in her machine would have fried you up in seconds. And if you really meant your pledge, the magic would have enslaved you to her will."

Malja laughed. "Right. Sure. You guys aren't very good at conning people. I mean of course I'll believe in fire magic. Everybody knows magic is based on the elements. And while you're fake wall trick is arguable, I'm sure many would reason it out for themselves — but sniffing me and suddenly knowing what happened and then throwing in magic that can enslave people. Nobody's going to believe that."

Willie didn't change his attitude at all. "There's far more magic in the world than you'll ever know." Malja thought of how Tommy had made her talk so bluntly. "If you give Cole what she wants, you'll see some of the worst."

"Then you tell me what I want to know."

"And what is that?"

"Cole knows where Jarik and Callib are. Finding them is why I came here. That's all I want."

Old McKinley coughed hard. As he hacked away, Lonnie rubbed his back and looked at Willie with a hopeless expression.

Willie rested a hand on Old McKinley's shoulder when the coughing fit ended. He turned back to Malja. "I can't tell you where to find the magicians."

"But you do know. Until now, you've been Cole's second-in-command. From what I've seen, you still are in many ways. It's not possible that she would hide that bit of information from you. So you choose not help me."

"It's not that simple."

"Then I guess I'll go see Cole."

"You can't go to any of them. You don't understand what they're trying to do. Cole, Jarik, Callib — they've all gone too far."

"Then tell me."

"How can I tell you of powerful magic when you don't even believe in the smaller stuff?"

Old McKinley groaned and raised a hand to Willie. After some whispering Willie nodded to Lonnie, who wheeled the old man away, but not before Old McKinley pointed a shaking finger at Malja. He almost spoke but started coughing, and Lonnie rushed him out before it could become another full-on fit.

Willie consulted Robert next. Robert didn't like what he heard but relented under Willie's stern eye. He dug into his coat and produced a vial of yellowish-green liquid. Willie took the vial and handed it to Malja.

"Tomorrow night," he said, "when Suzu comes for you, drink this. It only lasts a short time but it'll deaden many of your readings so Cole's machine will fail. The machine will say you speak the truth but its magic will be blocked."

Malja examined the sickly liquid. "Why would I trust you? This could be poisoned."

"Old McKinley said you'd take it. He said you're a great warrior and once you've thought through the strategies involved, you'll see we have no better alternative except to kill you. But we don't want to kill you. It would keep you out of Cole's hands and Jarik and Callib's, but then there'd be nobody bold enough to fight them."

"Do you always speak so vaguely?"

"Just drink it tomorrow. Cole will think she has control over you. She'll tell you everything and show you more. You'll see then. You'll understand. Then I expect you'll very much want to kill her."

* * * *

She spent the night alone. Fawbry had not been brought back. The idea that he might be dead weighed her down in between thoughts of magical machines, crazed old magicians, and strange liquids. Only her goal kept this bizarre place in perspective.

Listening to Shotgun snore while he should be guarding her only reinforced her will. She could have busted free many times, but that would send her back to the beginning — and Fawbry would be right about her creating a mess. Stuck in the middle of two power-hungry factions had brought her no closer to answers. Of course she would drink the liquid to gain Cole's trust. The real question was simply how much information could she get before blood had to be spilled.

Tommy flashed in her mind but she pushed him away. She knew what she had to do. It had to be kept that simple.

Chapter 16

Stuck in the stall throughout the day, Malja had nothing to do but rest, sit, and listen. She heard a lot of activity, more so than any previous day. They were preparing for something special. She heard Rev and Willie walking by outside. They were engrossed in a debate over which animals could be slaughtered for the party without damaging the needs of the farm. She heard plenty of guitars being tuned and plenty of joyful voices building in excitement as the day wore on.

But she couldn't be distracted by these sounds all day. At some points, her mind would wander. Inevitably, she would see and think of those she had killed. And she thought of the Black Beast.

She had not told Fawbry everything. She had spoken of Gregor's warnings and her rage-filled vows and all that one would say to dissuade another from the Beast. But the truth she withheld could not be hidden from herself — the Beast satisfied a part of her soul. Every step closer to her prey felt good inside like a brief intoxication. She would never turn away from it. The purity of her hatred promised an equal ecstasy when the bastard magicians fell. The Black Beast may be all that Gregor had warned, but it gave her so much, too. It gave her a purpose, a reason to live.

That was something Jarik and Callib had taken away. They denied her any chance to discover who she wanted to be. They molded her as they desired. But they didn't expect her to be so strong willed. She learned what she wanted and shunned the rest — but only of what they made available.

It all sounded good in her head, full of righteous bluster and woe-is-me anger. But underneath all that lay two stones of truth embedded in her bones. The first told her she could never get her fathers to see her as anything more than their failure. That's why they got rid of her.

The second stone reminded her of the coldest truth — she had been free from them since age ten. They wanted nothing to do with her and had no control over her actions. At some point, she had to stop blaming them and accept that all her actions are her own. But the Black Beast always answered that one with its raspy growl — *when they're dead.*

* * * *

That night, when Suzu arrived, he acted differently. He spoke with greater care and even added a polite "Yes, ma'am" and "No, ma'am" when answering her. He fumbled with the locks and walked with a stiff back that pushed his belly out even further.

"Wait," Malja said, clenching her legs together. "Before we go anywhere, may I ... you know?"

Suzu's cheeks reddened. "Of course, ma'am. I-I'll turn around, but don't try nothing. There's lots of people out tonight. You wouldn't get far. And I'd hate to see you get hurt."

"Thank you," Malja said. Once Suzu had his back to her, Malja downed the bitter liquid in the vial Willie had provided. Hoping the metallic taste wouldn't coat her throat long, she squeezed out what little pee she had so Suzu would hear. "All done," she said, and with a warm smile, added, "You're a real sweetheart."

Suzu giggled. "Follow me, ma'am. I'll get you there safe."

They walked up to the house, the party sounds loud but

not as raucous as before. Suzu's demeanor returned to his earlier formalness. Those mulling around the grounds whispered and exchanged darting glances. Whatever Cole had planned for tonight, it seemed everyone knew.

By the time they reached the office, Malja's body had become numb. The potion had begun to take hold. She still retained control; she just didn't feel anything as if all her nerve-endings had been frozen in a Korstraprime ice storm. Cole entered the room, showing no sign that Malja appeared any different.

"Well, my dear Malja, normally I'd be a better host, but the party's waiting on you," she said, dressed in a black gown with a white sash — ready for a party, indeed. "Let's just get the unpleasantness over with. Then we can go join the fun downstairs. That is, if you're ready to pledge to me."

"If it means I'll find Jarik and Callib, I am."

Cole beamed. "Well, bless your heart, that's simply wonderful." She wasted no time getting her machine. She pulled one of its crabbish arms outward and said, "You just hold onto this and speak the truth."

Gregor taught her about bravery and heroics once. It had been a summer morning and he cooked up talma root and tomatoes for breakfast. He said that true heroes act without self-regard in battle because they have controlled their fear. "See, sweetie, if you worry about getting hurt or dying, you'll be too cautious and too slow. The brave accept death, and therefore are free. After all, if failure means death, then you'll never live to regret failure. So, heroes charge in, knowing that if they live, they will win the prize, and if they die — then nothing. They rest."

Without pause, Malja grabbed the metal arm. "Cole Watts, I pledge myself to your service."

Cole concentrated on the machine, but she made no

reaction. Malja's hands tingled. "Try again," Cole said.

Malja cleared her throat and repeated, "Cole Watts, I pledge myself to your service."

Cole frowned, and Malja's hands tingled more. Her feet began to tingle as well. The potion was wearing off. It had to be. And while she knew in her heart that Gregor's words on heroism were true, the idea of dying in Cole's office instead of in battle turned her stomach.

"Thank you," Cole said in a monotone that gave away nothing. She packed up the machine and left it on the small table. Lifting her eyebrows and spreading her hands open, she said, "As promised, I will tell you where the magicians hide. You'll find Jarik and Callib in the City of Ashes."

City of Ashes — a massive cemetery of a city covering endless miles of the western mountains. Remote, difficult terrain, and inconvenient as a place from which to command. If Cole spoke the truth, they really picked the last place Malja would have ever looked. "You can be a little more specific. That city is enormous. I can't even be sure you're telling the truth. In fact, why don't you grab your machine and prove your honesty."

"Now, now. Patience. Once we're ready I'll walk you right up to them."

"I don't trust you."

"You don't have to. Just know that those brothers have hurt many people besides you. Some of us are willing to go far in order to see them pay." As Cole spoke, her eyes darkened. "I have no interest in betraying you. If I'm to harm Jarik and Callib, I need you."

"Then what are we waiting for?"

"First, we have to stop the Willie fracas. Once this group is united, we'll have our army. Then I'll show you the exact location of those nasty magicians' hideaway."

Malja sat back with a disapproving sigh. "You people

think magic can do anything. It's not like that."

"Oh, but it is," Cole said, her eyes firing up as she rose. "Before the Devastation, magic was used like most people think. Government and law kept it limited to the simple elements. They feared its power, so they controlled its users. After a few generations, magicians were born into thinking that's all they could do. But the Devastation came and wiped away the rules — no governments, no laws. Before, with billions of people, anarchy would have been madness. But with only a few scattered millions, anarchy is freedom. And that kind of freedom means nobody can stop a magician from reaching the fullest potential."

She walked into the dark hall. She turned, revealing her lovely profile, and said, "Come along now. Let me show you what I'm talking about."

Malja launched to her feet and rushed down the hall. Cole waited at another door. Colored lights seeped through its edges. Sorrowful, mourning music drifted in with the light.

With a suggestive roll of her shoulder, Cole opened the door. A vast hall spread out before them as if the house had been gutted of all its little rooms. A balcony wrapped around the hall, and Malja saw a stage at the far end below. Two guitarists and a drummer played a slow but powerful tune while a man who rivaled Suzu in size belted out the words. Like a Kryssta congregation at worship, the packed audience swayed and called and cried. They were a mix of humans, griffles, raggers, and cholohs — others, too that Malja had never laid eyes on before. She didn't know what to make of Cole's sympathetic vibrations, but she could see the magical way this music moved its people.

"It's called the Blues," Cole said.

"I should've guessed. They are the Bluesmen, after all."

"Watch now, dear. You're going to see something

amazing."

They went down a flight of stairs ending on a landing overlooking the stage. The music stopped. The crowd stilled. All eyes turned to Cole.

Four wide flags unfurled from the ceiling. Each pale-brown one dropped down about seven feet and flowed as if a gentle breeze cascaded from above. Malja first thought of magic, but then realized these were not flags at all. They were living creatures.

On an unspoken cue, Willie entered from the back carrying a guitar quite different from any Malja had ever seen. Rather than a deep body made of light-colored wood, Willie's guitar appeared to be a shallow, solid chunk painted with rich, dark colors blending into each other. Unlike a normal guitar, this one lacked a hole for the sound and was adorned with silver knobs and switches.

Willie stepped onto the stage. Robert wheeled out a large black box with a thick, black rope coming out of it. Willie picked up the end of the rope and stuck it into his guitar. He touched the box and suddenly the guitar came to life. Willie played a few notes and the sound wailed out of the box like a crying brother god. The crowd roared its approval.

Four Bluesmen brought out chairs and guitars — normal looking ones. They took up a steady, pulsing rhythm which the drummer joined in on. Willie played over this, his guitar making one long cry after another. Watching Willie perform mesmerized Malja, and she missed the moment when still other guitarists joined. Looking around the stage, she now counted twenty men playing including Lonnie and Robert. Others in the crowd also strummed. They clearly yearned for the stage but no more space was opened.

The noise level increased as did the tempo. Willie's

playing grew frantic, but his notes were precise. He pushed the others faster and louder. More energy. More power. The music broke down into a cacophony of dissonance. Despite the sheer mayhem of sound, the crowd moved as one to a rhythm Malja could not discern. Her skin prickled as sensation continued its slow return to her body. The music grew louder and the hair on her body stiffened. The higher notes that Willie hit shivered her teeth. She peeked over at Cole. The sexuality had vanished, replaced with a maniacal anticipation.

Following the erratic drumbeat, the crowd split down the middle, backing away enough to reveal a metal frame built flush into the floor. The wood inside the frame shimmered with each note Willie played. The air smelled of sweat and lust and something Malja could not place. As the air crackled with little electric arcs, it hit her. The smell — a memory of Callib attempting to teach Malja magic. Not the sour smell of violent casting, but a crisp aroma unique to special magic.

The flag-like creatures flapped with vigor, always in time to Willie's playing. Holes opened up — mouths that stretched enough to swallow a person. They sang in harmony — loud enough to remind her of Barris Mont. An enormous explosion of sound blasted the room as if the air itself had been shattered. Malja fell to the floor, covering her ears, controlling her breathing, trying hard to stay conscious. People passed out around her. She pressed her ears tighter. She closed her eyes to stay focused.

Somebody tapped her shoulder. She looked up. All was still. Cole rested her slender hand on Malja's head and pointed to the frame in the floor.

The metal frame pulsed an orange glow that kept time with the slow moan that the musicians had settled into. Inside the frame, the floor no longer existed. Instead, Malja saw a room as if she hung from the ceiling. A round table covered in fuzzy green material dominated the room while dark wood shelves and darker rugs filled the rest. Malja thought they had blown a hole into the floor and looked upon some basement room. Except bright, noonday sunlight cut across the table.

"What is this?" she whispered.

"This," Cole said, savoring each word as it crossed her tongue, "is real magic. This is a hole into another world." Raising her arms like a prophet before her people, she climbed down the stairs and crossed the stage. "Long ago, perhaps not as long as you think, before the Devastation, magicians who knew the truth the governments denied them practiced in secret so that their power would grow and their ways would not die. They sought to improve their dominion over the world. Like little children playing with guns, they attempted to open a doorway into another world. They succeeded. Only for a second. Then they lost control, and we've all paid for that."

Malja gripped the banister. "What are you saying? This is the magic that caused the Devastation?"

Cole whispered, "Don't worry. We've not caused another Devastation."

"Well, what have you done?"

"Sympathetic vibrations. We create our own magic — just like them."

"Who?"

"Those from the other side. They came to us first, opened a portal right here. It only lasted a short while but it was enough to start talking with us. They call their magic a séance and they think of us as ghosts. Through them, we learned the Blues music and their way of life. We pattern ourselves after them for we have seen what great power exists — after all they opened a hole to our world without destroying theirs."

A portal into another world. She had no idea if such a thing were possible or if this was a hoax. Gregor certainly never mentioned it.

From their ceiling view, everyone in the house craned to see into the portal. Malja watched as a woman wearing a pink dress walked in to the séance and set the green table. She moved faster than normal as if time itself moved differently on that world. The golden-pink hues of sunset cascaded across the floor and a few minutes later night arrived.

A commotion erupted behind her. Malja turned to find Fawbry being physically moved into the hall by Shotgun and another big fellow. Shotgun had looped a rope around Viper, and the weapon dangled at his side. Fawbry looked tired and frightened but not bruised or broken.

Cole stepped forward. "Malja, I've watched you grow for many years. I've waited for you to be ready, for you to be able to see this and understand it without fear causing you to ruin this incredible opportunity we have before us. The time has come. Watch closely now."

"Cole?" Fawbry said, his face lighting up even as Shotgun pushed him toward the glowing frame in the floor. "Cole, honey, it's me. It's Faw-Faw. Remember Faw-Faw?"

The crowd mocked him, and Cole spoke to them even as she offered Fawbry a solemn glance. "Those days are gone. The Bluesmen came to me so I could build them a way through. We want to do more than just talk to this other world. We want to travel there. We want to live there. Tonight, we may finally succeed."

Several people now sat at the séance table. They all held hands and one seemed to be chanting. Their jerky, rapid motions would have been comical under different circumstances.

A dark man in a fine, gray suit sat nearby. He strummed a guitar with a gentle hand. Malja looked around the stage at all the guitarists, all the suits — all learned from this other world. Impossible.

"This isn't real," Malja said. "If you had this portal, if you had this magic without a magician, you would've left the Freelands long ago. I don't believe this is anything more than a trick."

"My, my, it seems your pledge to me may not have been all that strong. I'll have to fix my machine. As for the portal — it is very real, and you'll now see our very real problem."

Shotgun moved Fawbry closer to the frame. "No, no, no. You don't have to do this to me."

"Watch, Malja. Watch what happens to Fawbry."

"Cole, my love, don't do this to me. Please."

"Love? You left me for a pack of griffles."

Malja said, "Stop this."

"Relax," Cole said. "We're not sending him through. But you need to see to understand."

"Let me go," Fawbry said, pulling back but not strong enough to stop them.

Malja wanted to rush in and save him, but her body had become numb again. She didn't know if she'd be fast enough or have enough control to help. Her thoughts swirled and her head throbbed.

While the one man held Fawbry tight, Shotgun grabbed his hand and edged him toward the floor. Blubbering, pleading, begging — Fawbry watched as they plunged his hand into the framed hole.

He howled — a ghastly, chilling cry that caused several in the crowd to flinch. Malja heard the hand sizzle and smelled burning flesh. When they pulled Fawbry back, only a cauterized stump remained. Gray wisps of smoke drifted up like paper-thin tendrils. Fawbry cradled his stump and rolled on the floor. Tears and spit and mucous covered his open-mouthed anguish, but he made no sound.

Though she tried to be cold and stoic, Cole winced at the few gasps escaping Fawbry. She took a breath, plastered on her faux smile, and said, "Now, Malja, it's time for you to understand just how special you are."

Two men took hold of Malja and pushed her toward the portal. Her head dipped and her body followed, but the men kept her upright. She yanked her arms back. The men held on.

Too numb.

Looking down, she saw the séance magic — silly and frightening at the same time. The men each grabbed one of her feet and the world flipped over. Vomit rushed up and out — burning into nothing as it hit the portal. When Malja finally regained her bearings, she was suspended over the portal frame.

She couldn't feel her arms and legs — she just floated like driftwood on a lake. She closed her eyes, enjoying the sensation. Until they dropped her.

Her body swung — both men clamped down on her legs — so that her head went in first. The shock to her skin jolted straight to her toes like ice cold water on burning hot skin. The sudden cold reignited her numbed senses, clearing her mind even as it tortured her body.

She screamed.

Opening her eyes, she saw those around the séance table staring at her — some amused, some terrified. They moved at a normal pace now. The walls were high like a prison but a tall window showed Malja another world — buildings pressed against each other as wheeled vehicles pulled by horses clip-clopped by. Streetlamps of flame lit the area. Two children smooshed their faces against the window, looking wide-eyed with her.

A woman dressed in veils and holding a heavy book rose from her seat. Those seated around the table paled and shivered, a few mouths quivering. The guitarist slipped out of the room, muttering a strange prayer not to the brother gods but to a deity Malja never heard of — Geezuz. The veiled woman raised one hand and said, "Oh, Spirit from the Afterworld, long we have tried to meet you, to see you as more than a voice. Oh, wondrous apparition, guide us, please. Show us the way to our greatest fortunes."

Something pulled at Malja's ankles. Before she could speak, her body receded into the ceiling. And she was back home.

The band launched into a lively tune, and Cole Watts gyrated and twirled to the music. The entire crowd roared its excitement. People toasted their success and guzzled their drinks. With the change in music, the portal spell collapsed — popping and clicking until nothing remained but an empty frame, the wood floor, and the strong aroma of vinegar. They shoved Fawbry on stage, and Cole danced around him. He held his stump and gazed in the distance like a slave enduring a master's punishment.

Malja felt the majority of her numbness had vanished. The congested atmosphere closed in on her but she didn't move. She suffered disorientation, and nausea crept up her throat. She waited for it to pass and wondered if after experiencing the portal, it ever would.

The song finished and Cole, perspiration beading on her skin, calmed the rowdy crowd. "I told you all the truth. I promised you that Malja would be the key, that she alone held the secret within her. Tonight she proved it. Tonight, our sweet Malja safely slipped into another world. Oh my, and will you look at her face. She has no idea. That's okay, dear, soon you very much will."

"Let Fawbry go."

"No, no. He's our insurance for your co-operation. Now that I've proved what you can do, I need to study you. I need to figure out the process, so I can build a machine to let all of us travel through. And when we have that, we can access all the wonders that the world has. We can be great powers of this world. Jarik and Callib will bow at our feet, and we shall destroy them. But don't worry. You're far too precious. We'll test the machine on Fawbry first."

No.

In seconds, the hall became a tumultuous cavern of violence. Two brutes had closed in on Malja, and she wasted no effort in dispatching them. Blows to the head. Blows to the gut. She fought through the crowd with one focus — save Fawbry.

Suzu blocked her path. She elbowed his chest, bending him over, locked his head in her arms, kicked back to ward off those trying to sneak up on her, and propelled Suzu like a siege engine tearing apart a tower wall. Three people were knocked aside.

"Malja, stop," Cole said. "You won't be harmed."

The fury state had taken over. Malja dodged, attacked, and surged ahead. A battle cry from the stage slashed through the commotion — Willie. He pulled a sword from the neck of his guitar and plodded towards her.

Watching Willie, Malja never saw the attacker on her left. Two punches to her stomach took her by surprise. She doubled over and saw Viper hanging on a rope — Shotgun. Instead of straightening up, Malja jabbed her elbows skyward. Though her right met only air, her left caught Shotgun with a satisfying crunch. Before he recovered, she tore Viper free and swung up to meet Willie's attack.

The blades clanged and a metal chip flipped through the air, flickering light in all directions. The sound echoed across the hall. The chaos ebbed as the crowd settled, backing up a respectful distance. Malja had experienced this before. The people wanted to watch a show. From the look in Willie's eyes and the strength of his attack, Malja suspected they would put on quite a show indeed.

Willie ignited a flurry of blows that Malja should have parried with ease — her spinning head and sudden exertions worked against her. Twice she locked his straight sword in the curve of her blade, but could not snap it loose from his hand. They circled, each feigning attacks to feel out the other's counters, waiting for the other to overreach. Malja knew a good fighter when she saw one. Willie took his time, searched with his eyes, moved with grace and agility. He displayed patience and balance. A good fighter — definitely. Perhaps even an excellent fighter.

Wrapped in her thoughts, she failed to notice he had taken smaller steps for the last few, closing their distance by her own doing. He jabbed forward. When she blocked, he used her power to spin in the opposite direction and land a blunt chop on her side. The hit shocked her. Before she could get over her mistake, he swung through, catching Viper and nearly disarming her. The momentum knocked her off balance and onto the floor. Willie's sword tip caressed her neck.

"Stop," Cole called out, her voice trembling.

Malja kept her eyes on Willie as she breathed deep, sweat drenching her face and hair.

"Malja? You okay?"

Fawbry? Malja searched for where his voice had come from. Fawbry must have snuck off during the fight. At the same moment as Willie, she found Fawbry, his good hand leveling a handgun at Cole Watts.

"Malja?"

"I'm okay."

Willie helped her to her feet. The cut on her side looked

worse than it felt and would hamper her until it healed.

Fawbry cleared his throat, and in his most powerful voice, he said, "Malja and I are leaving here. Nobody'll follow us. If anything happens, I'll kill Cole. When we feel safe, she'll be set free."

Willie said, "What about —"

"No talk. Get three horses ready. Do as I say or she dies."

"Kill her, then. We got on just fine before she came along, we'll be fine if she's gone."

Fawbry hesitated. Malja said, "Then we'll shoot someone else until we find one that matters."

"Come now, Malja," Willie said with a half-cocked grin, "Why do you think I went to the trouble to get you in here?"

"You *want* me to kill her? Then why are you fighting me?"

"You were hacking away at everybody. That, and I needed time to get my men in place. I figured everybody would want to watch us fight. See, Old McKinley is in charge now. Look around."

Malja, Fawbry, Cole, and many of Cole's supporters surveyed the still room. Willie's men guarded all the exits. Others formed a barrier around the portal frame. Still others occupied key locations should Cole's people try to fight. All of Willie's soldiers were armed, many with guns.

Willie sauntered onto the stage and retrieved his guitar. With great care, he slid his sword back into the guitar's neck. As he wiped the fretboard with a thin cloth, he said, "I thank you, Malja. We needed you to prove there was a way through the portal, and we needed Cole to show everybody how power-mad she really is. Now we can follow Old McKinley as he learns from your body the magic we will all use to leave this world for one far greater."

He kissed his guitar and rested it in its case.

Malja's lip lifted a tiny fraction. "Let her go, Fawbry."

"What?"

"Do it," she said and leveled her icy glare on Willie, "And then pick up Willie's guitar."

"No," Willie said, moving toward Fawbry. Malja lunged for the stage, hooked Viper around Willie's knee, and the arrogant bastard fell. Fawbry lifted the guitar and held it like a club.

Malja said, "Anything happens, Fawbry, and you smash that guitar. Then you destroy any others you can get your hands on." She closed in on Willie. "No guitar, no magic. Right?"

Shivering with impotent rage, Willie grumbled, "Let them go." A path parted toward the front door. "When I see either of you again—"

"I expect no less," Malja said, as she and Fawbry edged off the stage. To Cole, she said, "You're coming, too."

Before Cole could move, Willie said, "She stays. Break all our guitars and all our bones. Doesn't matter. Cole stays."

Malja saw truth in his eyes. He would throw away everything that mattered to him, fight until he lacked the strength to move, all to make sure Cole did not leave the farm. Old McKinley wanted to fondle her no doubt. Besides, politics don't end just because Malja wrecked the place. "Fine," she said. "You're on your own, Cole. I'd say I'm sorry I couldn't help you here, but we both know that would be a lie."

Cole rolled her eyes. "Just go."

Backing out, Viper poised for work, Malja and Fawbry exited the hall.

Chapter 17

All through the night, they rode. They had to go slowly or else endanger their horses with a nasty fall in the dark, but still they rode. From time to time, Fawbry would look back with anxious jittering eyes. Malja looked back, too. Even after they left the guitar by a tree, they looked back.

Malja wanted them to follow, wanted them to appear — especially Willie. Every minute they traveled further away, she thought about him. When they stopped by a creek to let the horses rest, she had decided. "I'm going back."

"What?"

"You go meet up with Tommy and Tumus. Look after them."

"You can't go back there. We almost died."

"I still don't know where to find Jarik and Callib. The City of Ashes is too huge. But Cole Watts knows."

"Cole Watts is dead."

"Not yet. She had a lot of supporters. If Willie kills her right away, he'll have a civil war on his hands. He wants to be their leader. So, he's got to convince them first. Rile them up until they only see her death as a release from her tyranny. He'll convince them that doing what he says is true freedom."

"How do you know what he'll do?"

"It's what I'd do."

Fawbry paused for a moment. "I don't believe you," he said finally. "You don't care about Cole. We could find out that information some other way. No, you want to go back because you're ticked off that Willie got the better of you. You want a little revenge."

"I want—"

"Go. I don't care anymore. You and your Black Beast and your screwed-up fathers and all of it — I don't care. I'm done with you."

Malja stayed motionless, her face devoid of expression. She stared at Fawbry until he broke eye contact. He shook his head, mounted his horse, and trotted off. She listened as the dull clops of horse hooves receded in the distance, and only then did she relieve her tension with a drawn-out sigh.

Fawbry had spoken a fraction of truth — it angered her that Willie had won their conflict. But she had no intention of hunting him down. Not yet. She sought Cole Watts. She sought information.

Riding back took even longer than getting away. Several times she heard noises and had to hide — Willie and his men might have tried to pursue them or simply patrol the area. Caution was critical. Malja exercised greater patience than she ever thought possible. By the time she edged toward the open compound, the noonday sun blazed overhead.

Sitting against a large rock, she observed the area through her spyglass. The farm appeared to be running in full force — just another day. Closer to the house, however, the tension ramped up. Willie stood on the porch with fists pressed against his hips like an arrogant general, while Lonnie and three others sat on horses, waiting for orders. Shotgun paced behind Willie, his weapon resting on one shoulder. Suzu flitted about, his energy revealing the true degree of fear simmering. Not Willie, though. No fear there. Just the controlled anger of the true warrior.

Whenever possible, Malja kept her attention on Suzu — who he talked with, what he might have said, where he went. Suzu was the main lackey. Sure enough, at length, he stepped out of the house carrying a tray of food and a glass of water — lunch. He headed for the stables. An armed guard checked over the tray before letting him in.

Well, well. No office prison for Cole. Malja hunkered down amongst the rocks. For now, she had nothing more she could do until night. Nothing but sit quiet with her thoughts spinning around Fawbry's words.

* * * *

She waited until the party grew raucous, until the only people leaving the house were amorous couples seeking dark privacy. Only then did Malja leave her position and scuttle in the shadows toward the stables. The sticky air warned of heavy showers, but the sky harbored only a few clouds. With any luck, the storm would arrive soon. Heavy rains would aid her escape.

Crouching low, she hurried across open land, stopping when she could press her back against the stable wall. She slid along the wall, reached the corner, and peeked around — still just a single armed guard. She released Viper from its sheath and readied to rush the guard.

Suzu slammed open the house door. He held a bottle high in the air and stumbled a few steps. "Long live Willie," he said before taking a tumble down the stairs and passing out.

While the guard watched Suzu, Malja took advantage of the distraction. She acted with swift confidence like a magic shadow stealing in the darkness. The guard never heard her approach, and in seconds, she had him out of view on the side of the stable. She raised Viper but the guard's face stopped her. He couldn't have been much older than Tommy. His eyes pierced her much like Tommy's eyes.

"Fine," she grumbled and hit the guard's temple with Viper's hilt. He passed out.

Taking a moment to check the area once more, she noticed the top half of the stall door above her was open. She climbed in. Peeking through the main stall door, she saw Shotgun's empty stool. The guard must have been all they thought they needed — after all, Malja would never dare come back. Not this soon, at least.

She crept across the stable in dark silence. Cole Watts had been tied to a gate similar to the way the Bluesmen had tied Fawbry and her only days before. She had been allowed to change clothes. Gone was her party dress. Instead, she wore a more practical pair of pants and a dirty men's shirt — clothes for field work. Despite the darkness, Cole's wet cheeks stood out in the cuts of light that broke in from the house.

Cole perked up. "Hello?"

"Be quiet."

"Malja? What are you doing?"

"Jarik and Callib. Where in the City of Ashes?"

Disappointment lowered Cole down. "I thought you'd figured this out. Thought you came back to try the portal on your own."

"I don't really care about your little magic games here."

"You should. It's little magic games that caused the Devastation. And it's little magic games that'll restore the world. It's where the power is to make a real difference."

Malja pictured the glowing metal frame, the green round table, the portal to another world. She had been given no time to think about any of what she had seen. *And not now either.* She checked to make sure nobody was coming. Shotgun and a man with milky-white hair weaved down the dirt path, but they stopped half-way, turned to the side, and pissed on the grass.

"I'm not interested in making a difference. I just want Jarik and Callib. Tell me where they are or I'll kill you."

Cole shook her tied bonds. "Look at me. When they finish their party, *they'll* kill me. If not tonight, then tomorrow's party. So, if you want to find your fathers, then you best get me out of here. I'll take you right to them or wherever you want, just get me out of here."

Malja hadn't slept in a long time and lacked the energy to argue. Besides, this situation could go sour very fast. Best to get Cole Watts out and get the information later.

Using Viper, Malja snicked Cole's ropes open. "Follow me, do what I say, no questions. Understand?"

"Since we're talking about keeping me alive, I'll understand anything you say."

Malja checked outside once more — Shotgun and White Hair had returned to the party. Malja led the way out of the stable. They passed the tailors — door closed. They passed the guitar workshop — a couple embraced against a post. They crossed the open land. Their feet crunching the dirt road echoed in Malja's ears, but she knew others could not hear it. Such sounds were illusions created by tension. All seemed to go well as they scrambled back up the hill.

Until the ground shook.

Cole looked back as men poured outside with guns and women screamed in drunken fear. Malja tugged Cole's arm, but Cole wrenched her arm free. Blood drained from her face.

"This can't be," she said.

Malja watched the chaos below. "What's wrong? It's just a quake. Isn't it?"

"No. They're coming."

Willie stepped outside and fired a round into the air to regain control. Malja couldn't help but think of the wasted bullet. The ground settled and Willie said, "See? Just a quake. Now everybody back to the par — Where's T-bone?"

Shotgun and Lonnie dashed toward the stables. Malja pulled Cole further up the hill. "Come on. They're going to find you've escaped."

"No," Cole said, resisting with her meager strength. "They're here. Your fathers are here."

The ground shook once more. The fierce fighting dogs whimpered and scurried away, tails tucked between their legs. The horses whinnied and kicked their stalls. Even the bravest Bluesmen moved closer to the house and Willie.

"Everybody calm down," Willie said.

Shotgun and Lonnie rushed back. "She's gone," Shotgun said. "And T-Bone's out cold round the back."

"It's okay, everybody," Willie said, but Malja heard the worry of a leader facing his first big test. "Robert, take three men and check the perimeter. Mud and Rev, get a few more and check all the out-buildings — make sure she ain't hiding out there."

"Right," the men said, but they never got to follow through on the orders.

The ground cracked open. A hole formed the size of Suzu. It buckled as something below pushed hard, swelling higher and growing wider until it exploded in a shower of rocks and dirt. Five maxdins punched around the hole until they could climb out. Eight feet tall, covered in bristling hair, and with more teeth than brains, the maxdins were Jarik and Callib's personal thugs. They lumbered on two feet, striking with sharp claws.

"They're really here," Malja said.

The maxdins pressed forward, herding the people away from the fissure in the ground. With another rumbling quake, the ground surrounding the hole tumbled inward. The maxdins let loose a low bellow that caused the skin to quake.

Two men rose from the smoke and dust. They ascended like graceful dancers and continued into the sky. A circle of ten magicians, male and female, rose beneath the two men — each cross-legged on air and locked in concentration. Balls of electricity spread around, casting the area in stark light.

Malja's stomach felt like she had been punched. The men looked nothing like the Jarik and Callib she remembered from childhood, yet she knew to her core they were. Both were bald and shirtless, and tattoos covered every bit of skin. Despite their age, both looked to be in their prime — young, strong, commanding. The only difference between them — Callib's tattoos formed harsh, block-like patterns whereas Jarik's formed delicate webs of intricate designs.

The Bluesmen had recovered from their shock. They aimed their weapons and approached with calculated steps, fanning out with impressive unity. Willie stepped down from the porch, putting out his hand to caution his men. With a similar gesture (and, no doubt, some magic), the magicians halted the maxdins.

"Welcome to the Bluesmen's home," Willie said, opening his arms and bowing.

Callib's mouth turned down with scorn. "Give us the portal frame."

On the hill, Cole dropped to her knees, one hand covering her mouth, the other holding her stomach. "They mustn't. Sweet child, they mustn't get that frame."

A gun fired. Malja couldn't tell who shot, but the release let loose all the others. Gunfire blazed like the dragon fire of ancient stories, but the bullets never reached their targets. Concentrated wind bursts like two-second hurricanes knocked the bullets away. The air in Malja's lungs chilled until she gasped a breath — she never knew magic could do such things.

The snapping gunfire ceased — eight weapons had jammed and the rest needed reloading. As if toiling through a tedious day, Jarik floated behind Callib and focused on Callib's back tattoos. Callib gazed upon the people below like they were bugs he longed to hear pop.

By an unspoken command, the maxdins attacked. Those unfortunate enough to have been standing in front of the beasts never had the chance to fight back. The maxdins scooped up their victims and devoured them raw.

"Take cover and fight back," Willie yelled. His men scattered for cover and enough distance so they could reload.

Jarik lifted his head to the sky and let out an ecstatic, pleasurable moan as magic rippled along his veins and tensed his muscles. Vines darted from the open ground — thorny, gray vines. They moved fast like hyperactive snakes, wrapping around legs and arms and weapons before the Bluesmen could react. A few vines squeezed their victims' throats and dragged the blue-faced bodies back underground.

"How did they do that?" Malja asked Cole. "How can a magician use another's tattoo? And so fast. They're so fast."

Cole shook her head like a child both afraid and in denial. "Don't let them get the frame. Not the frame. Nothing else matters."

Malja picked her way down the steep hill even as her mind raced to digest a fraction of the moment. Jarik and Callib — her fathers — hovered in the air unleashing carnage upon those who had become her enemy, yet her soul told her to defend the Bluesmen. Her mind warned her that she had not yet prepared for this, that despite years of searching she never dealt with any emotion regarding her fathers beyond anger. Still, her legs charged on.

Two maxdins spotted her assault. One tore off to meet her. The other first finished chewing an arm.

Malja leapt from a rock and surprised the first maxdin — it never expected her attack to be so high. She cleaved its head half-off. The other tried to rush her, but when she hit the ground, she rolled right up against its legs and severed the backs of its knees. The hairy beast howled while its blood muddied the ground.

The remaining maxdins turned toward Malja. They bared their numerous teeth and growled from the throat. Malja launched toward them, cutting every vine within reach as she approached.

Her eyes kept snatching glimpses of Jarik and Callib — the two frowning and a bit confused at her appearance. She trained her attention back to the maxdins. Still her eyes wanted to linger on her fathers. She wondered if they even recognized her or if they had been so consumed by her failure that they could not comprehend their daughter's current ability.

A maxdin threw its arms high above and stomped towards her like a towering giant squashing the villagers. Four gunshots rang out followed by something bursting. The beast toppled to the darkening ground. Behind it stood Suzu, his face as pale-gray as the smoke seeping from his handgun's ruined barrel. He had been lucky to get two shots off, let alone four, before the weapon busted. Shotgun and Robert disposed of the remaining two maxdins with several more gunshots.

A chorus of anguish rose from the circle of magicians floating underneath Jarik and Callib.

"Willie?" Suzu called out. He stood amongst the blood and bodies. The others also stood in the destruction while each passing second deflated them like leaking balls. They had beaten the magicians' forces, yet they acted defeated.

The right corner of Callib's mouth lifted and his eyes narrowed. He slid behind Jarik to focus on one of the spidery tattoos.

"No," Malja said. Ignoring her conflicting thoughts and roiling emotions, she sprinted towards her fathers and let out her war cry.

Callib took no notice of her. He remained focused on the tattoo. Jarik, however, flicked his hand at her as if shooing away a fly.

Yanked by an unseen force, Malja flew back twenty feet. The impact knocked the air from her lungs and slowed her from getting back up.

"Gahhh!" Callib said, and a sudden storm approached. A blast of wind and bolts of red magic smashed into the house. Those inside screamed and some abandoned the building in panic. Everything but the floor — walls, roof, stairs, doors, everything — cracked, splintered, and shattered. The cacophony washed out all other sounds of the house. Pieces blew off into the distance like a pile of dead leaves carried on a stormy gale. When the last of the house, a brick chimney, crumbled and blew away, the storm ceased.

Like a floating fortress, the mass of magicians cruised across the air until they hovered above the houseless floor. Jarik moved his hands in a circular pattern and the portal frame ripped out of the floor. It drifted toward Jarik like a hawk returning to its master. Callib stroked the frame as if consoling it — promising the worst had passed.

"Magicians!" a defiant voice called out.

Everyone turned toward the fields. Willie and Lonnie stood there with their guitars in hand. Between them stood Old McKinley. The old man's bent body and vacant expression clashed with the shock and hesitation seen in

Jarik and Callib.

"We've got what we came for," Jarik said, waving the frame. "There's no need for further tragedy."

Callib elbowed Jarik aside. "McKinley? Are you such an idiot that you'd try to face us again? Look at yourself. Drooling like a baby. You can barely stand. Where's your wheelchair? And you've pissed yourself. I can smell you from here. You're feeble and if you persist, you'll be dead."

"Stop this now," Willie said in a firm voice. "Give us the frame and go your way. You've done your damage. We can't hurt you with it. But we can't let you leave with it. We won't have another Devastation."

"Is that what you think?" Callib said, and as he launched into a speech of self-aggrandizement and false assurances, Malja heard a voice call from the side.

Cole Watts waved her over from the back corner of the stable. Malja wanted to hear her fathers and see what would happen, but the urgency on Cole's face and the fact that she had climbed back down the hill could not be ignored.

"What?" Malja said when she came closer.

Cole had her saddled horse waiting. "We must go now. McKinley — he'll kill us all."

"McKinley can't even control his bladder."

"He's still capable of creating powerful magic — but he's unstable. One of my greatest fears if Willie took over was how he'd handle Old McKinley."

Malja's tone lowered. "He's handling him like a loaded gun."

"And like any gun, there's a high probability this one will blow up in Willie's hand. So get on the horse, and let's ride."

Though Malja's head still rang from being tossed, she had enough sense to listen. She climbed into the saddle, and Cole got up behind her. She heard a growing argument from the field. Callib's rage and Willie's scorn dueled like master swordsmen. But Willie broke off his words, and he and Lonnie started playing their guitars.

Over it all, a craggy voice chopped into the air. "Malja," the voice called, and it twinged something in her brain.

"Brother gods, it can't be," Cole said. "Old McKinley is speaking."

"Malja, listen to me."

She heard Callib yelling, but Old McKinley's voice echoed in the hills.

"It's the music," Cole said. "They're making him clear-headed and letting his voice become louder."

Malja said, "Is that even possible?"

Though Old McKinley looked weak and emaciated, his voice echoed with youthful vigor. "You know me, Malja. You killed my partner after I murdered your dear Uncle Gregor."

She didn't doubt his words at all. The twinge in her brain recalled the voice as its owner had held her against the wall of the shack. Her face paled.

"I told you then that Jarik and Callib ordered the death, but that wasn't quite true. Jarik never knew. Callib is the one you want. And if you can see them right now, you'll be happy at the seething anger burning between them."

"Get this horse going," Cole said.

"Enough," Callib yelled, and Old McKinley toppled to the ground. Willie and Lonnie continued to play. Someone started blowing a mouth harp and other Bluesmen plucked notes to compliment the growing sound.

Old McKinley returned to his feet. "Malja — Callib is your true enemy. Just like he's always hated you, he's always hated me. I never did what he demanded."

"You're making it easy to want to kill you," Callib said. Again Old McKinley was thrust into the dirt.

The music raised in volume as others joined in. Those without instruments sang. The sound bolstered Old McKinley back up.

"They hired me, Malja, because they were too weak to do it themselves. That's their true secret. They're weak."

A red bolt arced from Callib's hand and pulled Old McKinley into the air.

Cole leaned close to Malja's ear and said, "They're using music to build up enough power to create an explosion. They're making themselves into a bomb. They'll release it, and we'll die with them."

Malja saw it on their faces. Solemn, resigned surrender. She kicked the horse into a strong gallop.

When they reached the rocks from where Malja had spied earlier, she pulled up the horse and looked back. The music drifted up their way. She swore she could feel the magic mounting in the air.

"I've got to go back."

"You can't. Old McKinley isn't telling you this for no reason at all. He's going to—"

The music ceased, and the softest of sounds like a puff of air from a thrown pillow met with the harshest of lights like a little sun exploding from Old McKinley's heart. A wall of heat rolled up the hill and smacked into Malja and Cole, knocking them off the horse. Cole covered her head and curled into a ball. Malja, however, looked once more.

The little sun continued to burn. She smelled rotten eggs. She had to turn away — the brightness hurt her eyes.

She heard a noise building like a wild animal working itself into a rage. The full force of a new blast reached them, smashed Malja to the ground, and burned across her back. Her assault suit protected her skin from damage, but it could not protect her head from being knocked unconscious.

* * * *

Malja's head throbbed. The morning sunlight penetrated her like needles poking through her eyes all the way back to her brain. Her tongue rubbed at the dry, pasty film in her mouth.

"Ah, you're up," Cole said, her voice echoing and magnified.

Malja wiped at her nose and closed her eyes. Sleep would be much easier than dealing with anything else.

"No, no," Cole said like Gregor would when she tried to shirk her daily chores. "We've lost too much time as it is. The only reason the world's still here is because McKinley's magic closed in that hole in the ground and put a sore beating on Jarik and Callib's pets. Best I can tell they're headed north."

Malja bolted up fast, fought back her spinning stomach, and said, "My fathers are still alive?"

"Dear me, McKinley isn't near strong enough to take down those two. Not even with two full bands playing behind him."

Gazing down the hill, Malja saw the flattened leftovers of a powerful blast. A clear, grassy circle marked where McKinley and Willie had stood. White blast marks streaked outward like salt strewn across the land. Bodies littered the area.

She turned back. Cole's eyes were still red and her face puffed from the exertions of mourning. "I'm sorry about all of this."

Cole carved a grin. "Not your fault, is it? Besides, there's no time for sadness. We've got to get moving."

"North?" Malja said.

"Your fathers have my frame. With their magicians hurt, they can't travel back the same way they came. The City of

Ashes is west of the Yad. Closest crossing is north. If they mix their magic with my frame, well, what do you think will happen then?"

Malja gave a weary nod and groaned as she pushed up to her feet. She patted the horse's neck and breathed in its thick aroma. She mounted the horse and said, "Let's go."

* * * *

Hours later, she should have stopped. The poor horse faired worse — both could barely stay awake, but the horse carried two people on its sore back. Still, Malja pushed on. She tried not to think. Too many quiet miles lay ahead. But too many had drifted by, and her mind refused to hold back.

Tommy. Always Tommy.

She wanted to wrap her arms around that boy, hug him tight, and kiss his forehead. She wanted to promise him that once Jarik and Callib were dealt with, she would build a home for them. It would be a small place in the woods, far from the chaos — a small place with a garden filled with fresh vegetables and an apple tree loaded with perfect, red apples.

Night descended as they staggered upon the way station. Malja found no sign of Tumus or Fawbry or Tommy. The fire ashes were cold. Some nuts and a bit of chewed meat littered the floor. On one wall, Malja noticed charcoal doodling — a big circle, some dots, an arrow pointing to some little circles, wavy lines. She touched the drawing and pictured Tommy standing in the same spot.

But they had gone now. They must have left before Fawbry had returned. They could have left days ago — and perhaps he followed.

Cole stretched out on the floor. "This place reeks."

"Smoke-cutter died in here."

"Good. I hate those bastards."

"Go to sleep. We'll move out soon."

Cole rose on her elbow. "You need to sleep, too."

"Don't worry about me."

"Are you guarding me? You scared I'm going to try to run away? You shouldn't be. Everything's different now. Your fathers — they're not right in the head. They're going to do far worse to this world than the Devastation. So I'm sticking with you. I think I'd like to have you there when things turn ugly. So get some sleep. I need you alert and ready."

Malja weighed the points and lay down on the counter. "If all you just said is true, then you can tell me where Jarik and Callib are going. Where in the City of Ashes? If I'm going to protect you, I need to know so I can plan the safest route."

Cole chuckled. "Rest well. I promise I'll take you there. You have my word. Tomorrow, I'll lead the way."

"Not tomorrow. We have to go find my friends first."

"We don't have time for that. We've got to stay after your fathers."

"You don't get a vote in the matter."

Cole rubbed her face, and with a frustrated exhale said, "And where are they?"

"I don't know for certain, but I have a strong suspicion. And the more I think about it, I'm as close to positive as I could ever be. It's the only place that makes sense."

"So where would that be?"

"Dead Lake."

Cole said nothing for a moment. She shook her head and turned over to sleep. "You've got strange friends."

Chapter 18

Malja awoke a few hours later, yawned, and put her head back down. Her body craved another hour or two, but her brain urged her to prep the horse. The poor beast might not survive if they maintained such a grueling pace, but Malja saw little choice. She hoped some extra care now would be enough.

Stretching her limbs, but not getting up, Malja inhaled, held her breath, and exhaled slowly. The fighter in her chastised such a lazy awakening. She should spring to alertness. But her body needed to recoup, and this was the best she could manage. Peeking at Cole to make sure she still slept, Malja scrunched her face tight, held it, and let all her muscles ease back. It was a little relaxation ritual Gregor had taught her.

I'm close, Uncle Gregor.

Knowing Old McKinley died did nothing to quiet her Beast, but it did fill a small darkness in her memories — like recalling a name after struggling for it. She hoped Gregor was pleased, but tried not to think about it. And before her mental image of Gregor could frown at her and point out how too often she tries not to think about things, she rose and headed outside to the horse.

The morning work helped busy her mind, but in case it wasn't enough, she thought about the hole into another world and the fact that she fell through it without dying. She should have been burned to dust but here she stood rubbing a horse. Perhaps Jarik and Callib had put some strange spell upon her. Perhaps Cole had done it with her machines. It was even possible that they all had conspired together when she was little.

And there was the other world itself — a world far more civilized, probably more powerful, and possibly more dangerous. Contact with this world had had enough influence to birth the Bluesmen. Malja's fist tightened at the thought of what such contact would do to her fathers.

As Malja finished with the horse, Cole awoke and readied to go. They headed out without a word.

Malja stayed alert. She listened for snapped twigs or a sudden break in the birds' melodious morning chatter. She searched the trees and rocks for a shadow or a glimmer or anything unusual. She sniffed the wind for signs of a camp or an ill-washed enemy.

"I wasn't trying to hurt you," Cole said after several hours. "I know how it looked, but you were never in danger."

"You burned off Fawbry's hand."

"That was a little personal. Besides, I had to act harsh for the Bluesmen. My place with them was tenuous. They needed to see that I had the strength and the will to follow through on my promises. Otherwise, they would never listen to me."

"I don't care about anything you want to say except for where I'll find Jarik and Callib. So let's just go to Dead Lake, make sure my friends are okay, and then head for the City of Ashes."

"You're in charge. Even if it means we'll lose your fathers. I just hope we're not going to see Barris Mont. You can't trust anything that bloated monster says."

A flock of gray and white minrits took to the sky leaving behind the skeleton of a dead birch. "What do you know about Barris Mont?"

Cole scoffed. "More than you, apparently."

Malja refused to be baited, so she let silence lap over them. That didn't stop her brain, however. Over the next hour, she reviewed her limited experience with Barris Mont, searching for any hint of his ulterior motives. Unfortunately, there were many — well, not hints, exactly, but plenty of signs to suggest he had lied or at least obscured the truth.

They camped early that night to insure the horse's survival. The following midday, they came upon the Muyaza village. Something bad had happened.

Nobody traveled across the river. No line of waiting passengers had formed. Two buildings had been squashed into rubble. Dark, soupy smoke billowed toward the clouds. Worse — a row of bodies rested at the shore and a few weeping families sat nearby. Others carried more bodies over using the river litters. Blood stained the food table.

As the two women neared the village, a Muyaza man noticed them and thrust a finger towards the hills. "Go," he said. "No cross."

"What happened here? Who did this?"

"No cross. Go."

Malja looked to Cole. "Jarik and Callib?"

Cole raised an eyebrow. "Possibly. But this world is full of violent people."

The Muyaza man continued to point, but said no more. To Malja, he looked like a sad Chi-Chun — so distraught he could raise only one arm. She surveyed the area.

"You," she said. "Magic do this?"

The man's face tightened. "You bad. Go. No come back. Ever." Wiping his hands in an exaggerated manner, the Muyaza turned his back on them and left.

Cole said, "They really love you here."

"Doesn't matter. We still have to cross the river."

"Considering what's just happened, I doubt they're

doing their usual patrols against bridge-builders and such. We could easily build a boat. They won't bother us."

Malja's stomach rolled at the mere thought of water travel. "A boat will take too long."

"Nonsense. We'll go back to my cabin. I have tools and machines that can help."

"Your cabin is days away. Besides, there's nothing there anymore. Fawbry burnt it to the ground."

"He what?"

"It was an accident."

"That Kryssta-loving fool. He did it on purpose. I know he did."

"I don't care. Get that into your head. I don't care. All I want right now is to get across that river, and it won't be done on any boat."

Malja set the horse moving toward the river's edge and then headed upriver. She hoped to find a shallow or narrow area to attempt the crossing. After only a few minutes, however, she heard the clumsy steps of someone following them without knowing how to do so properly. Wrenching the horse around, she saw a Muyaza man trip in shock. Not just any Muyaza. This one bore a white scar across his chest and had almost died under Viper's sharp curves. Tommy had stopped that from happening, and now she would see how Tommy's kindness was repaid.

Malja slid off the horse and pulled out Viper. The man scrambled to his feet. "No. Please. I help."

"Help how?"

"I take cross Yad."

"You want to help us cross the river?"

With an enthusiastic nod, the man smiled. "I called Skvalan. I take cross Yad."

"Why?"

Skvalan turned cold, his brutish muscles and stern brow

finally matching the bruiser she had dealt with before. He gestured back at the village. "I listen. You hate magic. I hate magic."

He choked up and Malja recalled the woman who had tried to stop him from confronting her. "Did they kill your wife?"

"Wife?"

"Your woman."

His eyes darkened as he nodded.

"How do we get across?"

Skvalan stepped close. "Wait for night. No Muyaza see. I open water."

"I thought only the old ones did that."

"I no good but I do."

Cole said, "That sounds so encouraging."

* * * *

Night took its sweet time coming. As the hours passed, Cole noted several times how far they would have been in making a boat. Each mention caused Malja a second of bitter reflux in her throat. If Skvalan backed out, they would have to use a boat. The seasickness alone bothered Malja, but listening to Cole gloat would near kill her.

Skvalan arrived an hour after the moon showed its face. He wore a heavy cloak, a satchel overflowing with fruit, and he carried a litter. He looked at the two women without visible emotion. "We go," he said and dropped the litter at their feet.

Malja wanted to yell at the man, but it would do no good and she needed him. With Cole on the front and Malja in the rear, they lifted the Muyaza on the litter. Skvalan took a cleansing breath and concentrated on his leg tattoo. Five minutes passed before the protective bubble formed, and it barely covered the three of them.

"Leave the horse behind," Malja said.

As they entered the river, walls of water pressed in. Skvalan grunted as if struck by invisible foes. He strained to maintain the bubble and their safety. Malja urged Cole to walk faster, but Cole had never labored under a litter before — she grunted and strained, too. For Malja, the litter was easy. She had carried many bodies off many battlefields. The water, however, worried her. It pushed against the bubble with steady force that they had to compensate against or be swept away. Fighting the Yad, swimming to shore — it had been hard enough the first time. She had no wish to repeat the event, particularly at night.

Though the moon provided some light, the darkness beneath the water blotted out most light. The river flowed around them in muted tones. Even the river's odors seemed less pungent in the night.

Halfway across, Malja asked if anybody needed to rest. "Just keep going," Cole said and Skvalan grunted. Though Malja approved of them both for toughing it out, she suspected Cole didn't want to stop for fear of not being able to start again.

They pushed on. Slick stones and uneven surfaces threatened to topple them at every step. Malja risked a peek at Skvalan. His body shook with his effort.

As if leaving a long, dark tunnel, they emerged from the Yad and reached the shore. Skvalan and Cole dropped to the ground, sweating hard and breathing heavy. Blood dribbled from Skvalan's nose. Malja handed them fruit and treated herself to a ripe apple. She gave them a short while to recoup.

"Thank you," she told Skvalan. "I owe you for this. Cole, let's go."

As they headed out, Skvalan followed. Malja now saw

the cloak and satchel for what they were — all his possessions. Skvalan must have seen her intention to turn him back for he reached into the satchel's side pocket and pulled out a long braid of dark hair. "Wife," he said. His fingers tightened around the braid as if choking the life from the bastard magicians responsible.

The Beast is in us all, she thought. She suspected he would follow them regardless of what she said. She might as well have him on her side. "Okay," she said.

Walking to Dead Lake sapped what little stamina they had left. Malja wanted to sleep. She had grown tired of being tired, but knew the luxuries of a soft, safe bed were long away. One look at Dead Lake told her that bed had moved even farther into the distance.

Trees had been toppled. Dying fires charred the ground, mixing their smoke with the growing fog coming off the lake. A Chi-Chun man hung from a tree limb, blood dripping into its own crimson puddle below. Further along the shore, they found more evidence of battle.

Skvalan tensed, and his head darted from side to side. Malja wondered if she had more of a warrior on her hands than she had given credit. Cole, on the other hand, held her nose against the harsh stink of the dead drifting like the fog.

"Stay close," Malja said. Clouds kept blocking the moon — she didn't want anybody getting lost.

She heard the mournful praying long before she saw the dark figure emerge. As they closed in, she spied a Chi-Chun woman bent over two bodies. The woman raised her arms upward and said, "Korstra, most powerful brother god, to serve you, we live and in serving, we are fulfilled. I offer you the souls of two cherished servants." She lowered her hands, touched the corpses, and began the whole thing over.

Only when they were close enough to trip over the dead

did Malja recognize the woman. "Tumus?"

Tears streamed down her dark skin as she faced Malja. "There was no warning," she said. "They just came in and started killing."

"Who? Tumus, who did this?"

"They never stopped. They kept moving forward like we were in the way." Tumus got to her feet and opened a secretive smile. "Don't fear. I left Tommy with Barris. They linked so Tommy could finish his new magic easier and in good health."

Malja didn't wait for Tumus. She might have strangled the Chi-Chun if given the chance. She stormed across the stony shore, each step making her angrier. Her actions, her choices, her orders — all of it should have made her wishes clear. She did not want Barris Mont playing with Tommy's mind. Her anger at the stupidity around her only fueled her anger at her own gullibility. She should have expected this the moment she decided to leave Tumus and Tommy behind.

Of all the carnage she had witnessed in the past, nothing compared to the bizarre setting she found at the dock. Numerous Chi-Chun corpses littered the ground like smashed scarecrows. Several horses lay dead amongst them. The corpse of Barris Mont rotted in the lake. Only a small portion of his bulbous form broke the surface like an island made for vultures and minrits. One damaged tentacle stretched from the water, across the dock, to the strangest part of all — a burnt hole in the ground surrounded by fallen trees, debris, and people, and all knocked away from the hole.

Cole said, "Something exploded here."

"No," Tumus said, but she wasn't correcting Cole. She was speaking to herself, denying what her eyes told her. Throwing her body onto the hole, her words grew louder and more painful. "No, no. Please, no. I'm sorry."

Malja chilled. "Tumus? Where's Tommy?"

"I-I'm so sorry."

"Tumus," Malja said, her voice snapping the Chi-Chun name but getting little reaction. She stood tall over Tumus, as if she could will the woman to speak. "Where's Tommy?"

"He ... he ..."

"Damn Korstra, where's Tommy?"

Screaming the words out, Tumus said, "I left him here with Barris! I left him here! I-I left him."

Chapter 19

Malja couldn't feel her hands. She slumped on the dock facing the charred darkness in the ground, and her hands just went away. Her face, too. Only the icy-hot spike of loss impaling her chest convinced her that the numbing was not a return of the magic she had drunk.

She tried to cry out, scream, make some sound — but she couldn't move. Her lungs could barely pull in enough air to keep her alive. Her eyes stung from not blinking. She stared at the black dust, the blasted dirt, unwilling to look away. When she exhaled, her breathing shook from her body like a broken machine.

She had promised him. She had held that little boy's hand as Wuchev's splashes blended with his terrified tears, and she had promised him. Yet the first moment he needed someone else, she broke that promise.

She could feel the excuses mounting and shut them down. "My fault," she whispered. She had left him with Tumus. Nothing would change that. No excuse could fix that. She had failed.

Callib's right. She remained there, staring, petrified in pain as her thoughts trundled over each other, spiraling her deeper into doubt. She had slipped off that morning, so Tommy couldn't cause her discomfort about leaving him behind — and in the Freelands, no less. Perhaps Jarik and Callib had been right to try to kill her. She left Tommy unprotected. *I'm a monster.*

She had held his hand. She had made her promise. And

now, she could only wet the ground with her tears.

"Who's Tommy?" Skvalan asked Cole. "Why she cry?"

Hearing Skvalan, Malja realized she was crying, and that blew her open. Every ounce of pain released like a blast of magic scorching the charred ground. She wailed and clutched at her heart. She kept waiting for everything to stop, to end, because the idea that life would continue made no sense.

But at length, her tears did stop. Her breathing eased. And a low, growling rumbled within her. Callib's not right, it told her. Jarik's not right. They're the monsters that murdered the only right one she ever knew.

Gregor.

She lifted her head and looked around. Cole and Skvalan meandered around, waiting for her to snap back, while Tumus cried on her own.

Sure. Wait for me. They're all helpless without me. The dead pain in her heart started to beat. *But if I say Left they all want Right.*

She had tried it their way. She had tried to be peaceful. She didn't slaughter the Bluesmen, she didn't kill the Muyaza, she held back all the time — especially with Tumus. The result — the Bluesmen had been decimated, the Muyaza refused to help her, and Tommy ... she had to stop thinking about that. Gregor had taught her to follow real evidence, facts not fancies. And Gregor was usually right. He believed in her. Maybe he was right about that, too.

Facts not fancies.

The only fact she had regarding Tommy — he wasn't at the dock. But her instincts told her that if he was alive, Jarik and Callib had him.

He is alive, she told herself, because the thought felt both right and necessary. Without it, no matter how angry she could be, she never would have stood again.

But she was standing. Angry, cold, even a bit dead inside, but standing nonetheless.

"We're going," Malja said, firm and strong. The others straightened and assembled. "Cole, you lead us to those bastard magicians. Mess it up in any way, I'll cut off your head. Anything gets in our way, it dies. This madness they brought upon me is going to end."

Wiping her eyes, Tumus said, "I wish to accompany you. I can help."

"No."

"Please. All I've known here is gone."

"I don't care."

"Let me help you. For Tommy. For what they did to him."

Viper flashed out and hooked Tumus in the back. Through gritted teeth, Malja said, "You did this to him. I charged you to protect that boy. You brought him here, to Barris Mont, knowing I didn't want that. The only reason I don't kill you now is because I think you'll suffer more living with your guilt."

She released Tumus. The Chi-Chun woman dropped to her knees and new tears bellowed out.

"We're leaving now," Malja said, turning away from Tumus. Cole cast a pitiful look at Tumus before heading toward the mountains and the City of Ashes. Malja felt no pity. Only one thought echoed in her head — *I've got a promise to keep.*

* * * *

Malja picked up the trail with ease — a wide swath had been cut through the trees and brush. Jarik and Callib made no attempt to hide.

Cole did better than Malja had expected. Hiking long hours with little break can be hard on the most seasoned soldiers. But Cole never quit and never complained. Skvalan held his own. Malja's expectations for him were high — after all, he had spent his days crossing the Yad over and over. He should be strong.

She spoke little during the day, letting the physical exertion work away the rest of her anguish.

That night, they circled their campfire and ate the stringy but nutritious meat of a dollad. Skvalan had caught the tunneler right before it burrowed to its freedom. Whenever he met Malja's eyes he raised the leg bone in his hand. She nodded the first few times, but his pride had become annoying. She concentrated on eating to avoid his eyes.

"I didn't see any signs of Tommy," she said. She didn't mean to say it out loud, but once started, she had difficulty stopping. "If they had taken him, he would've tried something to get my attention — drop something or leave a marker of some kind."

Cole and Skvalan exchanged looks of concern. Malja opened her mouth, ready to babble more, when a thought struck hard enough to make her smile. "If he's not with them, then he's out there somewhere. He might be just fine."

Cole touched Malja's knee. "Dear, you've suffered a loss. We understand that. If you want to turn back, it's okay. We can find some other way."

Malja's eyes flared up. "We're not going back. Tommy is not dead. I know it."

"All I'm trying to say is—"

"You just want out. Guess what Miss Watts? Everybody wants out. Nobody's ever happy with the life they were given. But some of us learn to live with it, to take control of it, and make the best of it we can. Others — they just want to cry over their wounds and go back."

Cole's face hardened. "Don't you dare lecture me, little thing." She threw her bone in the fire and plopped down next to Skvalan. "I may not have the Bluesmen under my control, but don't think I'm under yours. I have knowledge to keep me alive."

"Push me far enough, and I'll kill you anyway. I can search the City of Ashes without you. May take the rest of my life, but I'd do it."

"I believe you would. But I know more than just where to find Jarik and Callib. I know all about Barris Mont and I know the core truths of the Devastation. And I know where you come from. I've even seen your mother."

Malja shot forward, kicking through the campfire and releasing Viper in swift motions. Sparks lit up the darkness and reflected off Viper's blade as bright as the blaze in her eyes. Before Cole could react, Malja had Viper pressed against her quivering neck, a slick, trickle of blood marking the skin. Skvalan watched without comment and only mild interest.

"You'd better start sharing that knowledge now," Malja said.

"If I tell you, you might kill me."

"If you don't, I'll definitely kill you."

With her hands raised in surrender, Cole pulled back from Viper and used her worn smile. "Okay. You've convinced me." Malja held still a fraction longer while Skvalan reset the campfire. With her jaw jutting in a dare, she backed off two small steps. Despite her hands shaking, Cole continued, "You're not from here. Not this place. You were born in another world."

The words froze between them. Malja's mind pulsed with memories of the other world she had seen — the green séance table, the oddities outside the window, the people staring at her. "That was home?"

"No," Cole said, lowering her voice and her hands. "The world the Bluesmen talk with is not your world."

"How do you know?"

"Because I was there when Jarik and Callib got you. I saw them create a portal — just the two of them — and I watched you fall into our world. That world you came from — it's absolutely incredible."

Malja's mouth tasted stale and her lungs constricted. Gregor had said that someday she would learn the truth — no, that she would have the *chance* to learn the truth. "The important question," he said, "is do you really want to know?" Of course she wanted to know. But he only smiled as he served up breakfast and said, "Sometimes the truth is a heavier burden than the mystery."

Although Skvalan had built a hefty blaze, Malja could not escape the cold pressing in. "Tell me everything," she said.

Cole slouched as if the weight of sadness surrounding them had been placed solely upon her. "I told you magic caused the Devastation — the magic to create a portal. There's more. See, Barris Mont was alive back then."

"I know. He showed me. He had once been human."

"Perhaps. I wasn't there. But human or not, Barris planted the seed in all those foolish magicians' heads. Made them think they were better than all the rest. He knew of the other worlds, or at least he suspected, and he persuaded these fools to play with some very hot fire."

"Barris caused the Devastation?"

"Partly, yes. And you would think that erasing three-quarters of the world would give a person pause, but not Barris. He approached it like an equation that needed to be solved. He had no luck. Until one day, he met two brothers who were also budding magicians."

"He gave Jarik and Callib their powers?"

"He *unlocked* their powers. They had them from the start. But for all his ability to look inside a person's mind, that big fool had blinded himself to what Jarik and Callib truly were. Barris wanted to be right. He needed to be; otherwise, he had nothing to show for all the death he caused."

The campfire popped and the tower of wood fell apart on one side. Malja wondered how much more she could take before she, too, crumbled apart. "So, Jarik and Callib are trying to open a portal. But you've already done that."

"Patience, now. What you saw with the Bluesmen was nothing. Your fathers had accomplished that much long ago. They've been able to open portals to hundreds of worlds. What they can't do is travel to them. We all burn up if we touch the magic. Just like Fawbry."

Malja's stomach lurched. "But I don't."

Cole tilted her head like a big sister revealing the truth about boys. "No, you don't. Oh, my dear, sweet little Malja, life can be so unfair. Your fathers opened world after world, trying to unlock their secrets. They found many worlds with no magic at all — just machines. So they came to me. They wanted me to build many things — machines to stabilize the portals, machines to boost their magic, machines to test the portals, all kinds of things."

"And you did this, of course."

"Jarik and Callib aren't the types that really offer much choice, now are they?"

"I suppose not."

"Well, there it is. I built what I could, but we still couldn't get through the portals. One morning, they opened a portal, and it must have materialized right beneath your mother because she just fell into our world."

"Fell?"

"We all stood there, just stuck in shock. We'd never had

anything like that happen before. She had a baby in her arms — you. And she clutched you tightly like she knew what was about to happen. She stared at us with the widest eyes I've ever seen. Scared me into praying to the brother gods for a moment."

"What did she say? What did she look like?"

"She looked a lot like you — long, dark hair, strong face. If not for the fear in her eyes, she'd have been a striking woman. She spoke a lot, but it wasn't in any language I ever heard. Callib, though, he reacted like she had come to cause another Devastation. He saw something in that portal, and it scared him something awful. He shut down the machines and yelled out his magic. The portal sealed and sucked your mother back into it in the process. You, however, remained."

"She let me go?"

"No. The force of the portal stripped you from her arms. She screamed as it brought her back in. Most heart-wrenching thing I ever heard in my life. Callib stared at you like you were the spawn of evil. He wanted to destroy you. Dissect you, too, no doubt. But Jarik picked you up, and that was that."

"Then why did they get rid of me? If I'm the only one who can pass through the portal, if Jarik saved me, if any of what you're saying is true, then why toss me into the woods?"

Cole stifled a yawn. "Didn't know what they had, did they? I'm sure they wish they could take it all back just so they could use you. Now, I've told you enough."

"You sit there and tell me everything."

"You going to kill me? Then who'll tell you the rest? I gave you some of it, but I still have a few bits left and those'll keep me alive, thank you. So, now, I'm going to sleep. We've got a lot of hiking to do tomorrow."

Malja kicked her heel into the dirt and swore. As Cole rested her head on the ground, Malja joined Skvalan in squinting at the fire. She tried to stay angry at Cole, but the woman had given her more information than she ever had before. She saw her mother reaching for her like the campfire flames straining toward the night sky. Sleep would be a long time in coming.

* * * *

The rain began before sunrise — heavy, thick drops at first followed by drizzle, then heavy again. The ground became mush in seconds. Malja, Cole, and Skvalan hiked through the damp forest and over muddy hills, keeping their heads down and saying little. Being Muyaza, Skvalan cringed under the cold droplets, but Malja refused to baby him, and she suspected he would resent such help anyway. Skvalan would push through his cultural issue, if for no other reason than to prove his toughness and his worth to the group.

Malja required no proof from either Skvalan or Cole. Hiking mile after mile in chilling rain without the aid of horses proved enough. She only wished they could move faster. Jarik and Callib had hours on them, and the bastards could float over obstacles that slowed Malja's progress. She didn't fear losing them — with Cole's help, she would find them. But with the frame in their possession, Malja feared they'd have too much time to cast their spells.

Cole stopped. Massaging her hip, she said, "My, my, my. Take a look at that."

Malja trudged back and followed Cole's gaze. In the distance, nestled discretely behind a wall of oak, stood the ruins of an old mansion. Vines had engulfed much of its front helping obscure it from notice even more.

"We should keep moving," Malja said.

"Hold on. There might be supplies in there. At the least, we could get dry, build a fire, get warm."

"We're already too far behind," she said, seeing Skvalan's longing. "Stopping here will only make it worse."

"Maybe so, maybe not. Who can really know? But I know this — if I don't get a tiny bit of comfort, I won't be worth a thing in another mile."

Malja considered leaving Cole behind. She could find the City of Ashes on her own. Two powerful magicians couldn't be that difficult to locate — people talk, and Jarik and Callib were probably well-known in the city. She could do it. It would take longer, that's all. She took several steps up the path. A lot longer.

She kicked the muddy ground. "We'll rest for an hour, then it's back on the hike."

Cole had the sense to stay quiet.

Chapter 20

Skvalan broke apart another hand-crafted chair to feed the fire. They were in the foyer — a massive room of marble columns, curving stairs, and stained-glass. Two statues guarded the front door — the Prophet Galot on the left, and the magician Moonlo on the right. Moonlo looked gaunt compared to the well-fed image of Galot, but his stern expression spoke to the firm will power and unending faith that helped him write and spread the Book of Kryssta.

"Guess they couldn't make up their minds," Cole said.

"What?" Malja asked. Cole had been flitting about the mansion, commenting on its fine architecture and relatively good condition since they had arrived. Malja chose to ignore her as much as possible.

"The owners," Cole said. "Not very religious, I guess. Or maybe too religious."

"Sit down already. You're the one who said you needed rest."

"I know, but this place is amazing. People have probably walked by for a hundred years and never knew it was nestled back here like a buried treasure. You understand that? It's practically untouched."

"That's right. So we've got chairs to burn."

Skvalan tossed the last bits of wood into the fire and settled with his back against a thick column. Cole rolled her eyes. "Well," she said, drawing out the word like a disapproving parent, "the two of you may have no appreciation for the riches to be found here, but I do.

Enjoy the fire. I promise to return for some rest before we go, but first I've got to see what else I can find."

"No, Cole, you stay," Malja said, but Cole continued to rummage through a pile of discarded things in one corner. "We are too close to the enemy." Cole moved on to a small wooden desk with numerous drawers. "This is not the time for scavenging."

"Praise Kryssta and Korstra and whoever else you fancy, look what I found." From the bottom drawer, she pulled out two bottles of wine. The labels were torn and faded but the distinctive pyramid-shaped bottle meant they were Luntland — among the finest wineries before the Devastation. So fine that people still knew the name. "Here's one bottle for you and one for me. Now I'm off to check the rest of the house." With a triumphant gait, Cole sped up the stairs.

Malja and Skvalan wasted no time. A clean strike from Viper cut open the bottle. Skvalan found a light, metal bowl in the trash pile. Malja raised her first toast to Cole — an undamaged bowl like this was rare. If she had a horse, Malja would have loaded it with everything she could find. Instead, she and Skvalan emptied the bottle by the bowlful.

"You don't talk much," Malja said, resting her woozy head and watching the fire's smoke weave up to the ceiling three floors above. *Didn't mean to drink so fast.*

"No speak well."

"That's okay. I'm comfortable around quiet ones."

Silence settled between them. Sounds of Cole bumping through the house mixed with the drumming rain like the beginning beat of Cole's music magic, but between Malja and Skvalan — silence. Until Skvalan sniffed loudly and said, "We go soon."

Malja opened her eyes (she hadn't realized she drifted off). "I know. I want to go, too. But I'm starting to think

Cole is right. I mean, obviously, we don't have to track them. Cole knows exactly where they're going. And there's no way for us to catch them — we're too slow on foot. So, might as well rest and do the best we can tomorrow."

Skvalan placed his small pack under his head. "No good."

"I know no good. That's because I'm lying. I mean all I just said is true, but I'm not telling it all. See, I don't care if Jarik and Callib open another world. I don't even care if they destroy this one. I just want Tommy back. That's all. I should never have left him. That's why I've kept pushing us so hard. And now maybe Cole's right. She won't say it out loud, but maybe she's right. Maybe Tommy's in the middle of Dead Lake. Maybe he's dead."

Skvalan opened his bag and pulled out his wife's braided hair. "Wife dead. I see. Tommy no see. Tommy no dead."

"Don't give up, eh? Don't worry. I'm drunk and I'm babbling. Trying to convince myself. Prepare. Gregor always told me to prepare for the worst, because then you won't be disappointed. Trouble with that is you can end up lying to yourself. Jarik and Callib — I know them. I try to tell myself they were something else, but they're not. They're evil. And they raised me, influenced me for ten years. Maybe that makes me evil, too. Can a person overcome that? I know Callib wants to change everything, run the world his way. But he'll destroy everything good. Then they'll be nothing left for Tommy. So, I guess I do care if they cause another Devastation. That's something, right?" The fire crackled and Malja watched the sparks drift upward. "I do care."

Skvalan stroked the braided hair with his thumb.

"I've drunk too much. Don't listen to me. I'm just tired and angry and confused. And drunk."

Malja closed her eyes and felt her body drift with the

sparks and sweet-smelling smoke. Things had been simpler long ago. She woke each morning with one easy task — hunt for food. After that, the day was hers. If she could just let go of all her rage, just forget Jarik and Callib — they never existed. Only Gregor. He was her father.

But every time she tried, reality reared in her mind. Now she saw her mother reaching out for her. Now she saw Jarik taking her away. And now that bastard had taken Tommy. He must have. Any other scenario would have left a body or blood or some evidence. To leave nothing at all but scorch marks — that's the work of magic.

Even though she heard laughter from her mouth and her body shook, Malja also felt tears trickle on her face. "It's over," she said, jerking Skvalan from his own slumber. "I can act tough forever, and it won't matter. I care. I do. But we can't stop them if we can't get to them. You want to know why I agreed to come in here, why I got drunk, why I let Cole go running around? Because it's over. We lose."

Skvalan shook his head and spit to the side. He might not have understood a lot of her words, but Malja could tell he understood her tone. Perhaps the alcohol had gotten to her or the unyielding stress — whatever the cause, she felt tears. Not crying, pitiful tears but raging, frustrated ones. She wanted to pummel something, assert her strength, remind this Muyaza why he feared her not too long ago. She watched the fire cast orange and black against the walls. She didn't move.

Cole darted into the room, her face flushed, and said, "You must come see this."

If not for Cole's urgency, Malja would have rolled over and slept. Instead, she let Skvalan help her up. They followed Cole through the elegant corridors of the mansion. These weren't the sterile white of Barris Mont's old office or the decayed grandeur of Ms. Nolan's place.

These walls hinted at a youthful, new wealth with plenty of technological remnants that Malja had no knowledge of how to use. No wonder Cole wanted to snoop around here.

Cole led them into a wide open room of cool, smooth stone and sharp, musty odors. A blue, boxy contraption on four wheels filled up half the room. Cole ran her hand along the thing and slapped its metal body.

"Have you ever seen one in such good condition?"

Malja rubbed her head — she still felt a bit tipsy. "What is it?"

"Why it's a grounder, silly."

Malja inspected the grounder again, trying to imagine it as one of the rusting, hollowed out shells that dotted the world. "Didn't know they had wheels."

"They did, and a lot more. This one has been sitting here, protected from rain and wind and animals and thieves, just waiting for us. All it needs is some power and a little attention, then it'll run."

Skvalan nodded. "It is like horse?"

"Better than a horse. With this we can follow the old roads and even with stopping to clear overgrowth and as long as we don't suffer any major breakdowns, we'll reach the City of Ashes by tomorrow night. We just have to change the batteries." Cole hefted a pack of two large cylinders encircled with a coil.

"Well," Malja said, "unless one of you has suddenly become a magician and can produce electricity, this is all pretty useless to us."

"These batteries are in excellent condition. The best I've ever seen. Even if it takes us two days to find power, we'd still—" Cole stopped, her mouth agape, her eyes lost. "Willie?"

Malja turned around. Willie stood in the doorway.

But not Willie, too.

The creature had Willie's form but not entirely. One eye was clouded over like Old McKinley. And the corners of his mouth turned up like Shotgun. His stature belonged to Willie but his belly borrowed from Suzu.

With a guttural yell, Skvalan rushed forward. Thousands of insects, maybe millions, crawled out of the creature and covered him in a living armor — cockroaches, ants, tapats, silvers, and any number of bugs Malja could not identify. Skvalan punched the creature. The creature stepped back an inch — nothing more. Skvalan, however, clasped his fingers and grimaced as if he had broken his hand. A powerful back fist from Willie sent Skvalan tumbling against the grounder.

The insects skittered away. Some disappeared into his clothes. Others used his ears or nose as an exit. Some left his body for the walls and floor.

Willie lifted his arm. A jagged tattoo marked the underside.

"What is it?" Malja asked.

In a stunned voice, Cole said, "Magic I never believed in entirely — raising the dead. Jarik and Callib brought him back to get rid of us."

Willie stared at his tattoo.

"He has magic now?"

"He *is* magic. They probably didn't have time to be specific, so they just raised everything in the same ground as Willie."

"But he —"

"Dear child, are you going to stand here and let him get that spell off or are you going to kill him?"

Malja whipped out Viper and attacked. As she swung her blood-hungry blade, the insect armor reformed. Viper slashed through, splattering insects and knocking Willie back into the house, but drew no blood. Malja followed in and attacked again. Each hit knocked away insects and pushed Willie back further, but more of the bugs filled in the damage.

They entered a kitchen — sinks and counters remained as well as many metallic, boxy objects Malja had never seen before. She kept her focus on Willie. Even through her constant slashes, Willie maintained his focus on his tattoo — seeming to see through the insects.

Malja brought Viper around and attacked the tattooed arm. The insects clicked and chittered loudly. A new arm formed below the tattooed arm. This new arm also formed an insect sword. It deflected Malja's blow, spraying the walls with roaches and beetles.

The arm retaliated, and Malja went on the defensive. Blow after pounding blow pushed her abilities. Death had not lessened Willie's swordsmanship.

Malja tried to counter, but the attacks came too fast. Forced into blocking each swing, she struggled to find an opening. Her body tired, while his insects seemed stronger.

In a desperate move, she ducked under his swing and slashed at his legs. She lopped off the left at the knee. Willie broke off his assault, hopped backwards, and waited as the bugs formed a new leg.

Panting, sweating, and tired, Malja watched Willie like a wary rabbit sensing danger — still, but ready to leap.

"You can't beat me," Willie said. "I was too strong before and now, with my magic, you're hardly worth the time." The insects peeled down off his head and torso, creating an undulating mass around his legs. "But I'm a Bluesman, and we follow through when we're paid."

"You were never paid to kill me," Malja said.

"Just slow you down; hinder your progress." An electric ball burst into existence between his fingers. "Killing your friends should do that for me." He thrust his arm forward, shooting ball after ball of dazzling blue-white lightning. They sizzled and crackled toward Cole. Malja jumped in the way.

Before she could be hit, the ball broke into long, jagged strands. Each strand curved back as if a massive wind blew against it. The magic lit up the room as it passed over Willie's confused face and shot into a dark figure standing with arms outstretched.

"Tumus?"

The Chi-Chun woman continued absorbing the lightning and said, "Hurry. I can't do this for long."

Flinging forward, Malja hooked Viper into Willie's back and brought his innards toward her. He tried to summon his bugs, but Malja slashed, hooked, and tore with furious abandon — the insects could not move fast enough. Not when his focus fought in too many directions.

The lightning ended. Willie's hacked body dropped. The insects scattered.

Malja glanced at Tumus. Little sparks of lightning danced between her limbs, each time pulling a pained cry from her clenched mouth. *Good,* Malja thought. As fast as the thought arrived it brought with it the reason for her anger — Tommy.

Moving her lips the bare minimum, Tumus said, "Get away. Can't hold on to this much longer."

Malja didn't move. Cole, however, sprinted across the kitchen. "Wait," she cried, bringing the batteries to Tumus and showing her where to touch for recharging. As the magic drained from Tumus, she sighed like a child relieving a full bladder. Calmer, she recharged the second battery. When the last of the magic left her body, she dropped on the floor and wiped her drenched brow.

"You aren't welcome here," Malja said.

Tumus shrugged off Malja's words. "Korstra has

different plans."

"The brother god gets no say. Tommy's gone because of you. You're not welcome."

"Do not forget that I just saved your life. And do not believe you're superior to me. I did not try to get rid of the child. You did that."

Malja's hand tightened around Viper's grip. "I was protecting him. If he had come with me, the Bluesmen might've killed him."

"What makes you think we were any safer? Stuck alone in the Freelands? Yet we waited. For days. Barely any food. Every little sound a possible threat. Korstra looked over us, though. He was our true protector."

"Then let him protect you some more. You're not welcome, and I don't want you following us."

"I care nothing about what you want. I'm going to help save that boy."

Malja looked to Cole and Skvalan. Cole found something on the battery to draw her attention while Skvalan discovered the wonders of picking at his elbow. "They don't understand. They don't know you. You'll put Korstra ahead of all else."

"I will fulfill my duties. Korstra brought Tommy into my life, and I will get him back."

Malja turned away. As much as she wanted to lash out further, she knew Tumus was not to blame. Dangerous to a team, yes. But not to blame. "It doesn't matter," she said. "We're too far behind. Even with a grounder, we'll never get to him in time."

Tumus brightened. "So you do believe they took Tommy."

"Listen to me. We can't get to the City of Ashes in time. So go home. It's all over."

Struggling to stand like a newborn foal, Tumus let out a

muted yelp. When she stood, she took a boastful breath and said, "Powerful magic takes more than tattoos and time. It takes strength and energy. Creating a creature from bits of the dead is extremely powerful magic. Imbuing such a monstrosity with lightning magic *and* the power over insects is practically unheard of. No matter how strong Jarik and Callib are, the energy they expended to stop you will have weakened them extensively. Perhaps for days."

"You're saying they've camped out?"

"Or their followers are carrying them. Either way, they will not be capable of powerful magic for a little while."

"That's good information. Thank you. Now get out of here. Go pray to Korstra or something."

"You stupid fool. I will go to the City of Ashes. I will follow you if you won't allow me to be a part of your group, but I will go."

Malja's face blazed. She wanted to cut Tumus. Shaking her head, she reined in and stomped off to the foyer campfire. She paced the wide hall and kicked any debris that dared to block her path. Though fuming, an odd grin crossed her lips — she knew anger so well it had become an old, welcome friend. Something shivered beneath her rage, however. A sense of wrong, a sense of sadness and regret — an emotion tied to the name Tommy. She mashed it well with anger. She could swallow any emotion with anger. Normally that ended it. But everything surrounding Tommy kept resurfacing.

Skvalan walked in. "Grounder run soon."

Malja nodded.

Skvalan nudged the fire with a rock until it flared up. "Tumus come, too."

Malja squatted next to him and let out a tense breath.

"I love wife. I go. She love Tommy. She go, too."

Malja closed her eyes.

Skvalan said, "She helps."

"She's a zealot. That's why Tommy's gone. She refused to follow my orders and instead follows her brother god."

"What you mean? Zealot?"

"Forget it."

Skvalan rubbed his ample belly. "We go fight magic. We need magic. She has magic."

"Look, I know you want her with us, and I know that she can help. But I don't trust her. I can't."

"Trust Cole? I think no."

With a begrudging grumble, she said, "Cole's not so bad."

"Trust me?"

"You want revenge for your wife and village. I understand that better than you'll ever know. You, I trust."

Skvalan stopped picking at the fire and faced Malja. "We need magic. Tumus come. Trust me."

Malja made a bitter face. To stand her ground against Skvalan meant at best, creating a rift between each member of the team and at worst, breaking them apart. Being alone would be nice but would not be good strategy at the moment. "Fine," Malja said, a bit more aggressively than she intended. "She can come, but she'd better be careful."

"Good." He said nothing more as they waited for the grounder to be ready. For that, Malja was grateful.

Chapter 21

Riding a horse never bothered Malja, but just a few seconds on the sea could flip her stomach. Sitting in the front passenger seat of a grounder while suffering a hangover proved an odd mix of both. She felt fine, despite the constant bumps and swerves as Cole guided the vehicle along uneven macadam, overgrown dirt paths, and rocky, dried riverbeds — as long as Malja kept her eyes forward. Whenever she chanced a peek out the side window, her stomach would lurch its bitter, acidic contents straight up her throat.

At least twice every hour they had to stop to clear out a fallen tree or dig through a wall of rocks. These hindrances provided Malja with some time to relax her stomach. Even heavy lifting or hard work chopping wood felt better to her body than the unnatural motions of a grounder. She couldn't comprehend how people once used these machines all day long.

She was a bit thankful for her hangover, because nobody bothered her. Cole drove. Skvalan and Tumus sat in back. They spoke quietly throughout the day. Apparently Tumus knew the Muyaza language — a fact she never bothered to mention before. Had Malja felt better, she would have yelled for a while about it, but being sick saved her from that foolishness as well.

And it was foolish. She had no regrets about the previous night — she truly worried about where Tumus's allegiance ultimately fell — but this day, hours later and sober, she could admit that Skvalan also spoke some truth.

Tumus cared for Tommy and felt deep pain over what had happened. Yelling at the woman did nothing to help.

Cole brought the grounder to a halt and squinted off to the left. "I wonder," she muttered and got out. The others followed.

A few yards into the trees lay the wreckage of some vehicle. As Malja stepped closer, her eyes widened. It was the trader's flatbed.

Weyargo's mutilated body had been wrapped around a tree. Malja said, "I met him once. Nice man. He had a magician with him to power this thing."

Everybody glanced around. "Animals eat," Skvalan said.

"Perfect," Cole said. She had been dallying with the flatbed's batteries.

Malja perked up. "Can we use those?"

"Not directly, but we can drain some of the power to recharge ours. Shouldn't take too long."

Malja checked the sun. "Get to it. We don't want to be stuck here tonight. That dead trader'll attract plenty of attention."

Cole was true to her word. In less than an hour, she had managed to get a quarter charge added to their grounder's batteries. She complained that she had lost a lot in the transference, but Malja figured every little bit got them that much closer.

After a few hours driving, Cole pointed ahead and said, "Look at that."

They had crested a small rise and for an instant the trees parted. In the distance, they saw the City of Ashes. Endless rows of gray and black shapes sprinkled the mountains like rotting, jagged teeth.

"We probably can get another hour in before it's too dark to drive. Tomorrow, though, we'll be there."

They managed an hour and a half. Malja suspected Cole

pushed the extra time not because of good light, but rather out of a desire to finish this mess she had joined. Malja didn't mind. They had made the extra time without incident and were that much closer.

Later that night while Skvalan's deep snores creaked like an ancient wooden ship, Malja watched the City of Ashes and heard violence running wild in the streets. Flashes of magic and plumes of fire rippled along the city. The sounds reached across the sky like distant thunder.

As she settled in next to Malja, Cole said, "The few clans living there go crazy over territory wars. Jarik and Callib probably keep the peace a little better, but they're absent right now."

"I thought you liked anarchy."

"In the Freelands, yes. There are miles of nothingness separating small pockets of people. One government, one set of laws to rule all would never work in a place like that. But in a city where people clash together non-stop — well, just listen to that lunacy."

As if in response, a series of green bursts popped along the streets followed by two heavy booms like massive cannons.

"Did you want something?" Malja asked. She pulled out Viper and worked the blade with a good stone she had found on the ground. She would have preferred her whetstone, but that now collected silt at the bottom of the Yad River.

Cole clasped her hands in her lap, straightened her back, and curled her legs to the side as if posing for a sculptor. After all the hiking and trudging and fighting, Malja had forgotten just how beautiful Cole could be. "When we arrive at the city," Cole said, "we'll head west for several blocks until we reach the Kryssta temple. From there we go north until we find the Skyway Bridge. There's where we'll find Jarik and Callib."

Malja continued to run Viper across the stone, creating a rhythmic scratching like a machine needing oil. "Why are you telling me this?"

"I could tell you that you need to know in case something happens to me, or I could even say that it's all about stopping Jarik and Callib. But the real reason — I don't know exactly. Aren't I just a fool? I suppose I want you to keep me in the group, even though you don't need me for information."

"Being part of a group isn't very anarchic."

"Pure anarchy cannot be maintained for long."

Malja gestured to the city. "They're doing a pretty good job at it."

"Only when their Masters are gone." Cole shifted closer, lowering her body in an apologetic fashion. "I know you've got many valid reasons not to want me along, but when I watched you and Tumus argue ... well, you both fought passionately, because you both love this boy. The only thing I've ever felt that much passion for is my work."

"And Jarik and Callib have that now."

"Yes. I suppose I want it back, but it's more than that. I want to help you and be a part of something good. I know my time with the Bluesmen became a horrible screw-up. I know that. But my heart was in the right place. I just wanted to open up the possibilities for everyone, so magicians like Jarik and Callib couldn't rule over everybody."

"You want to keep the anarchy going strong."

"Please, don't fight me like Tumus. Sweet little Malja, let me do something good."

Malja drew her head back. "I don't know why you think I could force you to go."

Cole chuckled. "Thank you."

230-The Way of the Black Beast

They listened to the chirping night creatures and distant, random explosions. Malja sharpened Viper. Cole relaxed.

Many people had come in and out of Malja's life and she never minded much. Drifting through the world brought that about. As long as she thought she had a good sense of the person, she felt secure. The closer she came to Jarik and Callib, however, the more confusing the people around her had become.

Adding to her thoughts, Malja heard Tumus approach. "Can't sleep?"

Tumus huffed as she sat next to Cole. "That man's snoring is worse than listening to Barris Mont speak."

The others laughed loud enough to interrupt Skvalan's snoring, which only caused more laughter. The brief mirth didn't fool Malja, though. Tumus did not sit with them for companionship. As their laughter subsided, Malja pressed for an answer.

Tumus said, "I'm concerned about tomorrow."

"We all are," Cole said.

"I'm worried we're being led into a trap."

Cole's smile dropped. "You've the gall to accuse me —"

"Not you. Them." Tumus indicated the city. "Jarik and Callib had outrun us. They should have been to the city already and done whatever they wanted. Instead, they use exhaustive magic to send an abomination upon us. Why?"

Malja set her sharpening stone aside. "You think they wanted us to catch up?"

"It's a possibility."

"Yet you know I'm going in there anyway."

"For Tommy."

Malja inspected her blade. "Yes. For Tommy."

"Well," Tumus said as she stood, "I simply wanted to make sure we all understood. Good night."

After she left, Malja turned to Cole. "Still want to come

along?"

Cole's face darkened as she peered into the distance. Malja lifted Viper and stood in a ready stance. She sniffed the air and listened for snapping twigs or crushed leaves. Cole looked at the ground like a defeated child. "The fighting stopped."

"Jarik and Callib?"

"They're in the City of Ashes now. They're home."

Chapter 22

The batteries gave out a few hours into the morning drive. Malja's anticipation fueled her legs, and she suspected the same could be said of the others. Nobody complained. They moved like ants scaling a tree to get to some leaves — steady and strong with a goal firmly in place.

When the sun reached its highest point, they took a break, each member of the team settling under a tree or an overhang for shade. All except Cole. She stood at the path's edge, gazing across the wide vista.

Malja approached and offered a swig of water from a dented canteen. Cole's cheeks were damp — more than just sweat. "You okay?"

Dabbing at her eyes, Cole said, "It's silly, but I just started thinking about Faw-Faw. I was remembering how back then the two of us lived so free of any concerns. Our days were spent following our whims and our nights were, well, passionate. Now it's all just this."

"Sounds like it was a dream, and dreams don't last forever."

"I know. See, but then I think about chubby Suzu or Rev with his big voice and charming laugh and ... I'm sorry they're all gone."

Malja threw a rock into the open air and watched it plummet. "Let's get hiking. It's going to be hard. That'll keep your mind off the dead."

As they trudged through several hours, Malja found her own dead to be kept at bay by the hike. She focused on each breath, each step, each rock. As night approached, they came upon the city streets. No gates, no arch, no bridge — nothing to signify the start of the city but a few scattered buildings.

These first structures stood tall with little apparent damage beyond broken windows and the wear of ages. Some were brick. Others smooth metal. A rare few were made of the once-white material Malja saw in Barris Mont's memory. Now, the white barely showed. A fine dust coated every surface — a mixture of dirty ash and mountain snow.

Malja saw no signs of people. Not even a furtive peek from a window corner. Nothing. She listened for a slipped foot or dropped object or a hushed voice. Nothing. The place was a cemetery.

Cole led them down one street, and Malja tried to memorize the turn. Lampposts lined this new street along with plenty of evidence attesting to the horrid nature of the city's inhabitants. From each lamppost hung a body. On each body, the skin covering the head had been removed, the head had been hollowed out, and a candle had been mounted in the skull. The dim light provided unsettling shadows across the ash-covered street. Tumus murmured a prayer.

A few blocks further in, they came upon a humble building surrounded by waist-high grass. The buildings around this one structure had been razed to the ground. An altar poked out from the grass. A statue of Moonlo lay in several pieces.

"The Kryssta Temple," Cole said. They turned north. Cole pointed into the dark and said, "Straight that way, several miles, we'll come upon the Skyway Bridge."

On the next block, Malja noticed footprints in the dust. Just a few at first. But eventually enough that the others noticed, too.

"Are we being watched?" Tumus asked.

"Probably," Malja said.

They came upon a massive, circular fountain with the far end dipping back, tilting the whole thing toward the buildings. The street bent around the structure which Malja thought looked more like a lake than a fountain. The stagnant water reeked. A statue in the middle rose several stories — or, it once did. Now it was a pair of legs surrounded by piles of rubble.

As they walked on, bullet holes marked walls and doors. Burnt-out grounders and smashed storefronts lined the streets. A flyer teetered part way in a lone wall, as if unsure whether or not to crash to the ground. Craters pocked the sidewalks. Smoldering fires scented all the evidence of the previous night's fighting.

The deeper in they traveled, the worse the city looked. Graffiti marred the cracked and ruined walls — violent and pornographic images painted in mud, charcoal, and blood. Like old advertisements, the words CALLIB IS KING and JARIK RULES weaved around the pictures. Bodies with fresh wounds decorated walkways. Worse — body parts littered the streets.

The last of dusk's sunlight disappeared. Malja ordered they set camp for the night with two of them guarding in shifts. They picked the sturdiest-looking building and settled in on the third floor. Malja denied Cole's request for a campfire. "It'll attract too much attention." So, they huddled up and attempted to sleep in the cold mountain night.

Only Skvalan could sleep. The others shivered and paced and kept watch. They listened to the skirmishes ignite and fade out, but none of the fighting reached the scale they had witnessed during their approach to the city. Apparently Cole had been right — Jarik and Callib's presence helped tame things.

During one of the lulls, Tumus came up to Malja with a stern face. "I think you truly believe Tommy is alive, and that being so, I must tell you something you don't want to hear."

The first thought to pierce Malja's mind — *Tommy's dead and Tumus has known all along.* She came close to striking Tumus. Even repositioned her feet to provide a strong leap. But she recalled that Tumus also believed Tommy was alive.

Oblivious to Malja's reaction, Tumus went on. "I know you hate me and blame me for all this, but that blame is false. I did not seek to disobey your commands. Tommy did." Tumus stepped back from the wild glower in Malja's eyes. "Tommy asked me to take him back to Dead Lake, to Barris Mont. He said if I refused, he'd do it on his own."

"It's amazing he said all that," Malja said. She leaped to her feet and gripped Tumus by the throat. "Especially considering the boy hasn't spoken a word since I've met him."

Tumus did not squirm. She spoke calmly, though straining for air, and she bore her gaze into Malja with religious conviction. "He did not speak with words. He drew pictures on the walls."

Malja thought of the huge circle, the little circles, the arrows and dots she had discovered. She let go of Tumus and turned away. "He told you he wanted to go back? Maybe you misunderstood."

"No. We spent hours going over his pictures until I knew quite clearly his desires. He can feel the changes going on inside him. He knows he has potential, and permit me to say that he has astounding potential, but he's being kept back and he wants to learn how to control his powers. Barris Mont could help him, and Tommy wanted that."

"You think you know him better than me?"

"In some ways, yes. I'm not afraid of what he is, and I don't shun him for it, either."

"I do not—"

"It doesn't matter what you say to me. I'm telling you this, because if we find him, *when* we find him, you should be prepared that he's not the boy you're trying to make him."

Before Malja could say more, Tumus left her alone. Malja leaned against a windowsill and watched the empty street below. The half-moon cast its pale light on the debris, creating grotesque shadows and illusions of depth. Good light for hiding. She poured her energy into searching those shadows for enemies — better than thinking about what Tumus had said.

An hour later, as her head lolled to the side, somebody tripped and cursed while scurrying down the street. The noise startled Malja awake. She spotted the person in seconds. Not a person, really. A griffle. And not just any griffle. This one was small — a runt — and had several white tufts on its head.

Malja checked if anyone else had awoken. Both Tumus and Cole had finally fallen asleep. Skvalan, however, stared at her with sharp eyes.

She waved him over and whispered, "Keep watch. I have to check something out."

Skvalan crossed his arms and looked around. Malja couldn't tell if he was questioning her or foggy from just waking up. Finally, he nodded and slipped in next to the window. "Don't take long time," he said.

Malja hurried outside and down the street. Following the griffle was easy. The little creature made such a racket, a blind man could catch him.

They traveled several blocks west and turned south for a

few blocks more. The night air chilled Malja's nose, but her assault suit kept her body warm. She moved fast and kept her eyes searching for attacks. As much as the griffle's noise made him easy to follow, it also could attract unwanted attention.

Around a towering rubble pile, Malja saw the dancing orange light of a fire. She pulled out Viper and readied for what she might find — a horde of griffles, perhaps, or even some bizarre religious rite. She wasn't sure what she hoped to gain, but as Gregor would say, "Coincidence is just an excuse not to delve into the Why of something." That griffle could not be in this city by accident, not at the same time she sought Jarik and Callib, and she wanted to know why it was here.

As she rounded the rubble pile, she discovered her answer, and while she had no expectations, she never expected anything like this. Fawbry.

"Here, here, I've got food," the griffle said, jumping around while Fawbry lay with his back against a lamppost. He looked tired and bruised — his left cheek puffed and dark. His lovely coat, now blotted with dirt, lacked its usual sheen. "Eat, eat. Then read, Mayor, please read."

Fawbry patted the white tufts and nibbled on something dark and round. Before he could swallow, the griffle tugged at Fawbry's coat pocket. Fawbry grinned through gritted teeth and pulled out his little Book of Kryssta.

"Okay," he said. "Calm down. I'll read one more, but then we've got to get some sleep." He thumbed the pages until he settled on one. "Listen, now.

> *Though Time is infinite —*
> *Ours is a flicker of candlelight —*
> *It is ours to burn away"*

"Whee!" the griffle shouted and rolled on the ground. "That's my new favorite."

"Shhh," Fawbry said. "We have to stay quiet."

Malja surveyed the area one more time but still found no threats. She stepped into view and nodded at Fawbry. "Hi there," she said.

Fawbry and the griffle jumped to their feet. Fawbry fought against wincing, but his hand went up to his side and rubbed a sore spot. When he saw who had spoken, his posture dropped, and Malja caught a disappointed scowl flash across his face. But he broke out a smile.

"Malja. I can't believe I'm going to say this, but I'm happy to see you."

"What are you doing here?" she asked, not bothering to pretend smiling.

Fawbry glanced around. "Are you alone?"

"Are you?"

Opening his arms, he said, "It's just us two. Really."

Malja stomped toward Fawbry and raised Viper, poised to strike. "You better explain what you're doing here. How is it that you didn't know where Jarik and Callib were, yet here you are? That doesn't happen by accident."

Fawbry shrunk back. "I see nothing's changed for you. Calm down. No need for that. It's all easy to explain."

"Explain fast."

"Well, the short side of it is that after I left you, I headed west."

"Why west?"

"South is the Freelands, North is my family, and East ends at the ocean. None of those were good options. I couldn't go to Barris Mont without you. I wouldn't dare. So, I just wandered west for some time. A few days ago, I ran into two trogets. You ever seen them? Big brutes with horns running down their spines. They wanted to eat me. I tried to read them some of the Book of Kryssta because it worked with the griffles. Turns out it only kind of worked this time. They decided not to kill me, because they thought they might get a bigger reward if they brought somebody with brains to their masters."

"Let me guess — Jarik and Callib."

"They had me held near the edge of the city. Tufts and several other griffles ended up here after you broke up my little gang. He's always been loyal. So when he saw me, he helped me escape."

The griffle puffed his chest. "I did that."

"You looking for protection now?" Malja asked. "Is that why you're speaking nice to me?"

"I'm talking to you at all, because you've got that curved blade ready to eviscerate me." Fawbry put his arm around the griffle. "But we are on the run. So, we would appreciate your protection, of course, but I'm not trying to lie to you. I'm not trying to be falsely nice or anything like that." He raised his arm to reveal the stump where his hand should have been. "When I left, I was angry. I'm still angry. But I've never been outright stupid, either. I don't want to be here." He leaned close to Malja and whispered, "Frankly, I pretty much figured we were dead. I was just comforting the little guy and stalling. So if you can help me, if you're willing, then I'll gladly take your help."

Malja sheathed Viper. "You don't want to be here with me. I'll just make a bigger mess for you. Besides, I'm not leaving here. Not yet. I'm going after Jarik and Callib, and I'm going to rescue Tommy."

"Tommy? What happened to him?"

The genuine concern in Fawbry's voice, the worry bordering on fear, touched Malja. Hesitantly, she went on, "I think Jarik and Callib have him."

Fawbry exchanged looks with the griffle. "No, no, no.

This can't be. We were just sitting here reading from the Book about life and why we're here at all. I was trying to tell Tufts how I appreciated the risks he took for me, and how life is about doing for others, and that if you do that, if you help others, then good things come your way."

"Kryssta says that?"

Fawbry shrugged. "Everything I've ever done was for myself. Even helping you was just a way to stay safe enough to get to Barris Mont. And in the end, all it got me was the loss of my hand and almost being eaten by a couple of trogets. But this little guy here snuck in while those beasts slept, untied me, got me out, got me food, all because he believes in the Book and in me."

"Careful, you're starting to sound like Tumus."

"Look, I don't know what I'm thinking, exactly, but something's different. You suddenly show up right when we're talking about all this. Maybe Kryssta's trying to tell me that if instead of getting you to help me, that if I help you save Tommy, maybe things'll get better for me. No, that's crazy. I've been through a lot. My brain's not working right. But still, that's how I read it."

"Me read it, too," Tufts said. "We help. We get good things. We help. We help."

Malja didn't want to take him along, but she felt wrong leaving him here. "Cole's with us," she warned.

Looking around with awe, Fawbry shrugged. "Doesn't matter. This isn't about me."

With a frown, Malja said, "Okay. Follow me. And keep that griffle quiet on our way back. I'm tired, and I don't want to fight tonight."

They returned in silence. Malja tried to equate this Fawbry with the one who had left her back in the Freelands. Something had changed, and she thought it had to be more than just coming close to dying. That could change a person, but life in this world was full of chances to die. It could be a scary, altering experience, at first, but after awhile, even danger becomes routine.

When they got back to the others, they settled in for the remaining few hours of night. Malja surprised herself — she fell asleep within minutes.

* * * *

The following morning arrived to the shocked gasps of Cole and Tumus. Before they could ask a coherent question, Malja said, "I found them last night, and they're coming with us. This is about Jarik and Callib and Tommy. All your problems with each other get buried for now. Understood?"

Tumus glowered. Cole let out a sigh. But both women nodded.

"Good," Malja said. "Then let's get going."

The day passed in an arduous, silent hike. Miles of rubble piled against shells of once-towering buildings. The stench of rotting corpses flowed in and out, blending with the ever-present rich aroma of burnt wood.

Tufts had the energy of a child. At times, he would race ahead like a scout, or he'd circle members of the group — studying faces and embracing scents. Fawbry brought up the rear, keeping his distance from the others but staying close enough for protection.

By the time night approached, Malja saw something different from the monotony of destruction — an amber halo several blocks ahead. "Cole," she said, "what's that?"

Cole's features broke into an appreciative smile. "By Korstra and for Kryssta's sake, I don't believe it."

Tumus said, "Please don't blasphemy."

"That must be the factories."

"For what?" Malja asked.

"Everything. Jarik and Callib have hundreds of people and creatures living here. They need food, clothing, everything. Those factories use magic and muscle to provide."

"They run all night?"

Cole tapped her lips. "Perhaps they're making up for lost work from fighting while their masters were gone. Who knows? The factories, though, they're big. We'll have to cut west to go around them."

"How far?"

"Miles, I imagine."

"We don't have the time anymore. Jarik and Callib have had plenty of rest. Let's go ahead and scout what's up there. Then I'll decide."

Tufts hopped from foot to foot. "I scout. I scout."

"No. I need to see it myself."

Fawbry waved a finger. "No way am I staying behind. If I don't stick with you this time, bad things'll happen."

Tumus said, "What's he talking about?"

With a friendly pat, Cole said, "Don't worry. It's just some of Krysstanism coming through."

"Well, I won't stay behind if he's going. Korstra needs to be heard, too."

Malja raised her hands. "Stop it. All of you just shut up. You can all come. Just be quiet."

They proceeded along the streets, the factory lights brightening as they closed in on the location. Though they could hear the clangs and calls of people at work and see the warm lights surrounding the enormous buildings, they felt colder than any time before.

The buildings stretched off like a river and endless chimneys punched the sky. Fences of chains, wood, and scavenged junk marked the perimeter. Thick posts dotted the ground, each with a metal arm pushed out to the side. From these hung the flag-mouths Malja knew from the Bluesmen. They sang in unison — little soft songs that appeared to lull the workers through their drudgery.

Lines of workers left the main building to either walk in the yard or deliver materials to one of the numerous, smaller buildings. Many workers had been maimed or injured. A few weren't human.

Overhead, fluttering along the fence, several crazed-looking people with dragonfly wings kept watch. Each wore a vest strapped with two powerful lamps that cut through the dark with blades of light. Malja thought of Nolan's sister, Audrex, and how the bastard magicians had caused her insanity. Clearly, Audrex was not the only one they had experimented with.

"These people are prisoners," Tumus said, and Malja shared her disgust.

"Not quite," Cole said. "They're followers — prisoners only to their belief in the magicians' powers."

Malja scoffed. "Like the Bluesmen were to you."

"Maybe. However, dear, I never would have had to treat my people like this. We worked hard in our fields, but we did it together for the common good of all of us."

"*They* worked. You sat upstairs where no one could bother you. And somehow I don't think Willie would have agreed with you. In fact, he most likely ..."

Malja stared at the factory compound, her mind weighing out an idea growing within. Fawbry opened his mouth, but Skvalan stopped him with a sharp gesture. Skvalan's intense focus on Malja told the others to stay quiet.

Finally, Malja grinned. She pointed to a long row of homes cutting through the compound. Each home stood at least three stories. From the damaged fronts, Malja could see that each home shared a wall with the next.

"There," she said. "We get inside and cross the factory compound in no time. They'll never see us because they're busy working or guarding the workers or checking the perimeter."

"And we're upstairs where no one can bother us," Cole said with a bitter undertone.

"Might as well make some good out of what you did."

"Little girl, all the problems with the Bluesmen and with you, that was the fault of Willie."

"Willie didn't order Fawbry's hand burnt off."

Skvalan snapped his fingers, quieting the two. Fawbry looked both embarrassed and defiant. But Malja detected a little pride, too, in the way he placed his stumped hand around Tuft's shoulder.

Malja flushed with annoyance at the entire group, including herself. She thought she should say some words to bring them back together, to encourage them, but she stayed silent. Too late for that. They were who they were.

With Viper in hand, she led the group across an open street. Crouching as she scurried, she brought them behind half of a car. The ragged edges looked as if some giant monster had torn the other half off with powerful jaws.

Malja pointed out a gouge in the brick wall of the second row home. The factory fence began only one house further in. Nothing between the half-car and the gouged wall — no cover of any kind. Without a word, Skvalan shot off, sprinted across the open area and slid into the house. Tufts followed as if playing a game of warrior — hunched low, moving fast, his hand carrying an imaginary weapon.

"Okay, okay," Tumus whispered to herself.

Malja heard the mounting anxiety, and when Tumus jumped to her feet, Malja yanked her back down. One of the crazed dragonflies flew overhead, his stark light creating day for a few seconds. He snorted and giggled as he passed by. Malja's skin prickled.

They waited a short while, once the dark had returned. Malja took her hand off Tumus and watched like a hovering parent as Tumus crossed to the house. Cole, Fawbry, and Malja followed up before the next dragonfly guard could fly by.

The smell hit Malja as she entered the house — something only a day dead. A rank odor that never got easier to inhale. The factory lights seeped in enough to see. The dainty songs seeped in, too. *Good,* thought Malja. *Hopefully that means it's loud enough to cover our noise.*

The room had been picked over long ago. Only a pile of bricks, glass, wood, and dirt remained as an obstacle blocking entry into the hall. Using a wide plank, Malja dug out a gap large enough to shimmy through. Dust coated the air and tasted like moldy bread. Whatever died must have been buried in the rubbish pile. Malja pushed that thought aside and tried not to taste anything she breathed.

Once all six had entered the hall, Malja picked up the pace. Though they needed to be quiet, the faster they moved, the faster they would reach the other end. Besides, with Jarik and Callib so close now, she never could have moved slower.

Down the hall, up a flight of stairs, down another hall. Malja saw a finger-sized hole in the wall at the end. She peered in — an empty room in the next house, except for a stained, beaten mattress and a pot filled with liquid.

Malja used Viper to carve a larger hole. The others paced behind her, crossing arms, tapping feet, making little utterances that did nothing more than piss Malja off. She could have torn down the wall, but feared such an action would be too noisy. But after a few minutes of hard, sweating labor, she had managed only a fist-sized opening.

"Go away," Skvalan said in a brisk whisper.

Malja looked back to see Skvalan preparing to barrel through the wall.

"No," she said. "Too loud."

"Go away." He waved her aside, but she didn't move. To Tumus, he rattled off a few words.

Tumus said, "I think he wants to use magic."

Skvalan took slow steps toward the wall. He closed his eyes and concentrated. Malja stepped away as he approached. The narrow hall forced the others to slide around him so he could pass.

Malja wondered what other magic the Muyaza knew, but when Skvalan reached the wall, she understood. He only knew the one spell. The bubble formed around him and pressed against the walls. Wood creaked like an old ship in heavy winds.

Skvalan sat cross-legged in the hall. Malja wished they had something big enough for a litter — they could have made a battering ram out of themselves and the bubble. Instead, she watched as Skvalan pushed outward with his hands, forcing the bubble forward. Dust and chalky particles trembled around the hole Malja had carved out. Skvalan groaned as he pushed again, his hands shaking. A divot formed in the wood, growing bigger as the bubble moved forward.

The idea seemed good at first, but the harder Skvalan pushed, the more Malja worried the wall might crash down, giving them away. Before she had time to complete her thoughts, the wall burst open. Wooden framing snapped like broken bones poking out of skin. Flatter wood and soft filling crumbled to the floor sending more dust into the air.

For a few seconds, nobody moved. They all looked at Malja as she listened for sounds of alarm. Workers continued to trudge. Saccharine singing continued to mellow the yard. No screams or orders or attacks came.

One look at Skvalan told Malja they would not do this again. Sweat beaded on his face, and he had trouble getting to his feet. She hauled him up by the arm and slapped a hand on his back.

"Thanks," she said before ducking through the opening.

"Yeah," Tufts said, slapping Skvalan's leg. "Thanks."

They walked into a bedroom, down a hall, and found a door where the shared wall with the next house should be. Malja placed her hand on the door — cool to the touch. She pressed her ear against it and listened — nothing. As if handling explosives, she gently lifted the latch and pulled the door open.

A dark corridor stretched off. No door or windows offering glints of light existed. Just darkness.

Malja raised a hand to halt her friends. With Viper in front, she stepped into the dark. She paid attention to all her senses to discern if anything awaited them. Nothing to see or smell or taste. But she heard it — a slight, quivering exhale. Someone trying to be quiet, but too nervous.

With a graceful shift of her feet, she lowered her body, preparing to pounce. A twist of her hand repositioned Viper for maximum damage off her initial swing. She turned her hips, winding up like a top. She held all that built up power long enough to be sure of where to strike. And she let loose.

Three distinct strikes sliced through the dark. A surprised breath came followed by blood-filled choking. A body slumped to the floor sounding like a clumsy fellow dropping a stack of heavy books.

That's when the alarm sounded.

Chapter 23

Malja had expected the singing flags to blare out an obnoxious scream or perhaps to announce, in an irritating voice, that they had an intruder. Instead, they continued to sing and the workers continued to work. The alarm took the form of a high-pitched, rapid beeping coming from the dead man's belt — just like the frame in Cole's basement, the one that exploded.

Malja sprinted to the far wall and hacked away at it with Viper. Fawbry followed her, tossing away debris as it fell. Cole, however, did not panic. In the dark, she said, "It's an alarm, not a bomb."

A chunk of wall fell to the floor. Light streaked in revealing Cole bent over a torso while Tumus and Skvalan waited in the back. Tufts wrapped his little arms around Skvalan's knee.

"A quiet alarm is worse than a noisy one," Malja said and swung Viper into the wall again. "Means that whatever answers the call is expected to handle us without everyone knowing. It means that—"

Standing behind the group, a dragonfly-winged madman raised his arms. The lamps on his vest blasted the hall with drastic brightness. Malja shielded her eyes until they adjusted. She heard Skvalan yell, Tufts shriek, and the flat smack of Cole or Tumus hitting someone with a wooden plank. She could see the dark outlines of punches thrown and people tossed.

The Dragonfly faced Malja. He didn't kill the others. He read the team well. Malja saw it in the way he repositioned his body. He knew she posed the real threat. With his wings moving faster, creating an incessant buzz, he launched after her.

Fawbry dropped to the floor and covered his head. Malja had time for two quick thoughts. First, there was no room to evade the attack. Second, this was going to hurt.

She tried to bring Viper up to a useful striking position, but the Dragonfly slammed into her like a wild horse. Just as the impact on her front registered, the Dragonfly continued forward, using her to ram through the wall. Pain fired across her back.

They tumbled to the floor, spraying dust into the still air. They were in a wide room with a beautiful, tiled floor and tall windows lining both sides. Two huge lamps hung from the high ceiling, each decorated with glass bits now covered in cobwebs and grime.

Malja had no idea what the room had been built for, but as she shook off pieces of wall, she saw that the place was intended to impress. The Dragonfly glanced around, too, until they locked eyes. Malja raised Viper. The Dragonfly buzzed his wings.

Like before, he soared towards her with amazing speed. This time Malja didn't need to think. She had plenty of room. She sidestepped the attack and cut the creature through the waist. One swift slice. Two pieces of Dragonfly tumbled in different directions.

"Hurry," Malja called back. "More will come."

Fawbry's dust-covered face peeked through the wall. "Good to see things are as usual with you." With Tufts climbing on his back, Fawbry entered the room.

Skvalan limped in, his arm around Tumus's shoulder. Cole brought up the rear. Even in the dim light, Malja could see that Skvalan's body was not used to magic. But before Malja could speak, Tumus brushed by her and said,

"He'll be fine."

Halfway across the room, the tall windows behind them shattered. Four Dragonflies — two women, two men — flew inside.

So much for the quiet way. "Run!"

Malja bolted ahead to clear the way while the others hobbled as fast as they could manage. She hoped the Dragonflies would converge on her. No such luck. But her separation from the group confused the buggers enough to gain a few seconds.

She dashed into a small room with a wide bathing tub built into the far wall and a cracked seat with a hole at the bottom like a fancy indoor outhouse. She stepped into the smooth tub and swung Viper into the wall. Tile chipped off and the wall crumbled apart as if had been made of wet, clumped sand. The damp odor of rot wafted out. Malja stood still — the walls had looked so strong.

Skvalan and Tumus stumbled in. Malja heard the rapid buzzing not far behind. They stepped through the wall and continued on. Cole charged through next.

Malja said, "Get started on the next wall. I'll be right there."

Cole nodded and dashed off. Either she was a good soldier following orders or a scared mouse too frightened to balk. Malja was happy to take either one.

The buzzing grew louder. Malja flattened against the wall next to the doorway. She raised Viper and waited.

"I'm coming," Fawbry yelled, bursting into the room and through the wall, Tufts riding his back the whole time like a panicked version of a child's game. Malja waited as the buzzing closed in. When the first Dragonfly entered, she decapitated it. The others pulled back, hissing and buzzing. She leapt over the tub, through the wall, tucked her head and rolled. Popping to her feet, she hurried on.

Before she reached the end of the hall, she saw a new problem. The entire next building lay in a collapsed pile below. Malja waved toward the stairs. "Down," she yelled and the others obeyed.

Thumping down the stairs, Malja noticed Skvalan moving with a little more certainty. At the bottom, she pulled him ahead and said, "Will you be okay?"

Skvalan shook off the arm. "I don't stop."

"We've got to run the rest of the way. Understand? No cover. You fall, that's it."

"I fine."

"Good." She heard the confused buzzing above. "Everyone follow me. No stopping until I stop. Got it?"

She made eye contact with each one. They were ready. Maybe like dollops waiting to run from their burrows, hoping nothing tried to eat them, but ready nonetheless.

Malja counted to three. She kicked open the door and sprang off. Glancing upward, she saw them — two Dragonflies leaping from the open wall three stories up. They let out a churlish cackle as they descended in a frenzy of bloodlust and sheer, adrenaline-fueled excitement. She pointed onward and let the others sprint ahead.

The singing mouths clamped shut. Several Dragonflies hovered above, casting their spotlights on Malja's team. The workers halted and watched.

"Keep running," she yelled. They had another block to go.

Malja suppressed all sounds of her feet pounding the ground and her blood pounding through her heart. She ignored the lunatic symphony surrounding her and filtered out the confused calls of the workers. She heard only the buzzing wings.

The volume and tone changed. She kept running and listening, never looking back, just listening, driving her legs and listening. She waited for the pitch to alter as the Dragonfly swooped in to attack. It came fast.

She dropped to the ground and rolled forward. The Dragonfly passed overhead — close enough to touch. As Malja returned to her feet, she followed through with Viper, digging its point into her enemy. It cried out as one wing tore off. Malja sliced down and sprinted onward. She passed the trembling Dragonfly without remorse.

Tumus and the others had stopped running. Malja cursed as she rushed to catch up. When Malja reached them, she saw what had brought them to a halt. A Dragonfly woman stood before the fence. Her greasy hair draped over her lowered head as she stared at her tattooed arm.

"I'll handle this one," Tumus said and spread her arms outward.

Malja waited. She tapped her fingers on Viper's grip. The itch to attack grew stronger, but the Dragonfly's spell might be ready. She could be waiting for Malja to launch. Better to wait on Tumus while everything remained static.

Skvalan leaned on Cole. Fawbry bent over and coughed spittle onto the ground. Tufts hid behind the legs of one, then another, in the group. His eyes big with nervousness as he rasped out harsh breaths.

They were all exhausted, but Malja's body shivered with adrenaline. Her assault suit kept her going, too.

The fourth Dragonfly landed behind them, his body taut and ready to strike. Malja attacked, her muscles thrilled to be active again. She swiped low, hoping to cut the creature near the knees. This Dragonfly, however, read her intentions and took to the sky.

"Die! Die! Die!" the woman guarding the fence bellowed as a rush of fire flowed from her hands.

The nearby workers squealed and sought cover. Tumus

stood her ground, mouthing the name *Korstra* while the flames shot towards her. Though Malja had witnessed the Chi-Chun absorb magic before, she couldn't help but wonder if this time Tumus would fail.

As it neared, the fire curved toward Tumus. The Dragonfly woman raised her arms and the stream of flames reared as if it were leashed to its creator. Tumus turned her palms upward and the flames pulled down toward her. Back and forth, tugged one way then the other, the flames danced in the air like a pet caught between two masters.

Like all the others watching, Malja stood mesmerized by the display. When the Dragonfly man swooped in to hit her head, she never countered. The blow knocked her to the ground and brought sparkling lights to her vision.

She knew better than to try to shake it off. Even as she stumbled to her feet, the Dragonfly landed next to her, striking out with a fist. Though dizzy and off-balance, Malja swung Viper to block the attack. Her strike lacked power and went in a wide, wild arc, but its unpredictable wobble served her well. The Dragonfly pulled back.

In the short time he took to reconsider his next attack, Malja's head cleared. The two warriors came together in a brash display of solid weapon work meeting superior reflexes. The Dragonfly held no weapon because he had no need. Malja missed every swing. He was too fast.

But she could be fast as well. He came at her with fists and feet. She dodged most of it. Twice she willingly took a punch in the side hoping to use the closeness against him. The first time she gouged his arm. He wised to the trick the second time.

Caught between two fights, Fawbry, Tufts, Cole, and Skvalan all stood tight together, watching and waiting. Tumus continued to battle for control of the conjured flame, but Malja couldn't look long enough to tell who might win. She ducked and countered, but Viper slipped through air. She felt like a child practicing against her shadow.

The Dragonfly rose up at least twenty feet and hovered for a moment. He cocked his head to the right and opened his mouth. Rotting teeth and a sickly-gray tongue greeted her.

Thrusting his arm forward, he dived straight down. Just before hitting the ground he shot off away from Malja. She had braced for the hit, but the change in course left her confused. That is, until she understood his target had changed — Skvalan.

In a series of smooth motions, the Dragonfly threw Cole into a wall, knocked Fawbry into Tufts, and snatched Skvalan, taking him high above the ground. The weakened Muyaza tried to free himself but the Dragonfly held tight. Skvalan punched and wriggled. Nothing worked. In frustration, he let out a deep, guttural war cry.

"Let him go," Tumus yelled.

Malja watched on, stunned by the passionate power emanating from Tumus. The Chi-Chun spun her torso, her arms flowing like a seasoned dancer. The sudden shift in motion surprised the Dragonfly woman. She lost control of her fire and Tumus took over.

The flames funneled into her right hand. She raised her left and sent scorching bolts into the air. She had complete control now. The bolts circled Skvalan and the Dragonfly — only striking when they could do so without hitting Skvalan.

Malja felt Tumus's anger burn as hot as the magic above. Tumus turned back to the magic's source.

"Stand aside," she said.

The crazed Dragonfly woman giggled as if watching a silly puppet show. "Not until you're all dead."

Without further warning, Tumus released the rest of the flames. The Dragonfly woman never tried to escape. She welcomed the full blast with open arms and a sadistic smile. As it sent her crisp corpse smashing through the gate, Malja could still hear her foolish giggles.

All grew still. Only the sound of the brisk mountain winds blowing against the broken city infiltrated the area. The pungent odor of burnt air and burnt flesh drifted on this wind.

Just a few feet away, Malja saw Skvalan's body tangled in a heap with the Dragonfly man. No one moved. Tumus pushed Malja aside as she rushed to Skvalan. She dropped to her knees, crying, and carefully pulled Skvalan's body away from the Dragonfly man.

"We can't stay here long," Fawbry said as he settled up next to Malja.

"I know."

They waited. At length, Tumus composed herself, but she did not join the others. Instead, she raised her arms upward and in long, mournful tones, she said, "Korstra, most powerful brother God, to serve you, we live and in serving, we are fulfilled. I offer you the soul of a cherished friend." She lowered her hands upon the corpse, closed her eyes, and started again.

Cole looked to Malja. "She can't do this."

"She is."

"But these weren't the only guards."

"I know."

"There's bound to be more. If we stay ..." Cole's eyes and chin shivered.

Malja had seen plenty of people reach their breaking point. Cole was no warrior. She wasn't even a grunt soldier. She was a technician and a politician. That she had lasted this long impressed Malja.

"Keep yourself together," Malja said as she heard the distinct buzzing in the distance. "We don't go on without Tumus. We don't leave our teammates behind."

"But they're coming. We barely made it this far against just four of these nasty things. We've got to hide."

The buzzing had grown loud enough to pull Tumus's attention. The sound came from all directions — even above. Like a giant machine grinding its way through the city, a Dragonfly force of at least forty closed in on them.

Malja wiped Viper clean, rolled her shoulders, and settled into her battle stance. Cole's face dropped. With a worried whimper, Tufts scrambled up Fawbry's shoulder. Tumus joined them, grim understanding resting on her lips. Without a word, she handed Malja a strand of dark hair — Skvalan's wife. Cole looked at the determined faces of her allies and panic bloomed.

"Are you crazy? They'll kill us." Cole's hands shook and tears rolled along her nose. "I'll run. I can hide. I don't need you."

Tumus held Cole's shoulders. "Trust in Korstra."

Cole backed away, pointing a wavering finger. "You're both as insane as those guards. Come now, Faw-Faw, you don't want to stay here and die."

Fawbry picked up a rock as a poor weapon. "I've got to help Tommy," he said.

Tumus lifted her hands and started focusing on her magic. Cole looked at them with confusion at first, but a horrible understanding dawned on her face like a swimmer alone in the ocean seeing a massive wave towering over her. She spun to find the Dragonfly force hovering like a cicada-covered field — clear wings and incessant buzzing. She raised her hands in surrender.

One Dragonfly man landed. He wore a dirty red breastplate made from the hood of a grounder and held a machete in each hand. His cold face revealed nothing as he spoke. "I am the Factory King. You are trespassers and murderers. For you, there will be no mercy."

"I am Malja, daughter of Jarik and Callib."

A startled wave rolled through the Dragonfly force. The Factory King contorted his face and jerked to the side. He whispered to the empty space on his left. With a jerk of his head, he regained his self-control and said, "There are many of my subjects in this great world who would make such claims. But only the real Malja could defeat my entire army."

Cole dropped to her knees while keeping her hands straight in the sky. "I don't want to die," she repeated in a soft prayer-like whisper.

The Factory King laughed and pointed both machetes at Cole. The familiar burning rage Malja knew like a beloved pet snapped to life. In one rapid stroke, she cut through the King's arms. The machetes rang out as they hit the ground, but the King's screams challenged the sound. Blood gushed from his wounds leaving behind a crimson trail as he flew off.

"Put your arms down," Malja said, nudging Cole with her foot. "Grab the weapon."

Cole took a few seconds to react, but so did the infuriated army. By the time she took hold of one machete, Fawbry grabbed the other, and Malja had cut down three Dragonflies. The same panic that drove Cole to surrender now fueled her fury. She fought off her attackers with harsh strength and blind anger, but did little to reduce their numbers.

Malja moved in bursts of speed and grace. She knew her assault suit aided her; however, it could not manifest energy in her that did not already exist. Ducking one blow, striking another, feigning one attack, and following through on the next, Malja used all her skill to protect the group.

Streams of fire, bolts of lightning, and blasts of ice shot down from above. Tumus moved like a juggler, catching magic in one hand and throwing it back into the air with the other. Dancing left, reaching out right. Throwing magic without watching the result.

Fawbry did his best, but he lacked Malja's skill and Cole's rage. He parried what he could and struck a few enemies, causing an occasional cry of pain. When the opportunities arrived, Tufts leapt off Fawbry to claw at heads, eyes, arms, and wings. After a few lashes, he hurried back to Fawbry and readied for another leap.

Without warning and in unison, the Dragonfly force broke off. Malja, Tumus, Fawbry, and Cole stood back to back, weapons ready. The great cacophony of buzzing ceased as the entire army landed.

In the new silence, Malja heard her heartbeat drumming in her ears. Each deep breath she took sounded like a hurricane. She circled around her friends, waving Viper to keep the Dragonflies at a distance. Tumus pulled herself together and circled from the opposite side.

"This city is ours," a Dragonfly said.

Malja shifted her back foot, lowered her center of gravity, and cleared her mind. She turned Viper an inch more open. She searched for the one who spoke.

"Korstra will protect us," Tumus shouted.

A commotion broke out far in the back. Strange sounds like cheering and arguing filtered its way up. As it reached Malja's ears, her stomach hardened — not cheering, not arguing, but chanting. Over and over.

Zorum. Zorum.

Fawbry said, "Um ... Malja?"

"Shut up," she said. "All of you back away." She stepped forward to increase the distance between her and her friends. While she didn't know who or what exactly Zorum was, she had encountered enough battle in her life to guess. This had all the marks of their best warrior.

From the crowd of Dragonflies emerged a giant. Zorum stood nearly eleven feet tall with muscle so thick his skin tore in an effort to contain him. His wild hair shot off in all directions as if he had been struck by lighting. His Dragonfly wings lay flat and impotent against his back — a side-effect of whatever magic he had used to get this way. Blood dribbled from his oversized knuckles. Madness swam in his oversized eyes.

"I am Malja," she yelled. "This is Viper." Her voice overcame the buzzing. Her name stopped a few. Zorum's deep gasp halted the rest. She knew they sensed the tension, even those that didn't know her name.

Zorum saw the sudden pause in the group and registered his mistake. With a thunderous voice, he said, "Malja's a myth. You're just a wench."

"You're about to find out."

Without further preamble, they circled each other. The Dragonflies cleared around them and began to cheer. Roars of excitement followed each feint, thrust, and parry. They stood as one, bonded by an anticipation Malja could feel in the air. Those that knew her name, knew they witnessed the birth of legends. She thought she heard betting. It reminded her of battles long gone. Her lips cracked into a grin — just a second's break to smile, but Zorum seized the opportunity.

He charged, startling Malja into a clumsy block that left little more than a scratch on his arm. Zorum barreled forward again and grabbed Malja's free arm. He swung her around like a drunk spinning a whore, spitting laughter while his mates cheered him on. He smelled putrid, and part of Malja was grateful when he let her fly into the crowd. Several Dragonflies kicked and punched her as they tossed her back into the fight.

"I thought Malja was a great warrior," Zorum said. More laughter rippled through the Dragonflies. "Guess she's just a little girl with a big story."

Malja settled into a fighter's stance, breathing heavily but not empty of all her strength just yet. The corners of her lips raised — they always underestimated her. With a piercing scream, she launched her assault. She swung Viper over her right shoulder, guessing Zorum would block it with his magically enhanced arm. He did. So she reversed her motion, spinning fast and slicing horizontal across his thighs. Blood seeped down his legs but he showed no signs of suffering.

"Stupid," he said. He punched downward, his fist connecting with her back. The Dragonflies roared. She hit the ground, air shoved from her lungs, her head rattling at the blow. A thick hand took hold of her braided hair and yanked her to her feet. Zorum pulled back his fist, a brutal gleam in his eye, and let out a deafening yell — his breath worse than his body. As the fist sped towards her, Malja kicked straight out for his groin. Down he went, dirt spewing into the air around him.

He rolled on his back. She leaped over him, ready to stomp on his throat and end this. Instead of grasping his privates, though, like most males, Zorum stayed present in the fight. He caught Malja's foot and twisted her to the ground, once more knocking the breath from her lungs. Gasping, she rose to all fours only to feel a crushing blow on her head, sending her face into the cracked pavement.

Her head spun. She couldn't find her balance. The ground seemed to pitch and yaw under her. She saw Dragonflies urging her to fight, others laughing at her failure. She saw twisted faces and lustful eyes. They were beyond insane.

She saw her friends. They looked at her with pity and suffering and tears. They looked at her with defeat in their eyes. She attempted to rise but rolled on her back, staring at Zorum's towering figure.

"You see," Zorum said, but the words muddled in her ears as if spoken underwater.

She saw him shake with mirth while he displayed Viper like a conqueror and then let the weapon drop as if it were a harmless toy. Her eyes closed, and for a moment, the idea of sleep sounded ideal. More harsh laughter startled her awake. Fear wrapped a chilled hand around her heart — fear for Tommy.

Fawbry babbled, pleaded, but Malja couldn't decipher the words. Zorum dropped Viper and pointed at Fawbry who raised his stump in defiance. *Good, Fawbry.*

Malja rolled to her stomach. Zorum kicked her side — just strong enough to warn her to remain still. He stepped over her, one huge leg on either side. His deep voice rumbled the ground as he yelled at her friends bow down. She didn't need to look at them now. They had to be terrified. They had to be lost.

Then I won't be. Viper lay just in front of her head. No time for hesitation.

In a series of smooth motions, she snatched the weapon, flipped it so the curved blade faced skyward, jumped to her feet, and thrust straight up, sending the blade deep between Zorum's legs. She bellowed her rage as Zorum crouched and groaned in pain. His shock afforded her a few precious seconds — enough to step on his thigh and vault herself higher, slicing up through his gut and into his chest. Arching backward, she flipped her body. She pulled Viper along, tearing it out of him in a crimson spray, and landed on her feet.

Malja's head screamed at her audacity, pounding her brain against her skull with every heartbeat, and she fought hard not to pass out. Zorum gazed down in disbelief as his innards flopped to the ground. He couldn't even muster a final word. His body dropped like a soulless bag of rotten meat.

Shocked silence hung in the air. Nobody moved.

Malja stood still. Breathing heavily. Eyeing every Dragonfly she could see — there would be no more challenges.

Before she could speak a word, the Dragonflies prostrated themselves on the ground. Malja frowned. She'd never seen this kind of reaction before. But Tumus elbowed Malja, and the answer came to her without looking. She could feel their presence like the shadow of a predator darkening over sleeping prey. She peeked over her shoulder, knowing exactly whose appearance had caused the sudden change.

Jarik and Callib.

They floated over the wreckage Malja and her friends had wrought, looking every bit as strong and virile as they had at the Bluesmen's house. Bald, shirtless, tattooed — power radiated from them like a sun. Basking below them, their entourage of magicians floated and focused.

As they neared, Jarik turned his jaded but sad eyes upon Malja. She wanted to leap in the air, berate them for all the sorrow they had caused, and slay them with merciless blows. But more than just exhaustion stopped her. A strange emotion roiled underneath her hate — a desire to curl up and go unnoticed. Not a need to hide, but rather a hope to become small.

Callib leveled a stark, penetrating glare at the Dragonfly army and said, "You have made a mess of this place. If you can't handle the simple job of being guards, what good are you?"

"W-We're sorry," one Dragonfly woman said.

"I have made you all, and I can unmake you. Don't fail me again. Where is the Factory King?"

In a sturdier voice, the Dragonfly woman pointed at Malja and said, "She cut off his arms."

Callib faced Malja, and she felt the full weight of his gaze like a boulder sitting on her chest. It sent her mind swirling backwards — seven years old, caught in one of the many off-limits rooms, a broken beaker in her hand. She never could please Callib. It proved easier to disappoint.

"All of you will follow us to our home."

"I'm not here to follow you," Malja said, her brazen words surprising her as much as them. "I came to—"

Callib's hand sliced across the air as if he held a sword. "I know exactly why you came. Jarik may not have believed you were capable of patricide, but I never doubted."

"Malja," Jarik said, his voice firm but a tinge warmer. "Come with us. You won't be harmed. You may keep your weapons. Your friends won't be harmed."

"You can't hurt us anyway," Callib said.

"You've been gone a long time," Jarik said. "Ever since you came into our lives, we've worked tirelessly to find a way to send you home. Come with us and let us show you what we can now do."

"Besides," Callib said like a konapol lowering itself to strike, "we have Tommy."

Chapter 24

They left the factory compound with Jarik and Callib leading the way while five magicians brought up the rear. They moved at a slow, somber pace as if in a funeral procession. Indeed, Tumus and Cole both cycled through fear of the magicians and grief over the loss of Skvalan.

Malja's heart hammered against her chest, but not for the same reasons — she dealt with fear through force and she knew death too well to grieve. But her fathers were a different matter. She tried to quell the emotional tornado tearing through her, but each time Jarik looked over his shoulder at her, the storm grew stronger. Callib, thankfully, never looked back.

She caught a glimpse of Fawbry and a different sensation trembled along her skin. Battle left varied scars on a person's mind. Fawbry displayed an odd serenity. She had seen that look before — a man shaken enough by his experiences that he became so determined, so confident, all logical caution was abandoned. It was the look of a warrior believing in a righteous quest. Such things could be a great advantage, but could be equally dangerous and unpredictable. And such things tended to be temporary. One other explanation existed, and Malja hoped this to be true — that Fawbry was in shock.

The block they proceeded up barely resembled a city. Only a few buildings still stood — skeletons of brick, metal, and jagged glass. The rest littered the streets in uneven piles. The blocks ahead had become a trash dump.

Callib raised his left hand, glanced at the sawtooth tattoo there, and with a casual flick of the wrist, created four balls of light. The lights each took a corner surrounding the group and followed them as they moved through the dark, empty streets. Tumus and Fawbry gasped — neither had ever seen magic executed with such ease.

Malja, however, had seen plenty of it. She would not let Callib's little display intimidate her. *They are the bastard magicians, and they deserve all my rage.*

Only thoughts of Tommy kept Malja from attacking. Callib said they had Tommy, and Malja forced herself to wait until she saw the boy. Once she knew Tommy was alive and safe, she would let this tornado within her loose.

A grave smile crossed Malja's lips. Her thoughts were bold and full of pride. She hoped she could live up to them.

Ahead, the city seemed to disappear. For just a second, Malja's step hesitated.

Cole whispered, "It's okay."

The street ended without warning — just a sheer drop as if the ground had been gouged out by an angry witch. Malja could not make out the other end. Darkness and fog filled the chasm. Out of the darkness emerged what passed for a bridge — a haphazard framework of rubble slammed together by a drunk.

Jarik and Callib led the group onto the bridge. Its rough surface creaked under their weight. Half-way across, they stopped. Jarik faced the empty darkness. He raised his right arm and cocked his head so he could focus on the tattoo wrapping around his bicep.

Callib said, "This is where everything ended and everything began. This is the true location where the Devastation erupted. Others have claimed their paltry plots of land as the true location, but even Barris Mont's Dead Lake is not big enough."

"That's blasphemy," Tumus said.

"Not at all. The Devastation reshaped our entire world. It culled the weak and created opportunities for the strong. Magic of that magnitude would leave behind a grand mark. This crater is that mark."

"The Chi-Chun do not recognize—"

"I don't care what your little cult thinks. Here is where the Devastation began. A massive explosion of magic and fire that leveled the world. It blasted in all directions, even through the ground, and no doubt burst out in many places. Even your Dead Lake."

Jarik's body grew taut as if straining under a great weight. Callib turned his attention to the side of the bridge. With a brotherly smile, he patted Jarik's shoulders.

Malja stepped closer and peered over the edge. Under Callib's artificial lights, all she saw was a milky sea of fog.

Fawbry came up to her side. "Not very impressive."

But shadows formed beneath the waves. They grew larger, darker, thicker.

First, a tower broke the surface. This connected to the blocky architecture of a building out of Barris Mont's memory. It continued to rise, growing wider and gaining several smaller buildings at its sides.

Malja remembered the smaller, earthier house they had raised her in. More than anything else, seeing barbed wire surround the roofs and iron bars block the windows convinced Malja of the threats Jarik and Callib feared. They had built a fortress to live in.

The building continued to rise causing Fawbry to audibly gasp. He leaned back, gawking at the building's height. The bottom level finally came to rest flush with the bridge. The lesser magicians wasted no time getting through the entrance's massive double doors. Several looked back at Jarik and Callib like dogs eager for permission. Others rushed ahead for sanctuary.

Jarik exhaled and let his shoulders slump. Malja expected the entire building to plummet back into the chasm with the magicians screaming all the way down, but it held steady. Apparently, moving the building required much stronger magic than parking it.

Callib kissed the top of Jarik's head. "It still amazes me when you pull off that spell."

"It's getting easier. A few more times and it won't take half what it takes out of me now."

"With Malja here now, my dear brother, we won't need this place. We'll have castles all over the world."

As they stepped inside the building, a disturbing thought flashed through Malja's head — *we might not get out again.* She clenched her fists and sneered. She should be thinking like the warrior she was — not some prissy weakling worried about breaking a bone or losing a limb.

The foyer of this floating city block could have had no other purpose than to intimidate. Huge columns rose upward to meet the ceiling seven stories away. The walls were uneven like a cavern yet they had a geometric quality as well — long, flat rectangles like crystal sticks cut at irregular heights.

Two mammoth-sized statues made up the far wall. One of Jarik, one of Callib — each sitting upright as both the guard and the ruler, each scowling as they looked upon all who entered. Between these statutes was a normal-sized door. Guarding the door stood one maxdin — eight feet tall, coarse hair, claws and teeth.

The softest sounds echoed and amplified and mutated in the open space, surrounding visitors with strange, deep tones that chilled the skin. Malja had seen many extravagant rulers build many extravagant homes, but this surpassed any of her experiences. And while this foyer succeeded in composing awe and a sense of power, Malja wondered if this boasting through architecture undercut their strength as well. The most fearsome warriors she had ever fought almost always downplayed their appearance — choosing to dress like a commoner rather than in something that showed off muscles or weapons or power.

Whatever the case, Malja had had enough. Despite the turmoil spinning her stomach and the weariness aching her bones, she found it easy to pour herself into saving Tommy. Jarik and Callib, her fathers and enemies, lost importance to her. The portal frame that could open up other worlds but Cole feared would bring about another Devastation meant nothing. Tommy was the sole thought that stood in Malja's brain unmarred by conflicting ideas.

"Where's Tommy? You said you had him, bring him to us."

Jarik said, "She is plucky."

"You should know the only reason I haven't cut you both down is because of Tommy."

Callib raised his top lip as if smelling something vile. "Be careful how you estimate yourself," he said, opening both hands towards her. "You are no more than a rat."

Malja's hand reached back for Viper even as her nerves jangled across her body. Jarik pushed between them. "Callib, control yourself," he said.

"Control myself? If you had shown more control years ago, we wouldn't have to deal with her now." Callib broke away, throwing an angry charge of electricity into the air. "*No, Callib, I promise, she's dead.* But that wasn't true, was it? Cowardice got the better of you. You took one look in those little girl eyes and just had to leave her instead of doing what you should have done. And now look at this mess."

"Just because I didn't handle it the way you wanted

doesn't mean I didn't handle it."

"Leaving her for dead is very different than what I ordered you to do."

"Your mistake is thinking you can order me to do anything at all. We either work together or you can—"

Callib flapped his arms as he headed through the door by the statues. The maxdin straightened when the magician neared. "Enough already. Calm down. I'll get the boy prepared. When I come back, try to be more civil."

Jarik closed his eyes and took a cleansing breath before facing Malja. "Wait here," he said.

As he walked out of the foyer, he gestured to the maxdin and the creature followed him, ducking low to get through the door. Cole crossed her arms and snickered. "My, my. Those two boys are gonna kill each other."

"They've been together longer than I've been alive," Malja said.

"Family can have more conflict than anybody. Let's hope we can use that to our advantage."

Malja nodded and held back the urge to cheer on Cole. The woman had found her courage once more, and Malja did not want to make her uncomfortable by pointing it out. To avoid the possibility, Malja walked back toward the entrance.

She could not see the bridge. She pressed her hands up to the glass — a strange experience, unbroken glass — and squinted. Though she never felt so much as a slim vibration, the fortress had left the bridge and now floated in the dark fog. The house had become an island.

With an echoing clang, the door between the statues opened. Nobody came out.

"Guess we're expected to go," Malja said.

"Oh, how dramatic," Cole said, melting into her superiority like an old lover. "For all their supposed

270- The Way of the Black Beast

greatness, these two have a lot to learn about presentation."

Despite her bravado, Malja caught Cole's eyes darting around like a bird looking for an escape. *Well,* she thought, *that's okay. A good fighter always feels nervous before a big battle.* Tumus looked worried, too. For a Chi-Chun of Korstra, however, Malja expected less fear and more of that overconfident arrogance she had come to enjoy. Fawbry merely stepped toward the door. Not a word spoken. Even Tufts noticed — the griffle chose to walk several paces behind.

They proceeded down a corridor marked with numerous closed doors on either side. The walls were stone and arched overhead. Narrow alcoves filled in the spaces between doors — focus booths, each filled with a hard-working magician.

At the far end, an open door led to one of Jarik and Callib's workrooms. Large enough to fit a mid-sized boat, the room bore the magicians' conflicting tastes quite well. The ten-foot windows along one wall belonged to Jarik. They had red drapes that touched the floor and little animal wood carvings around the frames. Callib had been in charge of the workspace. In one corner, a wide desk covered with papers and books; the rest of the space left open for experiments — practical and utilitarian.

Malja took it all in with the expectation of battle. She noted exits, defensive positions, and areas to avoid. To her left was Cole's portal frame. They had rigged it upright with large cables connected to it. The cables led to the second large object — a chamber composed of mirrored walls and hanging metal rods. More cables snaked along the floor from the chamber to the third object — a dark cylinder about six feet high and three feet across.

Both Jarik and Callib stepped forward. Their bodies glistened with sweet-smelling oil that reminded Malja of

Gregor's cooking — particularly when he fried a myrit. Even their bald heads had been covered. The oil brought to life the vibrant colors of their tattoos.

Warnings spiked in Malja's head. "Where's Tommy?"

Callib turned away but not before Malja caught the sinister amusement on his face. He stepped into the mirror chamber, reflections of him on every wall, and adjusted several of its components. Jarik gestured toward the portal frame.

"Patience," he said. "We wish to show you what this is all about. We are not monsters. Sure, we've made mistakes. We are far from perfect. But, where others bemoan their failings and wallow in self-pity, we improve ourselves."

With surefire steps, Callib walked up beside Jarik. "Go get started," he said. "I'll handle this."

Jarik hesitated, the desire to explain pushing against the need to perform. With a muted nod, he acquiesced. Callib gave a little shake of the head and snickered as Jarik entered the mirror chamber.

They're like nasty children, Malja thought.

Jarik took a wide stance in the center of the chamber and focused on the mirror to his side. From here, he could see the tattoos on his back — the oil making even the smallest ones clear. As he worked on the spell emblazoned on his right shoulder blade, doubt trickled along Malja's skin. They might be nasty children, but she now saw that they were *smart,* nasty children.

Callib walked up to Cole and offered a ridiculous bow. "You have my sincerest admiration."

Cole frowned. "You have my portal frame, and I'd appreciate it kindly if you return it."

"I see the time away from us has not changed your humor. Well, I'm sorry, Ms. Watts, but we cannot return the frame. In fact, it is our deepest wish that you help us build an even better one — one that will help us connect with other worlds in more substantive ways."

"You can wish all you want but I—"

"We have glimpsed into hundreds of worlds. Hundreds. Each containing knowledge and riches that would better our world over and over forever." He raised his index finger to stop Cole from speaking again. "I understand why you're angry. But I think after you see what we can accomplish today with your frame, I truly believe you will have a new desire to help us."

With her head high, Malja said, "You get nothing from us until we see Tommy."

"You stupid brat," Callib said, spit flying from his twisted lips. "You never could wait. Never could just let us present things to you the way we had chosen. You want Tommy? You *have* to see him? Very well. But I warn you, this'll only make it harder on you."

Callib looked at a tattoo on his hand. He closed his eyes and whispered words Malja did not know. With a childish snarl, he jerked his head toward the dark cylinder that connected with the mirror chamber. When he opened his eyes, the cylinder became translucent. Inside was Tommy.

He stood in a knee-high, thick, green sludge. Green water filled the rest of the cylinder like an algae soup. Tommy's body swayed in an unseen current, his eyes closed.

"Don't worry," Callib said. "The boy is fine."

"Fine?" Fawbry said. "He can't breathe in there."

Callib pulled back, uncertainty crossing his brow. His eyes widened, and a devious grin formed at the corner of his lips. He eased back with a predatory grace. He looked at Tumus. "You didn't tell them."

Malja's eyes shot to Tumus. The Chi-Chun woman's face betrayed her. Malja said, "You have something to say?"

Tumus looked from Callib to Malja — neither appeared safe. "W-When Barris Mont connected with Tommy, he ..."

"He what?" Malja said, her skin and muscles burning with the desire to attack, to shut out whatever might come.

"He ..."

Callib cleared his throat in a loud, unnecessary manner. "Perhaps I can help. You see, when Barris realized that Jarik and I were approaching, he knew our purpose. We had come to take his power. So, he tried to trick us."

"No," Tumus said. "It wasn't like that. Barris saw a great power in Tommy, but the boy had been so abused in the past, he was too mentally damaged to unlock it safely himself. Barris simply wanted to help the boy."

An icy hand took hold of Malja's heart. "What happened? What did that bloated bastard do?"

Tumus opened her mouth but only shook her head. Callib said, "He transferred himself into the boy. That's why you're precious Tommy is still alive. Barris can breathe underwater, so now Tommy can too."

Malja pressed a hand against her chest as if her heart had been ripped out and she wanted to staunch the wound. *Stay focused,* she thought. *Mourn later.* Rubbing her eyes, she opened her mouth but no words followed.

Fawbry stepped closer to the tank harboring Tommy. "Barris took over Tommy's body?"

"No," Callib said. "They share it. And now that we have the boy connected to our chamber, we share it."

"You're using him?" Malja said, her voice cracking. "For what?"

Callib opened his arms and nodded to the portal frame. "For you." He walked into the mirror chamber and positioned himself similar to Jarik.

While Jarik appeared to be in a deep trance, Callib acted more like an impatient child. He moved about the chamber, using different mirrors for different spells. He focused on his knees, his spine, and his feet. Spell after spell blended with Jarik's singular, powerful conjuring.

The cylinder containing Tommy brightened and pulsed waves of heat. Cole pointed behind them. Malja saw more bright light as the occupied focus booths pushed their magic into the room.

"This is a lot of energy production," Cole said. "It feels like a bomb. Be careful."

"I'll do that," Malja said, her anger refocusing her even as it took on a tinge of Cole's caution.

A cracking sound like wood splintering under heavy pressure ignited the air. The cables wriggled, jolting with power. With a sizzle, an airy pop, and the smell of burnt leaves, the portal frame opened.

Jarik and Callib exited the chamber, triumphant and sweating. They both gestured for Malja to look into the frame. She stepped forward a little — enough to peer into the frame without being too close.

She saw a room made of dark woods. Shelves crammed with books covered most of the walls. A window provided Malja with a glimpse of wide, hilly grass and a vehicle passing in the sky across a huge, ringed moon. In the room, she saw the desk with blue-green lights floating above it. A woman sat behind the desk, touching the lights as if they had substance.

Jarik stepped closer to Malja. "This is your world. You came from here. You were born on those soils. And that woman is your mother."

Jarik's words slammed into Malja's head like an avalanche of stone. Everything around her — Cole, Fawbry, Tumus, Tufts, the mirror chamber, Tommy, her fathers, the fortress, the City of Ashes, the entire world — it all disappeared into darkness leaving only Malja and the portal frame. She felt as if she floated in darkness, cut off from her body's senses.

She watched the woman in the frame, searching for any resemblance, any sign to verify Jarik's claim. The woman did look like Malja — thick, dark hair and a strong body. Her face shared some of Malja's structure, and the way she concentrated on her work bore the same determined focus Malja knew well. Like Malja, the woman wore a black assault suit that fit her perfectly.

The woman looked up, her face mirroring Malja's shock. All her actions occurred in slower time. Even as she hurried around her desk and stepped closer to the portal, her motions were slowed. Her hair bouncing in the air, the chair falling backward, the papers on her desk fluttering — all moved gracefully as if underwater. She covered her mouth, but could not hide her tears.

Malja's world slammed back into focus. She looked to Jarik and said, "Can I go there?"

With a joyous laugh, Jarik said, "That's why we did this. Long ago, we wronged you. We made a mistake."

Callib leaned in. "We simply want to make things right. Go home, Malja. You've been gone far too long."

Malja glanced back at the others. Their expressions couldn't have been more different. Cole gazed upon the portal and the machinery that helped make it possible, and her hands rolled the fabric of her shirt. This small action kept her from leaping forward to examine the wondrous technology.

Tumus, however, could not take her eyes off Tommy. Her valiant chin jutted out, and her body stood firm. Malja knew exactly what she was thinking — how to save Tommy.

Fawbry lacked expression. He stood as if holding on through boredom, waiting for Malja's command to act. She knew for sure now — he was lost in his own mind for now.

I'm alone. Malja took a few steps closer to the portal frame. *I always have been.*

Except if she reached out across worlds she would find a warm hand awaiting her. One like her own. She could leave this destitute, unraveled world of misery and violence, and replace it with a cozy library, green fields, and flying machines. She could have the warm embrace of a parent who never abandoned her.

She took a few steps more.

Jarik looked on with a bittersweet expression. His mouth tightened as if to hold back from blubbering an apology. He hung his tattooed head and laced his fingers. Callib bowed as he gestured toward the frame as if to say *Accept this gift and please forgive us.*

There were no more steps to take.

She gazed into her mother's brown eyes. Tears glistened and dribbled down her mother's cheeks. The woman put out one hand, yearning to touch. Malja raised her left hand and held it just before the frame. She scrutinized her mother's features like inspecting herself after a battle. She saw the old scars and the healed bones — her reflection yet older and more worn.

It was like being inside Barris Mont's magic once more — observing herself from the outside. Except this was no memory brought to life. All she had to do was step forward.

Gregor would tell her to seize the moment. "If I could have my way," she could hear him say, "you would never fight. You would never have to. A little bit of order, and we could all just peacefully live our lives." Yes, Gregor would tell her to jump through the portal, to wrap her arms around her mother, and to never once look back at this blood-soaked world.

But she did look back — just one last time to say goodbye. She saw Cole and Tumus enveloped in their personal euphoria. She saw Fawbry grin — happy for her with unbridled affection. Tufts giggled for no clear reason. She saw Jarik and Callib smiling like the fathers they should have been all along. And she saw Tommy — his submerged body swaying and peaceful, a pleasant look on his face that promised he would be thrilled for her to go through the portal.

For a second, her shoulders slumped. She lifted her head, filled her lungs with air and strength, and said, "Goodbye."

She whirled around, unsheathed Viper, swung it over her head, and using the strength of both arms, destroyed the portal frame in one thundering blow.Sparks of electricity and magic shot up toward the ceiling. As pieces of the frame clattered on the floor, Cole and Tumus snapped out of their blissful daze. Fawbry and Tufts looked confused.

Malja turned Viper toward Jarik and Callib. Jarik had a stunned expression, but Callib seethed with rage. Cole rushed over to the portal frame, caressing it like an injured baby. Tumus watched Malja like a bodyguard unsure of what her employer required.

"You liars! I almost went," Malja said, her grip solid and unwavering. "So tell me this much — was that woman even my mother?"

Callib shrugged. "How should we know? All the women from that world look the same."

Malja sidestepped to the right. "This was your plan? Open the portal frame and cast a spell that drugged us all into bliss. Trick me into going in and then what? I'm gone and the world is yours?"

"The world has always been ours."

Jarik finally looked away from the destroyed portal frame. His expression cleared, replaced with cold stoicism. "Well, once again, you disappoint us."

Malja flinched, and the involuntary response disgusted her.

"We made it easy for you," Jarik continued. "That may not have been your mother, but it was your world. We all could have gotten what we wanted. You would have gone home and escaped from here. We would have learned how you can travel through the portal frame and saved decades more of research."

"You made it too easy," Malja said, inching toward Tommy.

Callib turned to Jarik. "You should have listened. I've always been right about her. But you promised me she would make it so we could travel to other worlds. We should have killed her from the start."

Malja said, "Now we're getting to some truth. You did want to kill me from the very first, when my mother dropped onto your floor clutching me in her arms. I've been thinking about this. Why, I've wondered, over all these years, why didn't you just blast me away with some magic?

"I guess when I was little, Jarik kept you from harming me. You need each other's tattoos, each other's magic and power, so you had to compromise. As I grew up, you saw the warrior in me, and that meant I didn't have the magic you wanted — the magic that Barris Mont had. That extra bit of power you needed to accomplish a stable portal. So you planned to kill me. Jarik promised to take care of the unpleasant details and then told you he had killed me because if you knew that he had left me in the woods and that I had survived ... well, Jarik knows your anger quite well. For some time after you didn't know I was alive. Then one day you learned about Gregor. You couldn't kill me because of Jarik, and you couldn't kill Gregor yourself because of Jarik. So you hired Old McKinley to do the dirty work. You had Gregor slaughtered and hoped I'd fall apart without him.

"But the question remains: why am I still alive now? Surely in the last few years you heard I was looking for vengeance against you both. Jarik no longer needed prodding. He wanted me dead, too." Another few steps brought Malja into range. "The only answer I can come up with — you fear me."

"If you believe that, then you're as stupid as you are insolent. When we learned you were alive, we couldn't have cared. It was only when we learned that Cole and the Bluesmen were looking for you, that she thought you might hold the secret to traveling through the portal that we decided to use you if the opportunity arose. But we never sought you out. We didn't have to. You were searching for us. It was just a matter of time."

"No, you saw something in my mother's eyes that first day. Something that terrified you. That's why you wanted me dead. That's why you went through this nonsense about sending me home. Get rid of me without facing your fears. And you've been afraid for years of this very moment. Because whatever you saw in her, you see in me. The only thing I can think of that would scare you so greatly is power. You don't try to harm me with your magic because you know I can defeat you."

"Never!" Callib lunged toward Jarik and grabbed his hand. "You think you're so strong," he said, pulling Jarik's arm close enough to stare at the tattoos. "You think you're special. But you're not. You're nothing. And like a spoiled child, you destroy the gifts we give because they're not perfect."

"Malja," Cole said, "he's stalling for his spell."

Malja stepped forward, but Callib said, "You don't want our stable portal. Fine. Now you can feel what an unstable portal is like."

With a flick of his wrist and a deranged howl, Callib let loose a massive blast of magic. Hot, white light burned from his eyes and fingers. It shot out of him like a volcano, breaking through other parts of him until it flowed from his entire body.

Tumus raised her arms to absorb the magic. A small tendril from the blast knocked her to the floor. The magic pouring from Callib and Jarik did not seek out Malja. Instead, it struck the open air behind her.

A sound like ripping cloth magnified a thousand times cut into the air. Hurricane winds churned up from nothing, all of them blowing against Malja. But the wind wasn't really pushing her as much as pulling her. Something was yanking all the air away and trying to bring Malja with it. She planted her feet firmly, but still the forces made her step back.

Callib's harsh, satisfied look chilled her. Cole and Tumus and Fawbry had anchored themselves on parts of the portal machinery, but their wide, shocked eyes told her something ugly awaited her. With a terrified squeal, Tufts lost his grip. His body soared across the room and disintegrated upon the portal.

"No," Fawbry screamed, but the howling winds drowned him out.

Malja peered over her shoulder and discovered what an unstable portal looked like. Then Callib's storm knocked her off-balance and tossed her through the portal.

Chapter 25

Freefalling through a bitter, cold sky, Malja's stomach rose up in her chest. The wind stung her face. For the first time in her life, terror reached down her throat and ripped out a piercing scream.

She fell. Mindless to all around her. Knowing only that she screamed.

When her throat finally balked, she managed to regain some self-control. She started to think.

I'm in another world. Clouds blanketed below her obscuring the ground. Nausea swirled inside her as she dropped.

She closed her eyes, but that didn't help. She rolled onto her back feeling the cold against her like an icy chair. When she opened her eyes, she saw the jagged portal hole receding into the sky. With only the racing wind in her ears, she watched as the hole snapped shut.

Before she had time to consider the implications of that, she passed into the clouds. Moisture beaded on her assault suit and dampened her hair. Thunder rumbled close by.

She broke through the cloud cover to discover a world of raging storms. Rain and lightning thrust toward the ground, and she dropped with it like some banished god. She kept waiting to see a mountain or a forest or a city some large object which would kill. Instead, she saw water.

In all directions spread a vast ocean. The tear that escaped her eye drowned on her rain-soaked cheek. She would die in the water, every bone shattered upon impact but still aware as she sunk beneath its murky waves. She

282-The Way of the Black Beast

might even feel the nibbles of fish as her chest burned for air.

She hoped some important event from her life might flash in her mind or just some pleasant memories of Gregor. She would have been happy to consider a lost opportunity or a regretful moment. But her mind blanked at the endless expanse of water below her.

She tried to makes sense of how this could be — how her life could be so abruptly ended — but it only made her feel pointless and small. Like staring at the stars after reading her astronomy book. She became so absorbed with her lack of final moments that her mind didn't register the ripping sound overtaking the storm. She didn't notice the dark maw open below her. And as she slid through, she only thought how nice it felt to be out of that storm.

Chapter 26

The rain stopped. The wind ceased. But still Malja fell. No longer day. No longer outside. She fell from the top of a high, vaulted ceiling.

The floor zoomed up and with it came the knowledge that she had returned to Jarik and Callib's fortress. Before she could smash to her death, before she could even think about it, the air around her thickened like a stew left overnight. Her body slowed until she landed with a gentle touch, the cool floor a gift against her outstretched body.

Though her life had been saved, her stomach still rebelled. She managed to get on all fours before throwing up. When nothing else could leave her system except long strands of spittle, she gasped and coughed. Wiping her mouth, she looked upon a sight that made her question if she had indeed returned to her world.

The cylinder that had imprisoned Tommy lay in shambles, its brackish liquid drenching a portion of the floor. The mirror chamber had been shattered, littering the area with reflective shards. Tumus and Cole watched Malja with gaping mouths while Jarik nursed his bleeding jaw. Fawbry stood by the cylinder brandishing a metal pipe dripping wet. He had used the pipe to smash open the cylinder. But it was seeing Tommy that confused Malja the most.

His lanky twelve-year-old body faced Callib with a warrior's strength. With one arm raised and eyes narrowed, he pushed back against Callib's magic. Fire, electricity, black smoke, noxious gases — all balled up between the two magicians.

There. She finally had admitted it. Tommy was a magician.

Callib roared under the strain as he attempted to heap more and more magic upon the boy. Though Tommy's arm vibrated and sweat dribbled down his back, Malja saw a fighter with greater stores of power yet to be tapped. No. *Not a fighter — a magician.* He's a magician using powerful magic which will rot his mind until only insanity prevails. Perhaps he had heard her thoughts for he turned his head in her direction and raised his other hand. The door leading out burst open.

Tommy lifted the corner of his mouth and pointed to the door. Malja thought she saw a tear run down his cheek, but she couldn't be sure — trenches of sweat cut down the dirt on his determined face.

"Malja, come," Cole said from the doorway. Tumus tried to pull Malja away.

With Viper in hand, Malja said, "No. I won't let a boy sacrifice himself for me. I'm not leaving until this is over."

Drawing on all her speed, strength, and accuracy, Malja raced forward. She held Viper's grip at her stomach so the crescent-shaped blade pointed out from her side. *Run straight past him and let the blade do the work.* She came in fast and silent, hoping Callib's attention would be focused exclusively on Tommy.

But Callib saw her.

"You," he said, saturating the word with all his disappointment, fear, and hatred. Malja didn't see the motion, but she felt the pain as Callib sent a red bolt in her chest, blasting her onto her back. Tommy thrust magic from both hands, and though the ball of magic shimmered, it held.

Malja stared at the ceiling, stars dancing around her

vision. *Stars*. Stars, magic, madness — it all connected for her. After a few moments to catch her breath, she rose to her feet with a satisfied smile. She had a plan.

She pointed Viper at Jarik. "I've always known you were the weaker brother. Right to the end, you make Callib do all the hard work."

"Watch your tongue," Jarik said, blood on his chin. "Standing up to my brother has kept you alive."

Malja turned to Callib. "Then you must be the weak one, hiding your shame behind all this bluster. Makes sense — you made Jarik get rid of me, hired Old McKinley to get rid of Gregor, never doing the jobs yourself."

"Be quiet," Callib said, keeping his focus on the growing mass of magic.

"You did all these things that Jarik never knew about. Haven't you ever wondered what he's done behind your back? Or do you just think he's too worthless to bother worrying about?"

Callib straightened, his eyes opening in paranoia. "What is she talking about?"

"Liar," Jarik said. "I've always been a loyal brother."

Malja looked unconvinced. "Except when you went against Callib's orders and let me live. And now look where we are? Seems to me the both of you are trying to get the better of the other."

"It's not true," Jarik said, blood sputtering from his lips. "Don't listen to her. She's just trying to turn us against each other."

"You're right, Jarik. Callib is the weaker. Wielder of powerful magic but, like you, insignificant in the end."

Callib's face twisted as he struggled against Tommy's magic. "Lies!" he said. "We are special. We are the most powerful, most unique beings in the universe. We are far more than mere magicians. Could a silly magician hold battle with another while talking with you? I think not." To prove his point, Callib sent a strong surge of energy into the ball, and Tommy slid back a few feet. "We are gods. This world belongs to us. We will dethrone Korstra and Kryssta, and all of Corlin, all of Geth, will bow down before us. We are the new brother gods."

Malja walked straight at Callib. "Brother gods? You can't even defeat a little boy."

"We are gods!"

Before Malja could change her course, before Tommy could conjure some help, Callib swept both his arms in her direction, throwing the concoction of magics at her. Though most of it dissipated from the sudden change in focus, enough made its way to hit Malja.

A stone wall of sound slammed into her — deep rumbles and high-pitched squeals. Her feet went out from under her, sending her reeling to the ground. Viper careened into the air. Her head hit the floor sparking a dazzling array of colors before her eyes.

Her disorientation lasted only a moment, but by the time she had recovered, the room had grown quiet. Callib stared off, his face frozen in disbelief. Malja's eyes darted to the left. There lay Jarik, wheezing as blood pooled beneath him, Viper lodged in his chest.

With cold, patient steps, Malja approached Jarik. They locked eyes. Jarik's paling skin flushed with life for just a few seconds. "Callib was right about you," he said. "Worthless. Disappointment."

"You can't hurt me anymore," Malja said, placing her foot on Jarik's shoulder as she gripped Viper. "But I can hurt you."

She jerked Viper free. Jarik screamed. "That was for Nolan's sister, Audrex," she said. She raised Viper over her head, but before she could strike, a blast of energy tossed her several feet away.

Callib hurried to Jarik. "It's not possible." He cradled his dying brother and made no attempt to hide his streaming tears. "We're gods."

As Malja jumped back to her feet, Callib lifted his hand and pointed a warning finger. From the corner of her eye, Malja saw Tommy preparing to defend her, and though she couldn't see Tumus, she knew the Chi-Chun woman also readied her magic. Malja held Viper at her side.

She stepped forward, and Callib thrust his arm. But nothing happened. Concentrating all his energy, Callib tried again. A few sparks fizzled from his fingers.

In a somber, respectful tone, Tumus said, "Their magic was tied together. As Jarik dies, so does their power."

"That's not possible," Callib said. "I was a magician long before Jarik."

"Once you started linking your power with Jarik's, you entwined your abilities forever."

Callib's dumbfounded eyes gazed upon Jarik's face. He stroked Jarik's cheek and nodded. "It's okay. Perhaps it's best this way." The floor lurched to the side and dropped three feet. Callib let out a short chuckle that brought a perverse gleam to his eye. He looked from Malja and Tommy to Tumus and Cole and finally, to Fawbry. He let out a barking laugh. "Jarik's dying," he yelled. "Jarik's dying, and he's the one holding our home in the air. We're all going to die together. One big, happy family."

With each successive laugh erupting from Callib's chest, his face twisted into a grotesque, maniacal mask. Like a sigh, the fight left Malja. There seemed no point now. Jarik and Callib were no longer who they had been.

"Malja," Cole said, her voice shaking more than the floor.

The left side of the building tilted for a second before

leveling out. Malja sheathed Viper as she ran over to Cole. Tumus, Fawbry, and Tommy followed. Together, they rushed through the door and down the long hall lined with focus booths.

Several of the booths had been knocked open by the building's sudden drop. The magicians inside were dead. A few bore the serene expression of someone asleep or in deep meditation. But others died in horrible agony, clawing at the booth doors until their fingernails were no more.

"How could this have happened? We never heard anything," Tumus asked.

Cole said, "Sweetie, Jarik and Callib linked everyone together to create that stable portal. When the whole contraption blew, well, there are always side effects."

Malja skidded to a halt. "What? You're saying I killed them?"

"No, no, dear Malja, no, no. You were inside the portal when this happened. Callib did it, when he struck out at Tommy, when he tried to stop the boy from saving you."

Malja didn't know whether to believe Cole, but the whining sound of bending metal and a turbulent thumping in the floor reminded her feet to start moving again. They left the corridor and hustled through the enormous foyer. Bits of wall and ceiling dropped like hail crashing into the floor and spitting up debris.

Tumus reached the other side first. She pushed the large door open and stood in the doorway, blocking everybody's progress. She looked back at Malja and shook her head. "We're too late."

Malja caught up and peered out the doorway. Although the building sank slowly, the bridge was still at least twenty feet higher up.

From behind, Fawbry let out a short yelp. Everyone looked at him. He looked back, a bit dazed, a bit unsure.

"What's going on?" he asked.

Cole laughed, wrapped her arms around him, and kissed his reddening cheek. "You went a little crazy, Faw-Faw. Kind of shut down for awhile. But you're back now, and you've helped save Tommy."

"I did?"

Malja said, "Yes, yes, you helped. You're a hero. But if we don't get out of here, you'll be a dead hero. So let's go. We have to climb."

Cole said, "Not at all. You don't think I spent all that time working for Jarik and Callib and I didn't learn any thing, now did you? Those boys would have a backup plan just in case something like this happened."

"You think they planned for us to come and destroy them?"

"No, but they would've planned for Jarik being incapacitated, seeing as how he's the one keeping this place in the air."

"Fine, fine," Tumus said. "So what's this backup plan?"

Cole leaned her shoulder against the wall and thought. Nobody spoke, though all of them stared at her. Fawbry shivered as he looked around. Tommy slipped his hand into Malja's. She clenched it tightly, but kept her attention on Cole. If she even glanced at Tommy, she knew she would start hugging him and possibly start crying. She wasn't sure she would be able to stop.

"A crash room," Cole blurted out. "They probably built a crash room — a reinforced section of the building that could withstand most types of impact. If they were in trouble, they could lock up inside it and just wait the whole thing out."

"Great. Where is it?" Fawbry asked, his voice climbing pitch with each word.

"If I were designing it, I'd put it at the bottom of a

normal building, but this one is floating — so, I guess it would be in the middle since an impact could come from any direction. That way they'd have plenty of cushion on all sides."

The building reeled to the side, sending everyone scrambling to stay upright. Tumus braced herself in the doorway. Shattering glass and tumbling rocks echoed against the walls. Malja planted her feet in a wide stance. A moment later, the building settled.

Holding tight to the doorjamb, Tumus leaned out. "I think, maybe, we can—"

Malja grabbed the back of Tumus's clothes and tugged her back inside. "No time for debates. Cole, lead the way to the crash room. Everyone else follow."

"Look here, I don't know for sure there is one," Cole said.

"Do your best," Malja said, "because any minute now, Jarik is going to die, and this whole place comes crashing down."

"I'm just not sure—"

"Cole!"

"Okay, okay. My goodness, you don't have to be so rough."

Malja gestured to the crumbling building. Cole said nothing as she headed back through the foyer and into the focus booth corridor. She stopped without warning.

"Damn," she said, staring at the floor.

"What now?" Fawbry asked.

A wide blood trail painted a path from the far end of the corridor into one of the unused focus booths. Cole said, "Callib dragged Jarik through there. He's taking him to the crash room. We're too late."

"We can't be," Fawbry said.

Malja kicked the booth at her right three times and

cursed. She took several deep breaths before speaking. "You're sure we can't find this crash room in time?"

"By the time I find it, Jarik and Callib will have it sealed up. I'm sorry."

"Then we climb. Get high enough to cross to that bridge."

"One of these doors should—"

Malja kicked down one door, then another. Fawbry had reached the third and tried the handle. The door opened to a stairwell. With a bow, he gestured toward the stairs as if inviting her to a dance. His hands shook, but Malja appreciated his attempt to not panic.

"Hurry now," Malja said, making sure everyone went ahead before going upstairs herself.

Climbing stair after stair, adrenaline pumping her legs faster than the muscles wanted to work, Malja listened to the building fall apart around her. She heard Tumus praying in short puffs. She could see the concern and bald fear on Cole's brow. And Tommy — Malja only wanted to think as far as knowing he was with them and alive.

"This door, I think," Cole said.

They entered an octagonal library. Books lined the walls and the air smelled musty. Two tables dominated the floor. Pieces of yellowing paper and moldy covers were spread across the surfaces. Some papers had been laid out like puzzle pieces that didn't quite fit. Others were stacked for later use.

"What a shame," Cole said as she led them through the room. "All this effort to rebuild lost works of knowledge, and now it's going to be lost again."

With a glimpse at the table, Malja said, "Keep moving."

Cole did as commanded, though her eye lingered on the half-completed texts. Fawbry rushed ahead, and at the far end of the library, he pushed aside two sliding doors that opened onto a narrow landing. Cole followed, leaned over the railing and by the relieved drop of her shoulders, Malja knew they were high enough.

Malja took a look for herself. She judged the distance as no more than fifteen feet and dropping. "Get ready," she said.

Cole swung her feet over the railing. Malja lifted Tommy into a similar position. She held him tight against her chest and felt his right hand pat her arm.

The building jolted and Cole lost her balance. Rather than tumble, she had the presence to push off. She hit the road and crumpled into a fetal position, clasping her ankle and crying.

Tommy wriggled in an attempt to dislodge from Malja. "No," she said. "Just a few feet closer first."

He glowered at her.

"We're sinking slowly. It'll be fine to just wait."

He shook his head and pulled up his sleeves to reveal the tattooed skin. Dark, thick-lined tattoos covered his arms like winter clothes.

Malja stepped back, unsure of what she thought of the sight. It revolted her, but it was also Tommy — she couldn't look upon him and feel that way. She leaned in to view the details, and he leaped off.

"Tommy!"

When he hit the surface, he tucked into a ball and rolled to a safe recovery. He glanced up at her, smiled, and went to Cole's side.

"I-I can't do this," Tumus said. Her dark skin took on a sickly hue. She shook her head over and over. "Korstra help me. I can't do this. I'll never make it."

"It's okay," Fawbry said. "I don't want to jump either, but you don't have to. When the building sinks some more, we'll be just about even with the bridge. We can just hop right off."

"No. I can't do this."

"And I thought Korstra gave you such strength. You going to let a Kryssta-loving fool like me show you up? Come on, now. We're close enough. Watch." Fawbry hopped off, hit the ground with a grunt, popped to his feet, and waved back. "Easy," he said.

Malja pressed against Tumus's back. "You can do this. It's just a little step to safety."

The building dropped fast. Malja and Tumus fell to the floor which dipped enough to slide them back into the library. Books tumbled off the shelves. Malja's cheek hit a table leg and the copper taste of blood coated her tongue.

"Tumus, we have to go now."

Tumus had wrapped her arms around a chair. "I can't. I'm sorry. I've never been in the air like this before. I can't."

"You must."

"Go without me. I'm not afraid to die. Korstra can have me."

"That's it," Malja said. She got to her feet and crossed to Tumus as the building leveled out once more. "If you aren't afraid to die, then shut up and come with me." She tore the chair away from Tumus, squatted down, and lifted Tumus over her shoulders.

The floor shivered. Malja lined up with the doorway and kicked the chair against the railing. The shivering grew to a rumble.

Letting out a primal scream, Malja sprinted forward, her tired legs straining under the added weight of Tumus. She stepped onto the chair, then the railing. The building sank rapidly. As Malja pushed off, she watched the bridge pass before her eyes. She reached out — metal and concrete scraping along her chest, Tumus screaming in her ear —

and latched onto the bridge as Jarik and Callib's building tumbled into the darkness below.

Malja hung from the bridge, her fingers finding the slimmest purchase, while Tumus clung to her back like a baby cholloh. Fawbry stretched out toward them, but they were too far down. Malja let out an aggravated moan. Her fingers slipped.

That was it. She just slipped for a second, but gravity gave no quarter for such mistakes. They fell backward. Malja watched Fawbry's anguish as he reached uselessly for her. Tumus let go, weeping from the sudden darkness that enfolded them as they lost sight of the bridge.

Falling to my death twice in one day. If her body hadn't been so tired, she might have laughed.

A distant, thunderous thump reported the destruction of Jarik and Callib's fortress. A long fall. Too much time alone with her thoughts. Too much time to pay the dead their due.

Heat suddenly. First a slight warmth. Next came a full-blown hot air thrusting up from below. An explosion. The air lifted her like a doll, effortlessly throwing her into the sky. The bridge came into view and just as fast disappeared below her.

"Just kill me already," Malja yelled.

The heat beneath her dissipated, and as her body crested, she felt a familiar sensation along her arms like fingers tapping up and down her skin. Instead of falling back, her body shifted toward the bridge and descended in a peaceful, controlled manner. She looked down to see Tommy guiding her and Tumus to the ground.

When she reached the bridge, Malja and Tumus went straight for Tommy. He lowered to the ground, breathing hard like he had jogged several miles. His body shivered as the sweat covering him chilled his skin.

Malja wrapped her arms around him and kissed his forehead. She didn't wipe the tears from her face or muffle the sound of her bawling. All she wanted was for Tommy to know, to feel within his bones and heart and, if such a thing existed, his soul — that she needed him. She loved him.

"Thank you," she said. Tommy matched her grip. Feeling his small hands pulling her closer sent her into another fit of tears.

"See?" Fawbry said to Tumus. "Easy."

Tumus prostrated near Tommy's feet. Her hands shaking like a bowstring just shot. She mumbled to the ground, but Malja distinctly heard the name *Korstra.*

When she lifted her head, Tumus smiled and said, "It's over."

Malja wanted to believe that, but she heard an odd buzzing that sent uneasy pulses through her. As the sound grew louder, she let Tommy go, wiped her face, and stood. Viper itched at her back. She let the weapon free, the sight of it sobering Tumus.

"What's wrong?" Cole asked.

"Listen," Malja said. By now they could all hear the horrible buzzing of Dragonflies. "Be ready."

Fawbry lifted Cole, while Tumus carried Tommy. Despite her exhaustion, Malja led the way with Viper as a warning to any Dragonflies suddenly getting brave. She used all her energy to keep moving and not stumble. If she showed any serious weakness, she expected the Dragonflies would swarm in on them.

As they progressed across the bridge, Malja kept searching the darkness. They wound through the mounds of trash and rubble, and still Malja remained alert. Several times her head swam. She feared she might pass out, but her will refused such an easy escape.

As they neared the factory fence, she could feel the eyes watching. Dragonflies buzzed overhead but none came close enough to be seen. Zorum's split body lay in a heap not too far away. That reminder did far better in protecting them then Malja's shaking arms holding Viper.

Two workers appeared with three horses. Their terrified gazes drifted between Malja and the billowing smoke from the destroyed fortress. That thick cloud would cover the sky for days.

One worker handed his reins over and dashed back to the factory. The other swallowed hard and held his reins out. He pointed into the distance. The message was clear enough — *Take these horses and go far away as fast as you can.* Malja had set them free from the factory life and they wanted to throw her out. As she snatched the reins, she growled and the worker sprinted away.

"Easy," Tumus said. "You just killed their gods."

Malja climbed atop a brown mare and closed her eyes for just a second of relief. She didn't think she had the strength to endure another fight. She barely had the strength to open her eyes again. Fawbry mounted a horse and sat Cole across, protecting her wounded ankle with care.

Tumus tapped Malja's knee and handed Tommy to her. Malja slid the boy in front and wrapped her arms around him. His unconscious body limp and unreactive. Without a word, Tumus walked away and mounted the third horse.

Before they entered the fenced-off factory, Cole pointed them westward for several blocks. The detour would add another day's travel most likely, but Malja didn't mind. They avoided the factory workers and any other Dragonflies in that area. And they had the time. After all, there was nothing left to do.

* * * *

Tommy still didn't speak, but the recent events had left their mark. Each night they made camp, he labored as hard as ever with the others, but when they finished, he curled up next to Malja, insisted she place her arm around him, and moved little until morning. Even while he ate, he did so from this position.

Malja tried to give the boy what he needed, but it did not come naturally. Besides, part of him was Barris Mont. She'd look in his eyes, searching for a flicker of that creature, and grew angry no matter what she thought she saw. After a week of travel, her conflicted feelings must have become apparent for Tumus chose to approach her one evening after everyone else had fallen asleep.

"He's all Tommy. You don't have to worry."

Malja saw no point in pretending ignorance. "Easy for you. You loved them both. This boy is double the prize for you."

"You know I don't see him as a prize. Korstra, in his infinite wisdom, found a way to save this boy's life. Barris gave himself up to Tommy, and while he lives on in the boy's body, he has no control over anything. Tommy is entirely Tommy. He merely has the essence, the power, of Barris Mont."

"This is supposed to make me feel better?"

Tumus grinned. "You need to forget about Barris. Just see Tommy. Nothing else has changed."

"I don't know. The magic he created to fight with Callib was ... if I hadn't actually seen it ... and you're saying that's all him. No Barris?"

"I'm saying that the boy is still a boy. And he still needs you."

"You wish it was you."

Tumus stroked Tommy's hair. "A little, yes. Yet I was not the one who saved him from slavery. I was not the one who protected him from the wilds."

"Some protection. He would've died, if left to me. You were the one who took him to real safety."

"Ahh, so that's it."

Malja closed her eyes and faked a yawn. "There's no it."

"You blame yourself. You think that you failed and that's why Barris is now within Tommy. You think you should have been there to stop it or perhaps never have let Tommy be in that situation in the first place."

"You couldn't be more wrong," Malja said, but she couldn't convince herself, let alone another.

Tumus clasped her hands. "I'm sorry you don't believe in Korstra for you would find great comfort and understanding if you did. You'd see that you cannot control the world, that even a brother god could not predict such things. If he could, he would have saved his beloved Elatria. I guess the best I can tell you is that this is not your fault. It is the will of the world. It is the way of life."

"Yeah? Well, life is tossing the Black Beast upon me for not being a good parent to Tommy."

A few days later they reached the well-kept mansion where they had found the grounder. Cole's foot had been wrapped and babied as much as possible — now, she could hobble along for several hours without tiring. They spent the night under the comfort of the mansion's roof, and Cole wandered its halls longer than she had spent at any stop since she broke her foot.

As Malja readied to go to sleep, she heard a strange noise. The size of the mansion caused sounds to bounce around, but she was sure she had heard a voice. She followed the echoing sounds until she reached the kitchen. There she found Fawbry and Tommy playing the Reflex

Game. A wide smile covered Tommy's face as Fawbry tried to feign an attack. Backing out quietly, Malja left them to their game. She finally slept soundly.

The next morning, as they prepared the horses, Cole called the group together. "I'm not going," she said. "I want to stay here."

"What? Why?" Fawbry said.

"Bless your heart, you still just want to be with me, don't you? Sorry, Faw-Faw, but it'd never work. We were good for awhile, but I've got plans and you'd really be better off going home."

"Kryssta, you're an infuriating woman. All I asked was why. I'm not professing my undying love."

"See that? Your undying love. You've got to move on."

While Cole and Fawbry continued to verbally spar, Malja thought about the mansion. Filled with ancient technology that begged the attention of someone knowledgeable, there was a graceful logic to leaving Cole with it. One thing gnawed at Malja, though.

"What plans?" she said, interrupting Fawbry's next insult.

Cole raised an eyebrow. "Excuse me?"

"What is it you want to do with this place?"

Cole walked over to Fawbry's horse and fussed with the saddle. "Oh, nothing to worry about. It's not like I'm going to start a group of blues-playing assassins or anything."

"That's right," Malja said in cautious tones. "That would be a dangerous and foolhardy thing to do."

"Why, Ms Malja, I think you're threatening me. Oh, don't give me any of your looks. I never was built for leading armies or anything like that. That's your area. I just want to get back to the simple things — building machines. Just because we all live by our own rules doesn't mean we have to live without comfort. It's not as if the two are mutually exclusive."

Malja stayed silent a moment, thinking it over, weighing the woman Cole had been with the woman she had become. Malja extended her hand. "Good luck. I think I'll actually miss you a bit."

"My, my," Cole said, shaking Malja's hand. "You'll have to come back and visit someday. You, too, Tumus. And Tommy. You're always welcome."

Fawbry swung up onto his horse. "Don't worry about excluding me. I wouldn't want to come back here if my life depended on it. Not unless you've got a new hand for me."

Cole raised both eyebrows, grinned, but said nothing.

Two nights later, Malja woke from a dream she could not recall. Tommy whimpered and nuzzled her side. Tumus sat by their campfire and asked, "You okay?"

Malja nodded. "What are you doing up?"

Tumus hesitated. Stretching out her legs, she said, "I'm trying to figure out what I should do next."

"Korstra's not telling you?"

A loud laugh broke from Tumus, and Tommy started, looked around and fell right back asleep. "Sorry," she said. "No, Korstra's not helping me out here. I've got to figure it out on my own."

"Any ideas?"

Licking her lips, Tumus said, "I think so. I'm going back to Dead Lake. Jarik and Callib hurt my people, killed many, and left them in disarray. Without Barris around, there's bound to be a mess, and I think I could do a good job helping clean it all up."

"You've been gone a long time."

"The Chi-Chun are not often fast movers."

Malja smirked, thinking of how most Chi-Chun could spend hours standing in one place. "We should pass the lake soon," she said.

"Then I have time to change my mind."

But Malja knew as she closed her eyes that Tumus would stay behind at Dead Lake. Malja's life did not join well with most people. If not for Tommy, Tumus would never have come along in the first place.

Sure enough, at Dead Lake, Tumus slid from her saddle and sifted her fingers through the soil. She washed her hands in the cold lake waters and breathed in the lake air as if she had entered a holy shrine.

Little had changed. Debris littered the ground and birds pecked at the few remains still scattered about the land. Barris Mont's enormous body could not be seen. Malja guessed that scavengers had consumed much of it before the rest slipped back underwater.

"Guess you're staying here," Fawbry said.

"It's best I do. Korstra wouldn't want me traveling with a Kryssta-lover like you."

Fawbry let out a shocked gasp. He jumped to the ground, stormed up to Tumus, and let his face open into a wide smile. He wrapped his arms around the woman and ignored her protests while he hugged her.

"Never thought I'd miss a Korstra fool, but I'll miss you."

When Fawbry broke away, Tumus faced Malja. "Don't pretend you'll miss me. I'm just glad we got through all this without killing each other."

"He's going to miss you," Malja said, jutting her chin in Tommy's direction. "That means I'm going to miss you. And, maybe, I just might miss you a little bit on my own."

"I couldn't ask for more," Tumus said before turning her full attention on Tommy.

Kneeling before him as if he were a king, she pressed his hand against her wet cheek. Tommy looked to Malja for guidance. She motioned with her hand — *make your own decisions.*

He tapped Tumus on the shoulder, and when she lifted her head, her broad smile set them at ease. She hugged the boy.

"You will always have a home here," Tumus said. "Promise me you'll come to visit."

Tommy covered his heart and nodded. He tapped his chest twice and brought his hand to his forehead — his military salute.

"Okay. Good." She brushed her cheeks clear and stood, but never let go of his hand. She gazed at the lake and grimaced as if the empty waters cut through her. "You could," she said, her voice quavering, "that is to say, if you wanted to, you would be welcome here ... to stay."

Malja pulled Tommy away, and to her joy, Tommy clutched her side.

Tumus held the boy's hand as long as she could, all the time speaking as fast as her mouth could move. "I'm sorry. Please, I'm sorry. It's just that part of him is Barris Mont and this is the home of Barris and I just thought part of him may want to go swim in his lake and feel his waters and know why he is the way he is now."

"Don't ruin this," Malja said.

"I know. I'm sorry. After all, I have Korstra. Who do you have besides Tommy?"

"We should go."

"Of course," Tumus said and blew a kiss to Tommy. "Please, come visit some day. I promise I'll be fine."

* * * *

They rode to the Yad in silence. Tommy made a few pleasant faces for Malja — reassurances that he was fine and that he wanted to be with her. But no matter what he did, Malja still felt doubt chewing at the back of her mind.

Does this parenting thing ever get any easier? she wondered.

At the Yad, three Muyaza came out to see Malja arrive. Much of their village remained in disrepair, yet some were back helping people cross the river's rough waters. Others worked on rebuilding their homes and fixing the broken litters.

One Muyaza waited for a moment, but when no other horses followed out from the tree line, he spoke rapidly to the others. They waddled off to the main part of the village and within a few minutes, the entire community came out. They were silent and somber.

Malja dismounted and approached with her head low and her posture as non-threatening as she could muster. An elder Muyaza stepped toward her. She offered the small lock of hair Skvalan had carried. The elder snatched it from her, clutching it close to his chest, and the entire community wept.

As the Muyaza turned away, Fawbry asked Malja, "Should we stay?"

"What for?"

"The funeral — assuming they have one."

Malja mounted her horse. "You're welcome to do as you wish. I don't go to funerals."

"That's because you're usually the one who did the killing."

Malja didn't bother answering. The Muyaza were gracious enough to get them across the Yad for free and that served as their final words. Once they had gone back into the forest, Malja pulled up next to Fawbry.

"Thank you for helping us save Tommy."

"Some help. I go crazy, and you're thanking me." Fawbry's horse snorted and this appeared to be the most answer she would receive.

"Well," she said, "I assume you'll be heading back north, back home, but if you want to stay with us, we'd be happy to have you."

Fawbry snapped his head around. "Are you insane?"

"Look I know things have not been easy with us, but Tommy likes you and I think—"

Laughter burst out of Fawbry like a colorful fountain spraying cool water. "Shut up already. You're insane to think I'm going north."

"But you hate me."

"Somebody's got to protect this boy from you, and I still have one hand. Besides, after I left you I almost died out there. And I ended up back with you, anyway. This is a dangerous world. Might as well have the most dangerous person in it on my side."

Tommy snickered and that brought a smile to Malja. "That's good enough as far as we're concerned," she said.

"Great." Fawbry clapped his hands. "So where are we going?"

Chapter 27

The town of Darmen had been built on a small hill and consisted of two roads crossing. Homes lined the north-south road. Here lived the Governor, some store owners, and a few citizens. The east-west road consisted of The Maple Tree Inn, the stables, a house of prostitution, a gambling house, three bars, another house of prostitution, and three homes belonging to the true rulers of the town — the Morlina Brothers.

The Star Bar had been built around the rusting shell of a bank vault which served to keep food cold. The metallic walls provided it with a unique atmosphere and unusual acoustics. Malja, Tommy, and Fawbry sat at a round table made from an old road sign — TORSKA BRIDGE 5.

"Got any apples?" Malja asked.

The gruff owner behind the bar, heavy beard and bald head, pointed to a small basket on the far end.

"Thank you," Malja said and helped herself to a ripe, red apple. The cold Korstraprime rains had been falling for three weeks, sending rivers of grime rushing through the town streets. Finding apples in such good condition was a treat. She bit into the fruit, licking its juice before taking the next bite, savoring the experience thoroughly.

Tommy dug into a cheese sandwich, his attention fixated on Fawbry's copy of the Book of Kryssta. Learning to read had proven easy for the boy, and Malja expected him to be proficient within a few months. She would have to keep an eye out for an astronomy book or else Tommy might become a Kryssta convert.

Fawbry said, "Um, not to upset you, but what in Kryssta's name are we doing here?"

"Having lunch," Malja said.

"But this is the Morlina's town. Coming here is like begging for a fight. I thought we were done with all that."

Malja took another bite of her apple. "How long have we been wandering around Corlin?"

The question took Fawbry off-guard. "I don't know. A few months, I guess."

"That sounds right. And what have we been doing?"

"Traveling. What's this got to do with being here?"

After one final bite, Malja placed the core on the bar and returned to her table. "We've been doing nothing. Just wandering. That's because we didn't have a purpose. Before, I had a clear reason for every action, every step in my life — get Jarik and Callib. But now there's nothing."

"I see," Fawbry said, his eyes more panicked with every word. "You were feeling bored and useless, so you thought it'd be fun to provoke some nasty men and cut them down."

"No," she said, calm and patient. "We're here because I finally know how to live in this world. For me. And I hope for you and Tommy. This is the first step."

"Oh, wonderful. Just what I wanted to hear. What limb am I going to lose this time?"

The bar room door opened with a blast of cold air. Four men walked in, each wearing a dark, rain-doused coat. The first was Arkam Morlina. The second was his magician. The other two were his thugs.

Malja's nerves jangled. Arkam was a portly, unimposing fellow on the outside, but his name and the violence his brothers had attached to it kept Malja alert. The magician ate far too much and smelled of raw onion.

"Are you Malja?" Arkam asked as his thugs spread out.

One edged behind her, the other slid along the wall in front. "I got a message you wanted to see me."

Fawbry nearly choked on his food. "You called this guy here?"

Malja stood in as non-threatening a manner as she could manage. "I'd like to discuss with you how you and your brothers are going to stop hurting this town."

Arkam stared in shock before breaking into laughter. "Are you threatening to take over here?" To his men, he said, "This is unbelievable."

"No threats," Malja said. "I don't want to hurt anybody. If you'd simply sit down, I'm sure we can figure out a way for you to live here peacefully, or if you don't like that, you and your brothers can leave and the town can take care of itself."

Arkam leaned against a wall and shook his head as if dealing with a naïve kid who needed to be shown who was in charge. "Do you know who I am?"

Malja raised a finger. "Do you know who I am?"

Throwing his hands in the air, he said, "Well, you've been funny, but you make no sense. I've got to go. Just be glad my brothers weren't the ones to get your message. If they had to get soaked just to listen to this nonsense, well, you'd all be dead right now." To Fawbry and Tommy, he added, "You both should run from her. She's going to get you killed."

Fawbry crossed his arms. "She's the safest bet we got."

"Come see me. I'll give you better."

Malja shifted her foot. "Don't make me hurt you. Please. Sit with me and work this out."

Arkam's face tightened. He motioned to his magician. The magician rolled up his sleeve and gazed on his tattoo — swirling smoke with bits of grit dotted throughout. Malja didn't have to look behind her to know Tommy had several spells ready to go.

Throwing his fist onto the bar, Arkam said, "Do you know what my brothers will do to you?"

Malja sighed as she saw Arkam's eyes signal his men. The one behind her died first. Malja jabbed Viper back and up, catching the thug just under the rib cage. The other one swung a short sword overhead. Malja sidestepped the attack and countered right through his mid-section.

Arkam backed up to his magician. "Y-You just killed two good men."

"These were thugs," Malja said. "They stole and raped and terrorized this town for you and your brothers. Now sit with me and talk. It can stop here."

Arkam kicked one of the bodies and slipped on some blood. He managed to keep from falling by holding onto his magician's sleeve. "You're all dead. You understand? Simple as that. All three of you are going to die."

The magician popped his head up and the ground quaked. Arkam bent over with a sadistic howl of joy. The bartender jumped from behind the bar, crying, with his arms raised in surrender.

"Fawbry," Malja yelled.

Fawbry leaped forward and tackled the bartender, bringing him to safety behind the bar. Even as the ground in front of her opened up, she listened for sounds that Fawbry had succeeded. She heard it in a giddy laugh — the sound of someone surprised to be alive. The sound that launched her into action.

She thrust forward. Viper sprayed blood off its blade as it sliced toward new victims. Before she struck Arkam, a thin stream of fire shot by her, igniting the somber magician. He screamed, but the sounds were never heard. A bubble of air had formed around him, containing the fire, the smoke, and the sound.

Malja brought Viper down and Arkam's right arm joined the bodies on the floor. With a flick of his fingers, Tommy closed the wound.

Malja placed Viper under Arkam's chin. A dark spot formed at Arkam's crotch. "P-Please. Don't kill me."

"There's only one reason you are alive right now. So listen closely. Your brothers are out of business. You go tell them that. And then, you leave this town and go to the next closest one. You tell everyone in that town that the great Malja is real, that she's sick of people like your brothers ruining life for everybody. You tell them that Malja is fair. Give up all this evil and all is forgiven. We've lived in crazy times. I understand. But fight me, and you'll die. Either way, I'm going to rid the world of all the scum like you. You tell them that, and then you go to the next town and do it again. And you keep doing it until you die of old age. Understand?"

Arkam nodded.

"And I'm going to be following just behind. If you stop, I'll catch you. So, get started."

He bolted from the bar, tripping on the fallen corpse of his magician and landing in the muddy streets.

"It's okay now," Malja said.

Fawbry and the bartender stood. "You do understand that his brothers are going to come fighting."

"Maybe not. I can hope for the best, right? If not this time, then maybe the next. Eventually these fools will get the message."

"But—"

"Tommy and I can take care of them. And I need you to keep the innocent out of harm's way."

"So this is the grand mission now? Clean up the country?"

Malja shrugged. "My fathers were Jarik and Callib.

Tommy has part of Barris Mont inside him. You were a warlord."

"I wasn't any good at it."

"And I ... I was consumed by hatred. We're responsible for a lot of this mess. Fixing it seems like the right thing to do."

Fawbry looked to the bartender. "Well, can I at least get a free drink for saving your life?" The bartender passed out. Fawbry shrugged, reached for a mug, and poured himself a drink. "I suppose this'll work well. Better than your myopic revenge thing."

"Much better," Malja said as she wiped Viper's blade. "The Black Beast is dead. Now, I'm the law."

About the Author

Stuart Jaffe is the author of *The Max Porter Paranormal-Mysteries, The Malja Chronicles,* the *Gillian Boone* novels, The Bluesman series, and much more. His short stories have appeared in numerous magazines and anthologies. He is the co-host of *The Eclectic Review* - a weekly podcast about science, art, and well, everything. For those who keep count, the latest animal listing is as follows: one dog, four cats, one albino corn snake, one Brazilian black tarantula, three aquatic turtles, one lop-eared rabbit, four chickens, and a horse. Thankfully, the chickens and the horse do not live inside the house.

For more information visit *www.stuartjaffe.com*

MALJA'S ACTION AND ADVENTURE CONTINUES IN

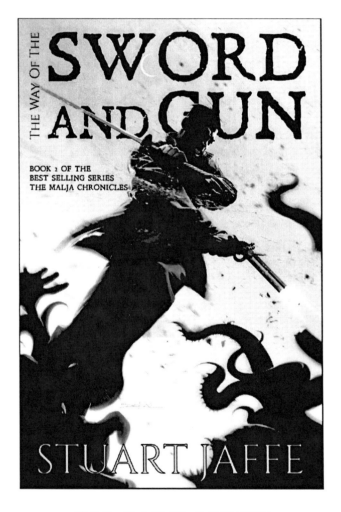

ON SALE NOW!

CPSIA information can be obtained at www.ICGtesting.com
Printed in the USA
LVOW07s2245230915

455409LV00006BA/867/P